FEARLESS INNOCENCE...

She stared at him, eyes sullen and dark. "You still think I shot at you on purpose, don't you?"

He met her gaze levelly. "The jury is still out on that, Moze. Why don't you button up that sweater and point me toward Dirty Fork?"

Moze hesitated, chewing at her underlip for a moment. Then she secured the lower two buttons on her sweater. "Maybe I'll just ride into Dirty Fork with you, show you the way."

"Seems fair. Only friendly thing you can do—after trying to kill me . . ."

TABOR EVANS

LONGARM

AND THE
BLUE NORTHER

A JOVE BOOK

First Jove edition published August 1981

First printing

Printed in the United States of America

Jove books are published by Jove Publications, Inc.,
200 Madison Avenue, New York, NY 10016

Chapter 1

He swung his legs heavily over the side of the bed. He sagged there with his head slumped forward between his shoulders, aware of oppressive midday heat, fiery sunlight rimlighting the drawn window shades, and most of all, aware of the naked girl sprawled in exhausted sleep on the rumpled mattress. He grinned faintly. She breathed through her parted lips, making a faint whistling sound that pleased him because it was as real and natural and honest as she was, as sincere as her total fatigue. She was a girl who believed it was more blessed to give than to receive, and when she gave she did it with all her heart and mind and gristle and sinew. A living, loving doll who truly enjoyed pleasuring a man. Exerting every ounce of his willpower, he kept both his mind and eyes off the radiant mounds and hillocks and planes of her ceramic-smooth body, but she called to him with fearful polarity, like some lovely succubus, a singing Circe, a ten-dollar whore, the hope of heaven—none of which she was.

"God, you're pretty," she whispered at his back.

He didn't turn his head. "I've still got to get dressed."

Her voice teased him like fingers scratching lightly at his back. "Even with your clothes on, you're pretty special, Long-arm."

"You got any idea what time it is?"

"I got an idea I don't care, and give me two minutes at that mast of yours, and you won't care . . ."

"It must be past noon."

"Half the day gone. All the more reason for coming back to bed. Too late to conquer any worlds today."

"I was due downtown at least three hours ago."

"What's downtown?"

He laughed and shook his head. "Beats me. But I sure as hell better go see, or I won't be able to keep myself in even the style I've had to grow accustomed to." He drew a deep breath. "Will you be here when I get back?"

She didn't answer and he grinned again faintly, knowing this was another of her tricks. She wasn't going to waste her breath reassuring him, if it went against her wishes. Let him suffer, let him wonder, let him worry and hurry back to find out for himself.

Sighing expansively, Longarm stood up. He heard her whispered intake of breath, but still did not turn to look at her. He could feel himself growing erect, just knowing she wanted him. Clamping his teeth tightly together, he took up his longjohns from the floor and hopped around, putting them on.

He was a tall man, lean and muscular, with the hard-boned body of a slightly aging athlete. There was a youthful vigor in his dark eyes and in his manner, though his face was seamed and brewed coffee-brown by raw winds and pitiless suns. Well over six feet tall, he towered like a bronze giant over the average male of the 1880s. The average enlistee in the recent unpleasantness between the States had been only five feet two. But Americans were getting taller, eating better, and winning a few of the battles against epidemic and disease, and Custis Long was a promise of what the best among them could be.

For a moment before he buttoned his longjohns, Longarm fingered at the pursed stitches that closed the latest wound he'd collected along the way since he'd long ago lit out from his native West-by-God-Virginia, in search of something he'd never found—though he came damned close to it, wrestling in that bed with Bonnie—and embarked on a trail that had brought him, with tortuous turns and twists, to this place and this latest job as a deputy U.S. marshal, earning the grand salary of one hundred a month plus expenses.

He grinned crookedly. Who'd ever have tabbed Custis Long as a man who'd reach such affluence on the lee side of the law? His grandma had always had a saying that pretty well covered the situation. "Nobody in this life truly knows what he's going to be," his grandma had said, "until he's already become it—and by then it's too late." A great old lady. Life had dealt her

2

a few hands off the bottom of the deck, but had never fooled her.

"Damn." A stabbing lance of such terrible intensity sliced through his gut from the ill-healed wound that he had to bite his lip to keep from crying out.

"What's the matter, honey?" Bonnie was truly concerned. She writhed on the bed, sitting up, but he remained facing away from her.

"Nothing, Bonnie. I just remembered something." Remembered? He'd never forget. Sometimes in the night he awoke in a cold sweat, thinking about it. Night shot, from the sneaking dark. He'd felt the impact of the rifle slug and glimpsed the muzzle flash at the same instant. He was knocked off his horse, and hellfire pain flamed through him as he fell. The first stunning numbness of the slug's impact was immediately replaced by a white-hot branding iron that chewed into his belly and made his toes curl with the agony. He'd still been conscious when he hit the ground, and then the pain overwhelmed his brain and knocked him out. At the moment he'd been thankful for the soft black pit of unconsciousness into which he plunged.

"That nasty old gunshot wound hurting you?"

"Only when I breathe."

She exhaled heavily, in deep sympathy. "I felt it last night."

"Oh? Was that you? What were you fooling around up there for?"

"It's bad. Not half healed. You ought to be in bed."

"I'll bet you say that to all the boys."

"Where'd you get it?"

"The bullet? On a job." He remembered the way he'd come slowly awake, after God only knew how long in darkness, a woman's soft hand on his fevered forehead, a woman-scent that was strange and pleasant to him, and him hurting so bad he couldn't care; not really care, with a hard-on and all. Jesus, he *had* been sick. Light lanced through his eyeballs and seared straight to the burning slash in his belly. Every move, no matter how slight, was like the stab of a merciless bowie knife in his side. It was not that it was the first bullet he'd survived; it was just that they never got easier. "A man don't get used to them," he said aloud.

3

"Come, let mama kiss it," said the warm, teasing voice from the bed.

He laughed over his shoulder. "Mama's too anxious." But his gunmetal eyes gleamed with reflected sunlight and inner warmth. He ran his hand through his close-cropped hair that bushed cigar-leaf brown between his fingers. His proud, well-trimmed longhorn mustache wriggled pleasurably. But the pain wasn't ready to release him yet. He had to go through it all, the recalled shock of impact, the ragged cut of the slug ripping its way through his flesh; the final flooding return of all the pain—of that bullet and all the slugs before it—and all of them ahead of him. And for what? A hundred lousy bucks a month and a pension in twenty years, plus all the lead he could carry, for God's sake.

"Why do I do it?" he said aloud, under his breath, mostly to himself. "What in hell am I doing here?"

Bonnie's voice chilled slightly and she stirred impatiently on the mattress. "What *are* you doing here?"

"Just lucky, I guess." He exhaled heavily. "Hell, Bonnie, I didn't mean you. It has nothing to do with you. I meant this latest memento of law and order. Law and order. Who gives a damn?"

"Not me. Just give me a warm bed and plenty to eat, and I'm fine."

"You're better than fine, baby. You're perfect. I really am lucky."

"Prove it."

"It's at least a month old and I'm still alive. I reckon I am lucky." He was remembering that saddlebag medic who had cleansed his wound, dug out the slug, and sewed him up.

"You're a lucky man, Marshal Long," the sawbones had said. "Lucky it was a high-velocity rifle that went right through you clean as a whistle, and not a pistol or shotgun—they'd have torn you up. You're lucky you got a nice clean hole through the fleshy part of your side." The doctor had gone on talking through the pain singing its dirges inside Longarm's fevered mind. "Why, you are lucky. You couldn't of picked a better spot for a body wound, if you had to have one. No inflammation. Yessir, I'd say you're one lucky hombre."

Longarm had laughed through the surges of pain. "Damned

4

if you don't make it sound like I got a prize instead of a bullet hole, doc. . . . I don't think you can sell me that one. This ain't the first slug that's winged me, you know."

The doctor nodded. "I saw your scars."

"And I reckon it won't be the last. I just don't see how a man can be so effing lucky as I am."

The doctor shrugged, unmoved. "You're breathing. Still on a payroll. Two or three months it'll be completely healed."

"Two or three months?"

"Just be patient, Marshal. Be patient and keep your bowels open."

It had been a full week before Longarm had been able to stand erect and totter around like a senile old man. And when he'd reached for the gun he'd holstered at his side, he'd gagged with pain and felt as if the top of his head were coming off.

The doctor had no sympathy. In fact he'd cursed Longarm for trying to get around at all. "You stupid bastard. You trying to undo my work? You trying to make me look bad, you son of a bitch? Hell, that bullet went through two muscles that wrap around from your belly to your backbone. Those muscles stretch near to ripping every time you move. You got to give 'em time to repair. You're in good shape, but hell, man, you can't get shot like you did without a *few* side effects."

He shook off the hurting memory and turned, catlike, from old habit, taking up his brown tweed pants from a chair. These trousers were just one size too small and he struggled, pulling them on until they fit as snugly as an extra layer of skin. It made moving in brushland a lot easier and a lot smoother, and that could save your life. The beginnings of an erection didn't make buttoning his fly any easier, but he managed to curse it shut. Then he bent over and found his boots where he'd tossed them under the old oakwood dresser. He sat on a straight chair and pulled on the low-heeled cavalry stovepipes. This soft leather footwear wasn't as perfect as Indian moccasins, but was more suited for running than riding. This was the way he wanted it. He spent more time afoot than he did in the saddle, and in these shoes he could outrun any cowpoke in fancy foot-pinchers.

Her voice snagged at him, playful and yet determined. "Must you go, Longarm?"

5

He didn't look up. Hell, he didn't dare look up. He was only human. In fact, he was human as hell, and this girl had been born tempting; he bet the doctor that delivered her had stroked her bottom instead of slapping it. He didn't even have to look at her to see her clearly in his mind's eye. She was etched there, a moving angel of beauty, and all woman. She was tall, slender, with thick, dark masses of curls about her face and neck and shoulders. Her eyes were taunting and saucy, and yet somehow as young as hell all at the same time, a deep violet gray, gleaming and bold and inviting. Her features were delicately cut, her bottom lip was full, made for kissing or nursing, and Jesus knew he wanted all she could give him. That body was firm, luminous with the faint wisps of daylight in the hot, dark room. She lay across the bed as she lay across his mind, driving him out of his head. With Bonnie, it was as it must have been with early man, finding a naked woman in his cave, and making fires with her long before matches were needed. He took in a deep breath and held it for a long time.

"Yes, I do have to go." He turned his back to her and slipped his arms into his gray flannel shirt. He fixed the string tie into a passable knot and tucked his shirttails into his pants, sucking in his breath. He took up his gunbelt and strapped it around his waist, adjusting it to ride on his hipbone. The rig holding his double-action Colt Model T .44-40 was cross-draw, and he wore it high; everything he did was part of his skill, the result of his learning the hard way. He drew the revolver effortlessly and held it out in front of him, feeling Bonnie's eyes on him.

He forced himself cautiously to inspect this most important tool of his craft. The barrel was cut to five inches and had no front sight, because he'd learned that revolver barrels can catch in open-toed holsters of waxed and heat-hardened leather.

"Like it or not, I got a job to do," he said between gritted teeth. "Whether it makes any sense to you or not. Hell, right now it makes no sense to *me*. But I *am* a lawman. That's all I am. That means I've got to go anywhere they send me, whenever they send me. That means I go if the rain is raining or the sun is shining, or I've got a bed full of the sweetest womanflesh ever clustered in one place in this sad old world.

6

That means I've got to go whether I can make you understand it or not."

"I could show you what really matters."

"I know what really matters, but I can't make a living at it."

She smiled tauntingly. "You get tired too quick."

"The hell. I read somewhere that a girl, no matter how insane she is for it, can't stand up to a man that's a good healthy sex maniac."

"Like you?"

"Like me."

"You're the one with clothes on. Come on, I'll prove I can take it far longer than you can dish it out. I could die trying."

He grinned. "I'll bet you could."

She sighed and lay still as he continued to resist her. He gave the Colt's cylinder a quick, close inspection, satisfied with five cartridges and an empty chamber. He had no intention of accidentally losing a foot, jumping from a horse, wagon, or moving train.

He shoved the Colt into its holster and finished dressing in his vest and frock coat. Into his left vest pocket he placed his Ingersoll watch, after winding it and holding it to his ear from boyhood habit. He left the watch chain dangling. Then he reached under the mattress at the head of the bed and took out a fist-sized, double-barreled .44-caliber derringer with a small brass ring soldered to its butt. He clipped this ring to the loose end of his watch chain and tucked the mean little pistol into his right breast pocket, the chain draping innocently across the flatness of the vest front.

Watching him, Bonnie exhaled heavily. "So you really are going, no matter what I do . . . or what I promise to do?"

He nodded. Positioning his snuff-brown Stetson carefully on his head, tilted slightly forward, cavalry-style, he turned and smiled down at Bonnie. But the naked girl wasn't looking at his face. She was staring at the revealing bulge of fabric at the crotch of his tweed trousers.

"Poor baby," she said. "What a sin, having to go off to work like that."

He bent swiftly and kissed her lightly on the mouth, liking the taste, but moving away before she could entwine those

7

arms about his neck. He let his gaze linger over the beautiful rises and valleys of her body. She writhed slightly, wanting him to look at her, wanting him to like what he saw.

He grinned down at her. "I'll be back to kill you."

She sighed and smiled, nodding. "I'll be waiting here to die," she said.

Longarm turned the corner at Cherokee and Colfax, passing the U.S. Mint on his way to the Federal Building. The high-slung sun tilted slightly westward, glittering in windows and glinting in puddles of standing rain.

He went up the steps and passed people hurrying out to lunch, talking and gesturing as they hurried. At the top of a marble staircase, Longarm paused outside a large oakwood door, gleaming with gilt lettering that read: UNITED STATES MARSHAL, FIRST DISTRICT COURT OF COLORADO.

When Longarm pushed open the door and entered the outer office, he could hear Billy Vail yelling from the inner sanctum. "George! Damn it, George, ain't that son of a bitch showed up yet?"

The red-faced clerk winced, clinging to the newfangled typewriter on his desk as if it were his only security.

Longarm gestured sharply downward toward the lean-shanked clerk, silencing him. The pink-faced junior bureaucrat only nodded, hanging on to the typewriter as Vail's voice rattled the windows. "Goddamn it, George, answer me when I speak to you—whether you know the answer or not. If I waited for you to know anything, I'd never hear from...Goddamn it, George, where are you, and where is that son of a bitch?"

Longarm pushed open the inner office door and leaned lazily against its jamb. "What son of a bitch is that, chief? Any particular son of a bitch you got in mind?"

Vail's head jerked up and his eyes widened slightly. He looked at the deputy marshal, nonplussed for less than the space of a full breath. Billy Vail had sat across too many poker tables at high stakes, stared along the gleaming barrels of too many outlaw guns, lied to many irate politicians, ever to reveal any inner confusion he might have felt.

The marshal half-crouched behind his pinewood desk as if about to pounce, outrage still gleaming in moist residue in the irises of his pouched eyes. At least fifteen years older than Longarm, Billy Vail wore his ill-healed scars like proud badges from long-past violences in memory-dimmed hellspots. He figured he'd ridden all the backtrails at least twice. He resented that he was falling victim to the one foe he could never outwit, outfight, or outlast: age. He resented that because of age only, he had been promoted out of harm's reach, away from the heady excitement of danger and conflict and encounter. He never even wore his gun to the office anymore. All his old enemies were in distant jails or faraway graves somewhere; he had outlived personal peril. Balding, desk-tethered, he was going to lard in belly and jowls, but in his imagination he remained as slim and hard and efficient as Longarm, and arguably faster with a gun. Foes learned that when Billy Vail drew his gun, he meant to use it. Sometimes he worried about Longarm; there was no better lawman, but Longarm had a way of thinking about things, and thought could put a lawman in deadly peril.

Vail's voice rasped like small-bore fire in the austerely government-issue-furnished office. There was no carpeting because Vail's grade didn't rate rugs, but the floors were polished to a high sheen because he had a cleaning budget the auditors expected him to use. He was permitted exactly three chairs— one swivel, one straight, and one red morocco armchair for guests—and two filing cabinets. A single window opened upon a sunstruck slice of the plaza. A 38-star American flag and a banjo wall clock shared wallspace with a map of the western half of the United States and a faded, framed photograph of the President.

"This here goddamn office opens at eight o'clock in the morning, Mr. Custis Long."

"Seems reasonable, gives you and George somewhere to go mornings."

"Don't bray jackass at me, Long. I show up at eight o'clock, I expect my deputies to show up at eight o'clock when they ain't on assignment."

"You must lose a lot of good men that way."

"You like your job, Long?"

"I've had worse."

"Damn right you have. Here we pay you like a goddamn

Persian prince, and give you an expense account so you can rob us blind—"

"You ever eat a ten-cent breakfast, Billy?"

"When I could afford it. You get your steaks. You got it pretty goddam easy, coming in here in the middle of the goddamn afternoon, needing a haircut, but smelling like bay rum or a whorehouse."

"I'm here, Billy."

"Yeah, and look at you. Look at your fly hanging open—"

Longarm grinned crookedly. "My fly's shut tight, Billy."

"But it could be flyin' open, that's the point," Vail said. "You'd screw a mare if you got hard up."

"You ain't tried it, Billy, don't knock it."

"Your screwing is your own business. Your taste in partners is up to you, but not on government time. Is that clear?"

"I think everybody on the floor is pretty clear on that, Billy." Longarm walked over and sank into the leather chair. He tried to bite back a yawn, but could not do it. Billy Vail's face flushed red, watching Longarm admit his fatigue—on government time.

"I got an assignment for you."

"Sure. How else could I earn my princely pay?"

"You know what the pay for most men is right now, Long? Less than two bits a goddamn hour."

"That doesn't include getting shot at, either." Longarm removed a two-for-a-nickel cheroot from his jacket pocket. He bit off the end of it and struck a sulfur match with his thumbnail. He stared across the desk at Vail through the drifting flame. "Mind if I smoke?"

"Filthy habit," Vail grumbled, but he didn't say no.

"I've earned some time off, Billy."

"The hell you say."

"You want to see the gun wound in my side?"

"Hell, no. I've seen gunshot wounds you could stick your fist into. You're startin' to pamper yourself, Long."

"The hell. An inch higher, that bullet could have smashed my ribs and ripped down into my intestines. An inch lower, it could have shattered my hip and crippled me for life. An inch to the right, it would have gutted me—belly and kidneys."

"What the hell, an inch to the left and it'd have missed you clean."

"Think how sick you're going to be with me collecting disability retirement."

"Over my goddamn dead body, you will. Now you listen to me, I'm going to take your word that you ain't up to snuff—even though I know you been out screwin' yourself blind. I got a nice easy little assignment—"

"Those are the most fearful words you could say to me, Billy." Longarm shook his head and sat forward in the chair, aware of the stabbing pain in his side.

"A piece of cake. A Sunday-school social. Hell, it's something even George could handle."

"Let George do it, then."

"You'd hate me for not giving you a paid vacation, Long. Hell, that's what this amounts to. A short ride from Denver. A little look-see. A little fresh air. A little paid vacation, that's all I'm asking."

Longarm held up a callused hand. "Stop. You're scaring hell out of me. The nicer you get, the sicker I get. I been on your little paid vacations before. They're a lot like a one-way trip to hell."

"Somebody's been cutting fence." Billy Vail sat down in his swivel chair, then got up and went to the slash of sunlight at his window.

Longarm shrugged. "Somebody's always cutting fence when his cows get hungry. You know that, Billy."

"This here is government drift fence they're cutting."

"Ridin' fence is for line riders, not a lawman."

Vail grinned at him coldly. "If I say you're a lawman, then by God you're a lawman. If I say you ride line, by damn you're a line rider." The rotund chief came back to his cluttered desk and shuffled some papers. "Hell, old son, this is just an easy ride down south to the Arkansas Divide. How lucky can you get?"

Longarm laughed at him. He blew a ring of smoke and watched it drift slowly toward the ceiling. "I've been on some of these prime vacations you arrange, Billy, and I'll tell you how lucky I've been. I've been lucky to get back alive."

Vail looked as if he might swell up and explode, but he

only shook his head and smiled again, though the smile never reached his eyes. "Now listen, son. This here is no tough assignment. I wouldn't do that to you, and you with a bullet in your side."

Longarm grinned wolfishly and shook his head. "There is just one thing wrong here, Billy, and that's the difference between what you and me call tough assignments."

Longarm realized he was in trouble, that he had spoken the wrong words. Vail nodded, face still flushed. He came around his desk and perched on the side of it, gazing at Longarm, eyes unyielding. "Tough assignments? Hell, I'll tell you about tough assignments. They don't hardly have them anymore, what with this country getting so civilized and people growing softer all the time. I can tell you about a tough assignment. I was caught once by them half-human little runt Paiutes up in the Basin country. Hell, I suffered every pain and indignity a man can suffer and survive. But I survived. We were tough in those days. Hell, once me and Doc Withers had to chop and build and then seal an Alaskan ice hut with melted snow and then crawl inside it to keep from freezing our balls off. We slept with our sled dogs for blankets and hugging each other close like we was newlyweds. Tough assignments! Shit, you don't know the meaning. Hell, I recall me and Doc Withers crossing a desert, taking turns riding the only horse left alive to us. I'd ride three miles, leave the animal tied up, and walk three miles whilst Doc took his turn in the saddle. But we made it, Long. By damn, we made it."

Longarm gazed at him in mock awe. "I'm real inspired, chief. I swear I am. And I'd take this assignment, but the truth is I got a hangnail—"

"Don't you smart-talk me, Custis Long. This here little job has got to be done, and by damn you're going to do it. That's U.S. Government drift fence they're cutting down there. U.S. Property. Just like destroying any other government property, it's against the law."

"What have those folks got against government bobwire?" Longarm inquired in his most innocent tone.

Billy Vail opened his mouth to answer him seriously, then stopped and drew his hand across his mouth.

After a long moment of silence in which Longarm peered

at his red-hot cigar tip as if it held the secrets of the universe, Billy Vail sighed and conceded, "We do have a couple little problems down there."

"I'll bet you have."

"Nothing to grab leather over, Longarm. Little things." When Longarm did not speak, Billy winced faintly and continued as if on a totally new tack.

"You know, the Goodnight-Loving cattle trail runs over the Arkansas Divide, and Texas herds are still moving up into the Wyoming-Montana ranges."

"Thought the Sioux Indian Wars stopped those long drives."

"Well, them feedin' ranges up there is opened up again after the pacification of the Sioux. Indians ain't your problem. Gettin' feeder-cows to graze, that's the problem of the ranchers and the old-time herders. Keepin' them bastards from cuttin' government bobwire is your only problem. It's that simple."

"If it's that simple, why are we in on it?"

"Because we got our goddamn orders to be in on it, that's why. That trail across the Divide is a public right-of-way, and nobody disputes that, and herders are welcome to push their cows along it—"

"Only the cows have grazed out any grass on the trail side of the fence and worn it down to dust and 'dobe," Longarm cut in.

"The public right-of-way is a good two miles wide between the government drift fences. A good two miles. I admit the trail narrows down to little more than a wide road in settled country, like around the settlements of Sun Patch and Dirty Fork. . . ."

"Dirty Fork?"

"Named for the mess some Indians made at a trail crossing when they came on some white people in wagon trains. Dirty Fork is not much of a town anymore, but they do depend a lot on passing herders for any income."

"So the local authorities down there in Dirty Fork and Sun Patch aren't cooperating with the government in trying to stop the bobwire-cutting?"

Vail gazed at the backs of his hands. He nodded. "That's right. Some of them ain't been real cooperative. The government is supposed to collect a modest grazing fee on every head eating public grass inside them fences."

"But they know damn well they can't do it. They know no Texan or anybody else is going to drive his cattle on a barren, dusty trail whilst grass waves green and lush on the other side of a damfool wire fence."

"All right. We concede that much. The government is supposed to collect, but nobody bothers to try to collect on casual grazing of passing cows. At least they never have before. But with the ranges shrinking southeast of Denver on the High Plains and along the Divide, Uncle Sam has had to set aside choice range for future homesteaders and local ranchers that are willing to pay grazing fees—usually no more than about two bits a head."

"Two bits?" Longarm whistled between his teeth. "With a big herd, that can add up to a lot of greenbacks. No wonder they're having trouble collecting from Texans ridin' with bellies stuck to backbones."

Vail shook his head. "Ain't the collecting that's worrying the government, Longarm. You ain't been listening. Like I say, there ain't no way to collect from drovers passing through on open range. That's why the Interior Department has strung bobwire fences west of and parallel to the Goodnight-Loving Trail. Hell, it had to be done if there was to be any decent public lands left. Passing cows are welcome to eat grass east of the fence."

"Only there ain't nothing but dry stubble on the trail side of that bobwire." Longarm shook his head, totally out of agreement with Interior Department policy.

"Damn it, Longarm, you ain't a loyal government employee, that's your trouble. How trail drovers feed their cattle ain't our problem here. Protecting government property is our problem."

"Bobwire fences."

"In this here instance, yes. Bobwire that protects government-owned lands."

"All I've got to do is stop Texas drovers from cutting fence when the only grass on a dry, dead trail is *west* of that fence, where grass is greening up and lush? Come on, Billy, what would you do if you were a Texas trail boss who already hates them damyankee bureaucrats up in Washington anyway?" He shook his head. "Right. You'd do just what they're doing. You'd cut fence."

"Maybe. Maybe I would," Billy Vail conceded after a moment. "But there's more to it than that."

"The story of my life." Longarm shook his head wearily.

"Them cuts made by passing drovers cause one hell of a lot more trouble than the Texans can be made to understand. Hell, nobody's begrudging the stolen grass. And Interior can afford to restring bobwire fences as long as the Glidden people keep turning it out by the running foot. Them drovers cut where they move in and they cut again when they finally move out on the trail again."

"What's wrong with Interior Department riders?"

"You mean them range inspectors?" Vail snorted derisively. "They don't have no real power to stop a man takin' a crap on government lands."

"But I can stop them?"

"I expect you to—with a modicum of trouble. You see, Longarm, the big bad trouble ain't the cuttin' of drift fences— goin' in or comin' out."

"I figured it was more than that—a *modicum* more," Longarm said.

Vail nodded. "The big pain is the growling and yelling of the legitimate local ranchers that *do* graze their cows on government land—with a permit. These legitimate ranchers have come to depend on the drift fence to keep their cows where they expect to find them, come roundup. They figure that's part of what they pay Uncle Sam for—to keep the cows on the graze. And you know very well, Long, a settled local businessman that pays for his permit to graze his stock is going to resent furriners passing through and fattening beef on grass that the local rancher has bought and paid for, plus cutting bobwire so the rancher's cows stray."

Longarm stuck his tongue in his cheek. "I see. It gets more interesting by the minute, Billy. All I got to do is head off a fence war between ranchers and trail drovers?"

"It won't be that bad, Long. Hell, you'll work with the sheriff at Dirty Fork. A Virginia gentleman and former town-tamer named Lawson Carr."

"I've heard the name. If Lawson Carr is sheriff down there, why don't he stop the wire-cutting and the trouble with the drovers?"

"Carr's doing all he can. He's a good man. But he can't enforce an unpopular law down there, especially not right now."

"What's wrong with right now?"

"Well, Longarm, it's election year. I mean a sheriff is a local politician first, I don't care how good a man he is."

"Sure. I see. You don't get any local cooperation because local authorities don't want to make the good ol' boys who control all the votes mad in an election year."

Vail exhaled heavily. "Well, I can see how the moccasin pinches Carr's foot. He is up for reelection. Even if he's the best sheriff in Colorado history, he ain't going to be much good if he ain't reelected."

"What you're saying is I can't expect any cooperation from Carr?"

Vail swung his arm at an invisible adversary. "No, dammit, I ain't saying nothing of the kind. You'll get every cooperation from Sheriff Lawson Carr. Within reason. I ain't saying that at all. I ain't even saying there *is* any big trouble between drovers and local ranchers."

"You just want it stopped before it explodes."

"It ain't that bad. You got authority where Interior's range inspectors don't. You can *act*, election or no election. I've got some warrants here that you can fill in and serve."

"On who?"

"Hell, how do I know? Anybody who spits on the sidewalk. You don't like the part in a man's hair. If he talks back to you. Hell, even if by chance you happen to catch somebody red-handed, cuttin' some Glidden wire, you might even cite *him*. I don't have to tell you your job, Longarm. We just don't want any trouble exploding down there in an election year. You may run into a few muleheads. Knock some sense into them. Hell, sometimes trouble in a place like this is nothing more than politics. Why, the Lincoln County War was Republicans against Democrats, Catholics against Protestants, for God's sake."

"I was there," Longarm reminded him.

"I know you was there. And I know you know how these things start and how they get out of hand. Hell, there wouldn't likely be a Colorado if them Protestants hadn't gotten themselves run out of the Midwest. Texicans called themselves rebels, but the truth was most of them was Irish Catholics, and Austin got his land grants from Mexico because the Mexicans figured that Irish-Catholic Texas would be a buffer between them and the Comanche–United States threat. Austin *was* a Catholic, but he still turned against the Mexicans. All I'm saying is that we got a little wire-cutting that can be nipped in the bud before it *does* flare into something big that nobody can handle without bloodshed. All I want you to do is to ride down there and spread the gospel. They're destroying government property, and that shit has got to stop."

Longarm had a quivering hard-on by the time he got back to his room in the hotel.

Breathing raggedly, he went along the corridor, put the key in the lock, and opened the door. A sigh of relief rolled out of him, from deep inside his taut chest.

Bonnie lay where he'd left her, and still naked. She had kicked off the twisted sheet, and perspiration lay in a glittering sheen over her breasts and rounded little belly and along those shapely legs. Her rich, dark hair was damp with perspiration too. Her thighs were parted slightly, topped with a fringe of dainty brown hair. His breath caught sharply because Bonnie looked as if she'd used her fingers pleasuring herself while she mentally relived all the excitement that had raged between them through the long night and most of the morning.

Her eyes were glazed with need and warmth and invitation. She licked her tongue across her full lips. "I thought you'd never come back," she whispered.

"You knew I'd come back," he said. He let his eyes graze over her lustrous body.

Her smile had all the confidence of a young girl whose knowledge of men is old as femininity. "I didn't believe you'd leave."

"I had to," Longarm said. "But I'm back now. I yelled back at old Billy until he agreed I could start my new assignment in the morning. Eight o'clock in the morning is what he said, but I wasn't listening too good. I was thinking about you, lying here in my bed. We've got one night to make up for all we've lost and all we may never have again."

Suddenly, Longarm was aware that Bonnie was studying him as closely as he studied her, except that her large, luminous eyes were fixed on his face. A faint pull of tension bubbled for an instant between her brows. She sighed.

"I've been lying here wondering what sort of girl you think I am," she said. "Do you think maybe you just told me?" Somewhat defiantly she said, "One night and goodbye."

He smiled down at her. "One *more* night, Bonnie. That's the magic word. One more night. I can tell you, Bonnie, what I think of you. You're as real and honest as a girl can grow up in this country. If you think I respect you less because of what we've been doing—and what we're going to do again— you're wrong. Maybe you're talking serious, about something lasting. That can't be. But not because of what you are, or what you are not, or what I might think you are. It's me. I wouldn't saddle the sharpest-tongued shrew in this world with marriage to me—or to any other lawman. You're too good for that kind of life, Bonnie, and be thankful I can think straight enough, with all that nakedness staring back up at me, to tell you true."

Bonnie sighed and smiled up at him. "Well, nobody can say you're not honest, Longarm. A woman takes you for what you are—while she can—and that's the way it is, eh?"

Longarm sighed. He did not smile. "If she's lucky," he said. "You think for one damn moment I won't sit by a hundred lonely campfires and see your face and your body in the flames? You think I won't lie alone—wherever I am—and wish you were pushed up close and snug to me? But that's what marriage to me would be, Bonnie. You lyin' alone in a bed, waitin', and me lyin' alone somewhere, wishing for you. That makes one hell of a marriage in my book." He shook his head and dropped the subject. "You hungry?"

Bonnie started to nod, then changed her mind, shook her head, the rich curls tousled on the white pillow. "Maybe later. Maybe a big sirloin steak."

He jerked off his string tie. "You got it." She lay and watched him remove his jacket, vest, and gunbelt.

She said, "Somebody knocked at your door a few times today. I let them knock."

"Man or woman?"

"How could I tell?"

"By the knock. You'd make one hell of a lawman."

"I don't want to be a lawman." She writhed on the bed. "I want to be just what I am."

The tone of her voice, the heat of her words, the light glowing deep in those eyes, struck Longarm like a fist in the belly. He felt his erection harden painfully. He could not remember when he'd ever wanted a girl so much—or so often. He forced himself to take a deep breath and exhale it fully, trying to calm himself.

He walked away from her, moving awkwardly because of the tightness of his tweed pants on his swollen staff. He heard her light, curious laughter behind him. He opened a bottle of rye. "You want a drink?"

"Do you need one?" she asked.

He exhaled. "I don't know. I came rushing back here to you. You weren't off my mind a total of five seconds while I was gone. When I was able to think anything, it was what I wanted to do to you, what I wanted you to do to me."

"You were reading my mind."

"I was driving myself insane. I came rushing in here, ready to leap at you. Now, when I look at you, I get the feeling I ought to slow down."

"Why?"

"For all those curves." He poured rye in two glasses, added water. He brought the glass to her. She put out her bare arm, but instead of taking the glass, she closed her fist on him at the fly and worked her fingers back and forth, stroking him. "Oh, my God," he whispered. He tossed off the drink in his left hand.

Bonnie took the drink in her free hand and sipped at it. He tossed his own glass behind him, hearing it strike the carpeting and roll along the floor. He watched Bonnie drain her glass and then he jerked at the buttons of his shirt.

"No," Bonnie whispered. "Come here, Longarm. Let me undress you." She got up on her knees on the bed, as unself-conscious in her nakedness as a young doe, and as lovely as

19

sin itself. Her breasts stood high, the nipples like bright cherries, rigid on the golden mounds. She fumbled for a moment with the buttons of his shirt, but quickly got the hang of it. Longarm shook free of the shirt and it fell to the floor. Bonnie was already loosening his belt and unbuttoning the buttons of his fly.

Somehow he managed to rid himself of his stovepipe boots without getting out of her arm's reach; she undid the buttons of his balbriggan longjohns and then peeled the garment from him as if she were skinning a banana. His rigidity rose to her view and she caught it in both her hands.

He sank to the bed with her, closing the last space between them; nothing separated them now. Her heated body was pressed tight against his and she fought to be closer. Her hands moved lightly across Longarm's face and throat and shoulders. She closed her arms about his neck and forced his face into the deep valley between her fragrant breasts.

Longarm's breath raged across his lips. She was kissing him, but he was aware of nothing except her breasts and her cherry-red nipples. That naked thrust of breast haunted him and he pressed his face into its resilient firmness, taking one of those bright nipples in his mouth, sucking at it thirstily.

She whimpered, crying out her delight. Her hands closed on his head, dragging him down harder upon her crushed breast. His tongue licked at its sweetness and the nipple hardened, as if it were a fruit bursting with succulence, rigid on his tongue. As he sucked, she screamed a little in sweet agony.

For a long time she held him there, nursing at her breast. Her hands moved on him in frantic pleasure. She kept moaning. "Harder. Oh God, Longarm, suck it harder. Hold them tighter. Tighter."

"I don't . . . want . . . to hurt you," he managed to whisper.

"Oh God, I want you to hurt me! I want you to eat me! Do it! Oh, do it before I die of need."

Still suckling at her, he heard her frantic breathing loud in his ear and burning his neck. When he lifted his head for a moment from her swollen mammary, he found her face flushed as red as her nipples, her eyes closed tautly and her mouth parted. She lay with her head pushed back. He moved his hand over the rise of her fevered femininity and down between her legs into her hot liquidity.

"Oh God," she whispered. "I hope you want me as badly as I want you."

He tried to laugh. "I want you bad, all right."

"Oh, that's nice," she whispered. She stirred against him. "Oh, that's so nice."

He pushed her under him and she lay with her knees bent and legs parted, watching him with sleepy intensity. He leaned down over her. Her arms came up and she pulled his head down. She parted her mouth wide when their lips met. He could feel the paroxyms of passion shuddering through her body like the tremors of an earthquake.

He lowered his body to hers and kissed her parted mouth and pressed her under him into the mattress. He drove himself into her and she gasped and crossed her ankles at the small of his back, locking him to her. She was panting wildly and her breath was hot and sweet against his bare flesh. Her hands reached for him, fondling him. Their bodies thrust and welded together as if they were truly one body, total and complete in that moment.

His tongue probed past hers, deep into her mouth. Her lips crushed together. Her slender arms chained him and drew him closer, her nails digging into his back.

He lay still upon her for one sweetly agonized moment, savoring the sweetness and the wonder of what they had together. Under him, she writhed helplessly. Her breasts rose and fell with her breathing and her urgent upthrusting, like ripe fruit precariously perched upon the soft peach-freshness of her nakedness.

She moved beneath him, thrusting and driving and holding herself up to him. It was as if everything were driven from her mind in this moment except the pleasure he brought her and the delight she afforded him in return. He heard her faint whispering, words she'd never learned at her mother's knee, an exciting and excited sound of aching enchantment.

"Please do it. Make me do it. Now. Now." She could not wait any longer. Tremors shook her whole body. Her fingers dug into him and her legs tightened like twin boa constrictors at his waist. He was afraid his bullet wound was going to be ripped open, but he suddenly didn't give a damn. What a hell of a way to die. She shuddered helplessly, completely enslaved by her passions, spinning out of control.

She went limp under him at last, totally exhausted, filled with delight and pleasurable fatigue that left her trembling. "Did you . . . like it?" she whispered. Her voice was throaty with her weariness.

"Couldn't you tell?"

She laughed, a low, lazy sound. "I could tell."

After a long time he heard her sleepy whisper: "Do you really have to leave me?"

"Not until morning."

"Do you suppose we can do it fourteen times by morning?"

"I don't know. Why?"

"Because that's what I want to be able to remember when you're gone and I'm at choir practice tomorrow night."

"Choir practice? You never told me you sang in the choir."

"You never asked." She smiled, kissing along his throat. "Just as you never asked my last name. . . . " She touched at his lips with her fingertips in a butterfly caress. "And I'll bet you didn't know I teach school—the third grade."

"You! A school marm? The Good Lord help us. . . . Too bad you can't teach your pupils the truth."

"The truth? What truth?"

"About sex. Teach them that killing and cheating and lying and stealing and raping are dirty and obscene and evil, and that sex is beautiful—that sex was the very best gift God could think of to lay on men and women, and that they messed it up, they made something dirty of it in their own minds."

She smiled, kissing him lightly. "You know I could never teach that."

"Why not?"

"Why not?" She reached down and caught him in her hand, holding him tightly. "What little boy would want to grow up to be a soldier? Or a politician? How'd nations make war if kids knew the truth about what really matters in this old world? Why, I could never teach things like that! Who'd build the bridges, or cheat the widows . . . or run for President?"

Longarm laughed, drawing her to him. "Who'd have the energy?"

Chapter 2

Longarm swung down from the Diamond K supply wagon. He gave the driver a little grin and half-salute of gratitude for the hitch from the depot in downtown Denver. The air was crisp and cold, too cold for the last of April and too crisp to be borne in a frock coat. He pursed his lips, blew out, and watched his breath smoke thickly in the rising breeze.

He glanced around at the big spread just south of Denver. Once it had seemed a long ride from downtown, but now there were already signs of civilization crowding in upon the great old ranch. Everything looked about the same. He was so accustomed to the Government-licensed remount and supply stop that he was barely aware of changes—if any—in the cow farm. Smoke boiled from the stone chimney of the ranch house and from the tin stacks at the bunkhouse and cookshack, adding to the sense of chill. The cold caused steam to rise from fresh horse apples just dropped. Beyond the corral, half-wild cows grazed in what looked like endless grass hemmed in only by a high blue dome of sky, dark blue hills, and faint violet peaks almost lost in the blue haze of distance.

He shifted his jacket up on his shoulders, the biting morning cold making him aware of sore muscles in his hips and along the backs of his legs; little Bonnie Brown last night had called muscles into play that he'd forgotten he had. But he was conscious enough of them today. It was going to be a while before he got Bonnie out of his system, for more reasons than that she was one of the best pieces of tail he'd ever bedded. He shook his head. He had to get Bonnie out of his mind. That girl could be habit-forming, like opium.

He sighed in regret and the residue of fatigue. He walked through ice-crusted puddles toward the barn. Suddenly a rau-

23

cous voice halted him in midstep, like a barb-strung snubbing rope.

Longarm glanced around in the chilled sunlight. The cattle pens, the corrals, the barns, the smithy were places of activity, every man on the place laboring diligently because this was a working ranch. Before he checked, Longarm already knew what pack of coyotes were not engaged in any physical activity more strenuous than jaw-clapping: the horse herders. These men were a breed apart. They worked hard when there was horse-cutting, roping, breaking, or hunting to be done. Otherwise they lazed around, holding themselves above the common labors of a ranch.

He even recognized the voice before he found its owner. Nate Dunaway's grating baritone was loud and sharp and rasping. He was used to yelling in high winds and lonely places; he was used to making himself heard. "Hey, Marshal Shortarm! Hold up there!"

Turning, Longarm set himself and watched Nate Dunaway and three of his elite pals waddling toward him like camels in deep sand. The four men were not alike, and yet they shared a number of traits in common: bowed legs, saddlesores and callused inner thighs.

"Hello, Nate," Longarm said without enthusiasm. Dunaway was taller than his cohorts, not as tall as Longarm but outweighing the marshal by at least forty pounds. Longarm doubted there was an ounce of fat on Nate's scarred and battered body; gentling horses kept him as hard as iron and gristletough. Nate was an ugly fellow with a close-cropped salt-and-pepper mustache and beard, hair stringing from under the sweatband of his battered Stetson, his nose broken and slightly askew, his narrow eyes seemingly set just off true. Longarm admitted it wasn't fair for him to judge Nate; but he disliked him cordially.

"Well, goddamn, Marshal Shortarm, if you ain't a sore for sighted eyes. What the hell you doin' this far from downtown Denver?"

Shrugging, Longarm removed the government chits from his pocket and handed them to the foreman. "Looking for a decent mount that won't fall dead before I ride him off the property—and possibles, if you got 'em."

24

"Oh, we got 'em." Nate checked the requisitions.

Longarm laughed at him. "Don't waste our time trying to pretend you can read, Nate. Just get me a horse and a sheepskin jacket and wooly chaps—it sure hell ain't spring yet."

Nate laughed cuttingly. "You just got pisswater for blood, Marshal Shortarm. You fellows know Marshal Custis Long, don't you? Sure, ever'body knows the marshal. I reckon it won't be long before ol' Ned Buntline hisself starts writin' books about the marshal here. Books like them fairy stories ol' Ned writes about Bill Cody. Jesus! I read in one of them books how the Indians called Cody 'Buffalo Bill.' The hell they did! They called him White Man Who Jacks Off Behind Choke-berry Bush." Nate raged with laughter.

Longarm kept his voice gentle. "You want to get those supplies for me, Nate, or you want me to take 'em out of your nose?"

Nate's curiously offset little eyes glittered. "I'd like that, Marshal. I'd sure like you to try that."

"You got it, uglier-than-me. Just keep pushing me."

Nate glanced at his grinning pals and laughed in that loud braying way he had. "Hell, just having a little joke, Marshal, that's all. What's the matter, Mr Shortarm? Is a man who makes a hundred green ones a month, like you, too important to take a little joke?"

"No, I came all the way out here just to listen to you bray, Nate."

But Nate wasn't through with the unfair inequity between his pay and Longarm's. He said, "Is it true, Shortarm, that the government pays you one hundred dollars a month for what you do? Just what *do* you do for that much money, Marshal, except kiss asses in high places?"

"What the hell, Nate, they pay you forty and found every month for doing this. Hard to find a man that can do my job, but anybody can bray like a jackass."

"Shit, man. You're right, it burns my tail that you make almost three times as much a month as I do. And for what? God knows, I have to work for my money. I don't priss around telling people to bring me a horse all saddled up and supplied. Hell no, I work for every goddamn penny I get."

Longarm shrugged. "Not my fault I got brains in my head and you got 'em in your ass, Nate."

"I never seen you do one fucking thing to earn the high pay you get. And a goddamn pension in twenty years. Ain't that right, Marshal?"

Longarm exhaled. "I'd like to stand around trading shit with you, Nate, but I'm in a hurry."

"In a hurry? To do what? Ride around and slap somebody on the wrist for stealing government property? Man, you do have one important job. You run errands for the bigwigs from Washington too, don't you, Shortarm? Hell, you must do *something*."

"Any kind of horse will do, Nate. Just so he'll get me past the sound of your voice."

Nate's taunting voice rode hard and rough over Longarm's. "You guard people too, don't you? Bigwigs? Hey, Summertime, how'd you like to know your life depended on this here critter and that play-toy on his hip?"

The coyote-thin horse herder called Summertime shrugged and grinned.

Nate persisted. "Tell me, Marshal, is it true that the President is coming out here to Denver this summer, electioneering?"

"I don't know, Nate."

"You don't know? A hundred-buck-a-month government man, and you don't know?"

Longarm tilted his shoulders in his jacket. "Hell, even if I knew, Nate, I'd never tell you a thing like that ahead of time."

Nate stopped smiling. "Why in hell not, Shortarm?"

Longarm shrugged again, giving Nate a briar-eating grin. "Security, Nate."

"Security?" Nate's voice rose, breaking. "You saying I'm maybe a security threat to our great President?"

"Your mouth, Nate. Your mouth is."

The three horse herders laughed, jostling Nate. The big man had to swallow back the bile that gorged up in his throat. He checked the government chits, and handed two of them to Summertime. "You and Slick get the great man here his sheeplined jacket and wool chaps and whatever else in hell he needs from supply. Cotton and me'll cut him out a gentle ol' mare that won't run out from under him."

Nate caught Cotton's arm and jerked his head toward the corral. Longarm sighed heavily. He knew what was ahead; he knew how Nate's small-bore brain worked. Nate truly resented the salary Longarm was paid by the government. It was like a burr under his saddle blanket. He couldn't get it out of his mind.

When Nate yelled his name, Longarm walked out to the corral. He knew for sure what was up when he saw the way Nate and Cotton held the dappled mustang's head snubbed down between its trembling forepaws. Longarm shrugged and tossed away his cheroot. What the hell, it was something that he had to get over with. He had to prove himself all the time; it went with the job, like the bullet wound pulsing in his side.

He took the bridle from Cotton, who was at least honest enough that he couldn't look the deputy marshal in the face.

Longarm shoved his left foot into the stirrup and half-threw himself into the saddle, fighting his boot toe into the right stirrup. Yelling, Nate released the bit ring and lunged toward the fence, scrambling up it.

Cotton climbed the fence too, getting out of harm's way. By now, word had spread and all work had ceased on the Diamond K. Men came running from all directions.

The quivering mustang jerked up his head and leaped toward the far orange ball of the sun. He came down hard, stiff-legged, and bounced all the way across the chewed-up corral. Men on the fence yelled. "Ride 'im, Marshal! Ride the son of a bitch!"

Longarm gathered up every inch of slack in the reins to twist the pony's head in close to his chest. He kept pulling on the line with all his strength. He hated cutting this horse's mouth, but it was hurt the animal, or get hurt himself.

The animal squealed in pain and indignity, sunfishing, side-stepping, and crow-hopping around the corral. Because Longarm held his head twisted in against his chest, there was only one way the mustang could buck—in a closing circle. The bit, cutting harder and harder into the horse's sensitive mouth, slowed the animal, discouraged him, got him to thinking.

Mindless with rage, the bronc pitched and yawed, circling as it bucked. Then, when the hated weight stayed on his back

27

and the bit cut at his mouth, the horse dashed against the corral railings, trying to scrape the rider off when he couldn't buck him loose.

But Longarm was ahead of him on this move too. He figured if you couldn't outthink a stupid, half-wild pony, you deserved to get hurt. He saw that the beast intended to rake his leg off, but he kicked free of the right stirrup and yanked his leg out of the way. He wavered there a moment without the security of stirrups. As the enraged dapple gray lunged sideways toward the left corral fence, Longarm gave fearful yanks on the cruel bit.

The mustang squealed, trying to lift its head enough to shake away the pain, and finding himself unable to do it. As the mindless horse barreled toward the rails, Longarm lunged free. Most of the spectators clapped, whistled, and shouted approval.

Panting, Longarm stood for a moment, watching the gallant little mustang circling the corral in a frenzy. Then Longarm turned, went to the corral gate, let himself out, and closed the bars behind him.

Men called to him, congratulating him. Longarm nodded toward the sounds, barely hearing them. He felt the same rage the mustang did, only his hatred centered on Nate Dunaway. He crossed the saffron sunlight toward where the grinning foreman stood.

"You got me a decent mount, yet, Nate?" His voice shook with anger.

Nate laughed at him. "Come on, Marshal. Just a little joke, that's all. Hell, nothing personal. I just wanted to see you do something to earn that hundred a month, that's all."

Longarm met the man's lopsided eyes levelly. He forced himself to grin, teeth gritted. "That's all right, Nate. Nothing personal." He brushed at imaginary straw on the foreman's boulder-thick shoulder. "I just want to be sure you earn your pay too."

He drove his fist straight into Dunaway's much-broken nose. The big man's eyes glazed over, and he said nothing.

Nate went on standing there for some moments as if bemused, gazing into the middle distance, placid and firm on his wide-set, stocky legs. Silence struck the ranchyard as everybody stared at him, waiting for the explosion. Then Nate's knees buckled and he caved in, pitching foward on his face. The stunned cowpokes waited with bated breath. He did not move.

The sheep-lined jacket felt good, and Longarm buttoned it to his throat. The slicing wind struck the wool chaps and whined away without cutting through them. He rode slowly, pleasantly warm and thinking about Bonnie, her thighs and mouth and hands; he felt as comfortable as a mountain goat and twice as horny.

Wind whipped in under the forward-tilted, flat crown of his hat. Longarm's face was seared with windburn before he'd ridden five miles south through the high-country pinyon forests, following the cattle trails and Cherry Creek south as far as he could.

It was a long day in the saddle, and he met few people. Those he met held guns in their laps and hurried their horses past, or grinned and waved and called out, "Nice spring day we're havin', ain't it?"

Longarm nodded and smiled and silently disagreed. He couldn't say why, but there was something in this penny-bright day that troubled him. He was a little surprised that native Coloradans didn't notice something amiss. Then it occurred to him that there were damn few native Coloradans around, unless they were reconstructed South Cheyenne or Arapaho. All these people—wheat farmers on their dry farms, cattlemen, nesters, and even lawmen like him—had one thing in common: they were all newcomers.

They were all pilgrims, and damned few of them knew what Colorado could do to a man and his dreams and his flesh and bones. Most of them, even Bill Cody and Wild Bill Hickok,had come off Midwest farms. The Earp family, like Longarm, had trekked out from West Virginia. When the North defeated the Confederacy, a lot of Southerners like Big John Chisum had emigrated to the West, cows and all, running away from ruin and defeat into a strange and terrible land. Even the feared gunslick Billy the Kid was a New Yorker. The first generation born and reared on the High Plains were still children. Texas and California and the far Northwest Coast had been settled before the Civil War, but the Great American Desert, between the High Sierras and Missouri, was carefully avoided by all thinking men—except the Mormons, of course, a driven people without any options. Nobody but emigrants with broken-down wagons stopped in the wild, broken country until the late sixties. A cattle boom was in the making on the High Plains, and dry-land farming was killing the open ranges, along with barbed wire and winter wheat, but it remained a raw new land of strangers.

He watched a fat tumbleweed cross his path and grinned faintly. Hell, even the tumbleweed was a newcomer. Sure, there were other weeds that tumbled in high winds, but Russian thistle had come in with the homesteaders, its seeds stowaways in the Turkey Red wheat and other European grains the immigrants planted.

He exhaled heavily. So maybe it wasn't so strange that nobody else sensed the doom in the cold, crackling, silent atmosphere. But his own feeling of impending wrong deepened as he moved south and east toward the humplands of the Arkansas Divide. He left Cherry Creek, the last water channel running north toward the Platte; the rest of the tributaries ran south into the Arkansas River and on into the Panhandle: Horse Creek, Pond Creek, Adobe Creek, Big Sandy. The country reared in upheaval here, dividing East and West.

Longarm glanced toward the silvered sun and the high, cloudless sky. He felt the wind shifting and he shivered slightly under his sheep-lined jacket, feeling a chill that had nothing to do with the cold.

He rode out of the dense forests of dark pines, where silvery trunks of tall aspens glittered among thick-chested evergreens, and came out upon the broken upthrusts of open prairie. Lofty peaks and the shadowed planes and gaps of the Rampart Range receded in the distance. He saw all the signs laid down as spring hurried north across the Divide, strewing lupine, blue asters, paintbrush, and sand lilies on knobby hills and along winding traces and ill-defined roadbeds. On these immense plains, trees grew only in the beds of dry washes, or in the crooks of stifled creeks. Long meadows of buffalo grass and grama stretched in swells and rises in unbroken tans, greening faintly with tattings and lacings of thin-stemmed daisies and sunflowers, and the winking nipples of wild strawberries. Mule deer darted like terrified shadows in open glades, feeding on clumps of wheatgrass and sage and rose of Sharon, and sniffing for precious water in the shallow water tables. In this early-spring season, the memory of snow masses clung to dark rills and rocks and shale outcroppings and rimrock cuts. The farthest green-and-tan slopes crept timidly upward to pine-covered high pasture and mountain promontory.

He moved deeper into the sage flats and rolling hills, where the country was changeless, like the swells of an open sea. A man easily lost his direction in scrubby ranges unfit even for sheep, on slopes broken with soapstone that the Indians used in making their pipes and pottery. Even on these open ranges, the land was tortured and broken and twisted by some long-forgotten upheaval. Short, deep canyons writhed through deep, red-rock outcroppings in pine-fringed foothills.

He sighed, gritting his teeth against the blaze of chilled sunlight. The only land more godforsaken was the Kansas country east of him. No wonder pilgrims took one look, shuddered, and kept going, or, if they were smart enough and strong enough, turned back.

He braced himself against the rising slash and cut of chilled wind across the open prairie—winds out of the north that old-timers said had started blowing the morning the earth was born and were blowing yet, eroding mesas and cliffs and sagebrush flats.

Out of the north? He drew rein, stopping the horse on a slight rise where buffalo grass whipped the animal's withers. Out of the north? This time of the year? That didn't make sense. Since he'd come out of the high forests, the wind had shifted to the north. That was crazy, because the usual south-to-westerly breezes were all that made life bearable as they warmed the High Plains even in earliest spring.

He gazed about him in the terrible stillness. There was an inescapable sense of something amiss in this strange change of weather that went beyond the numbing cold. Silence stretched thin and taut, fragile as icicles, a silence that seemed to be waiting tensely in the static atmosphere, where even the air crackled with electric charges. And yet that sky remained unchanged and unchanging, cloudless and an uncanny, nearly unreal blue.

He felt the horse quiver under him. He sniffed the air. He could almost swear there was a twister coming, only that didn't make sense either, on a clear day like this. Sure, spring was twister season, but there was a total absence of twister signs as far as he could tell; there were no thunderheads and none of the scary, brassy smell characteristic of approaching twisters.

He urged the roan forward, moving downslope, unconsciously shrugging the collar of the sheep-lined jacket higher on the nape of his goosepimpled neck. Another thing that bothered him was how totally, incredibly, and absolutely alone he was on this rolling, unbroken prairie. He'd not seen so much as a gopher or jackrabbit for the past hour. He may have passed sod huts unknowingly, because unless the farmer had the money and energy to erect a sunflower windmill, you could ride past a soddy and mistake it for just another mound in the grass-covered open plain.

He shook his head. This time of year the migratory birds—wild geese, whooping cranes, and curlews—ought to be heading north on a crisp spring day like this, too. Only they weren't. The skies were as empty as the prairie. Not even a solitary vulture soared on wind drafts, and even the normally numerous flocks of passenger pigeons were conspicuous by their absence. When he found a big snow-white arctic owl perched on an abandoned and petrified whiffletree, his sense of isolation and terrible wrong intensified.

He kneed the horse, suddenly wanting to find shelter. By his calculations he should be coming in on Sun Patch or Dirty Fork, or some sign of civilization, but he had a feeling of being stranded in a sea of grass, with a storm crackling somwhere unseen around him, and that damned winking owl staring holes in the back of his neck.

The sound of gunfire erupted in the taut stillness, as startling as lightning in a cloudless day.

The bullet buzzed past him. The slug was wide, but by less than a foot. It parted the wind next to his head and flew off into the cold air.

At first, stunned, he didn't know where the shot had come from. He dove forward, putting his head into the roan's mane at the crack of the rifle. He clung there, shivering for a moment. All he could think was that Nate Dunaway had trailed him down here. It was the insane, stupid kind of thing Nate would do.

He waited, but there was no second shot.

He slid slowly from his saddle, unsheathing his Winchester and pressing close against the chest of the roan. The animal still quivered, spooked. It was one hell of an upsetting sound, gunfire in that strange and eternal and silent emptiness.

Chapter 3

After the first bright, burning blaze of rage, Longarm calmed down slightly. He stood in the calf-killing cold, peering cautiously, trying to find the bushwhacker.

He moved cautiously, not wanting to alarm the sniper before he even found him in the open plain. The echo of the gunshot died away and there was nothing except silence and cold. Longarm's hand felt numb on the icy rifle stock.

He saw movement next to a gray outcropping topped by scraggly serviceberry bushes. Keeping the horse's body between him and the mound, Longarm called "Come on out of there, or I'll shoot ever berry off that bush and its roots out of the ground."

"Hold it, mister. Don't shoot me." The voice belonged to a woman, there was no doubt about that.

"Come on out of there," Longarm said, "and keep your gun in front of you where I can see it."

"All right. All right."

The girl came timidly around the mound, holding a rifle in front of her. A small horse followed, almost like a dog at her heels. "What do you want?" she said. There was no friendliness in her face, only a trace of fear in her eyes, and no other word of greeting.

"What do I want? What in the hell do you want?" Longarm asked in reply.

"I asked you first," said the sullen voice. The girl came slowly across the rough ground. At first Longarm watched her warily, and then with shock. She wasn't big, not more than five-three, but she had all the attributes that she would ever get—or need—to carry her from girlhood into womanhood,

34

and she was far more bountifully blessed than most other females at any age.

Despite the cold, she wore a denim shirt opened at the
collar, and a pair of much-washed and faded Levi's that she
seemed to be growing out of at that moment. Over her shirt
she wore an old cardigan sweater of wool, but it was ragged,
with a pocket hanging loose, and like her shirt, it was unbuttoned. Her blossoming body challenged the aged fabric of her
hand-me-downs in every direction and every way known to
nature. He tried to keep his eyes away, but his gaze kept
returning to the taut fullness at her bosom; it was clear she had
on nothing under that strained and aging garment, and that she
was totally unconcerned.

She wore no hat, but subdued her dark blond hair with an
Indian band of plaited leather with little daisies and bright
fireweed entwined in it. Her hair could have used a washing,
but even untended it was rich and thick and had a natural wave
almost to her shoulders.

She stopped a little way from him, on the brink of the worn
trail. She stared at him, unblinking, from eyes about the same
golden brown as her hair, and upturned slightly at the corners
under soft lashes, but glittering with a wary expression of
smoldering defiance. Yet, despite her sullen manner, there was
something almost shy about her, as most deep-country girls
were shy. Her dust-streaked face was a little too thin and her
downturned lips too full for beauty, but she was beautiful, all
right. Longarm met her go-to-hell gaze and wondered if she
had any idea how damned beautiful she was.

She stared up at him. "I asked you, mister. What do you
want?"

Her cold insolence enraged him anew. "You crazy little
bitch," he said. "What do you mean, what do *I* want? What
do *you* want? Why in hell were you shooting at me?"

The girl gasped, shaking her head. The shock that widened
those brown eyes was nothing that could be faked. She started
to speak, but could find no words. She shook her head and
kept shaking it. "Oh, Lord," she whispered at last. "I didn't
shoot at you, mister."

"You're the only one I see with a gun around here. Somebody shot at me."

Her mouth twisted. A look of hatred flared in her eyes, directed not toward Longarm but at herself, at the rifle in her hands, at her own stupidity.

She shook her head. "I . . . wasn't shooting at you, mister. Honest."

"You came close enough."

"Why . . . I didn't come close at all." She winced and waved her arm. "I was shooting at *him*."

Longarm followed the direction of her gesture and he stared, incredulous and doubtful, at a scarecrow flapping its empty coatsleeves amiably in the icy breeze. He went on gazing, amazed. There was nothing amazing about the scarecrow, but Longarm was astonished; the stick figure stood in a cornfield that was newly planted at a forty-five-degree angle from where they stood on the narrow trace through the grama grass.

He brought his gaze accusingly back to her face. "Nobody could miss that far."

"I did." She bit her lip. "I shouldn't have shot," she admitted after a moment, "but I didn't see you in the way."

Longarm laughed in spite of himself. "I wasn't in the way. I was almost behind you."

"I was practicing shooting at old man Estabrook—"

"Old man Estabrook?"

She almost permitted her lips to pull into a smile. "That's what I call the scarecrow over there. Only reckon I shouldn't, because I don't hate the scarecrow."

"As long as you keep shooting at it, it's perfectly safe," Longarm said. He glanced around, but found no soddy or hut to go with plowed field. "What are you doing around here?"

She shrugged. "I live around here."

"Where?" He found that he was beginning to doubt whatever she said, even on this brief acquaintance.

She waved her arm slightly northward this time. "Yonder."

Longarm followed the line of her pointing but discovered neither house nor tree nor soddy. "Where?" he said again, his voice hardening slightly.

"Up yonder." The defiance in her tone crackled in the clear air. He admitted to himself that she was a spunky little brat— he figured her at a well-developed seventeen or so—talking up to him though he was twice as big as she, and they were alone in this icy prairie.

In the distance he saw the area he supposed she referred to, a strange mesa rising out of the plains like a giant adobe anthill. Perhaps there was tableland atop the mesa, but he couldn't tell from this distance because two huge boulders reared near the summit of the steep incline. There could have been a house or a soddy or a mansion or even a town above those boulders; he could not tell because of the way they were situated. They effectively concealed whatever was above and beyond them on the strange mesaland tortured out of this tormented Divide. "You live up there?"

"Yes."

"What's your name?"

"What's yours?"

"I'm the one with the gun." He bit back a grin.

"I've got a gun too," she reminded him.

"But I'm the one could put a bullet in old man Estabrook's heart from here," he said.

"Old man Estabrook ain't got no heart," she said.

"You hate good, don't you? What did you say your name was?"

"Mozelle."

"What?"

"Mozelle. You laugh and I'll hit you with this here gun. If you got to call me anything, you can call me Moze. Everybody does."

"Who'd give you a name like Mozelle? Was it done in spite?"

"It was my grandma's name. And it was a perfectly good name in her time and back in Iowa and all. And that's my name, and I ain't heard yours yet."

"Long. Custis Long, ma'am."

"That ain't the prettiest name I ever heard, either."

"Then you can call me Longarm."

"Why?"

"Hell, why not? Because my friends do, and so do some people who take potshots at me—though some ain't that polite."

"What are you doing out here, Longarm?"

He drew a deep breath. "Why don't you button up your

sweater? You trying to freeze them nipples off before they're ripe?"

"Never mind me or my nipples. I ain't cold. I'm plumb used to cold, and used to being outside in all kinds of weather."

"I never saw a day quite like this. Day like this, most people run for cyclone shelters. They don't sit out in the open prairie shooting at scarecrows."

She tilted her lovely head, her dark golden hair shivering around her slender shoulders. She frowned slightly. "Is strange and still, ain't it? What you doing out here?"

"Am I mistaken? Ain't this a public road?"

"It's a public road, all right, but where you headed on it?"

He met her gaze, found it chilly and defiant, and shrugged. "I'm on my way to Dirty Fork."

He was caught in shock by the way Moze reacted to this simple statement of fact. He saw her fists clench on her rifle, saw her head tilt warily and her eyes grow colder than ever, more watchful.

"You ridin' west, and you trying to tell me you're on your way to Dirty Fork?"

He frowned, staring over his shoulder at the wan sun, a silver ball in the incredibly blue sky. "West? Are you crazy? I'm riding east."

"Either you're one hell of a poor liar, or you're lost, mister." She looked him over carefully. "You don't look like no pilgrim. I think you're lying. For your information, *Mister* Longarm, Dirty Fork is thataway." She flung up her arm and pointed in the direction from which Longarm had come.

Longarm stared down at the defiant little ragamuffin with the dirty face. There was no doubting it. Moze wasn't lying to him, not this time; he was lost.

He sighed out a deep breath, watching the vapor cloud out from his lips in the frigid, dry air. "Maybe you and me could strike a bargain," he suggested.

"What kind of bargain?" Her tone dripped her natural suspicion of all strangers.

Longarm shrugged. "Well, looks like I kind of lost the lay of the land—"

"Well, I can tell you, mister, I ain't the lay of the land, no matter what you think of me."

He laughed, shaking his head. "Good Lord, Moze—"

"I told you, mister. Don't laugh at me. Don't you ever laugh at me."

"I'm not laughing. Look, I'm not laughing." Longarm bit back the wisps of a smile. "I am a stranger, and I maybe have missed Dirty Fork somewhere—"

"That's God's truth."

"So maybe if you could point me in the right direction, and promise not to shoot me in the back, I'll be on my way."

She stared at him, eyes sullen and dark. "You still think I shot at you on purpose, don't you?"

He met her gaze levelly. "The jury is still out on that, Moze. Why don't you button up that sweater and point me toward Dirty Fork?"

Moze hesitated, chewing at her underlip a moment. Then she secured the lower two buttons on her ragged old sweater. "Maybe I'll just ride into Dirty Fork with you, show you the way."

"Seems fair. Only friendly thing you can do, after trying to kill me."

Dirty Fork wasn't much of a town, a couple of rows of slab-pine buildings shivering along a wide, rutted street where small, ice-crusted puddles left over from forgotten rains winked like eyes in the dry chill.

"Silver Palace is the showiest place in town," Moze said, riding slowly beside Longarm in the middle of the rutted street. The sinking sun sent long shafts of shadows from the buildings. "Biggest, too. Old man Estabrook owns it." At Longarm's quizzical look, she said, "Not the one you know. The *real* old bastard. Fondis Estabrook."

The Silver Palace reared like a haughty matron, the most imposing structure in the settlement and the only one with the memory of paint on it. Prairie winds had raked all the other buildings to the bare board, sandblasting them relentlessly and pitilessly. Though the temperature was numbingly low, all the hotel windows were open on both floors across the front, the faded curtains billowing, furling, and crackling with cold in the erratic breeze. Saddle horses and work wagons and surreys lined the hitching racks, and people moved along the boardwalks, hunched into themselves against the chill. A few scavenging hogs and tight-wrapped children grunted and yelled in alleys, and dogs barked in excitement, without menace. Indians crouched in abandoned doorways, like human litter flung there on icy winds, or they staggered in alleys between buildings, fortified against the cold by the white man's firewater, which was like a pleasant poison to the red man. Loiterers sought shelter in windbreaks, and smoked and talked without much passion or listened without much intetest; they'd said all they had to say a hundred times before, and they'd heard all their neighbors' stories until they'd stopped listening, even to themselves.

Wind crackled in sharp and chill on the wan April sunlight. It carried whispers of danger, of far places of the Comanche, the smell of sage and aspen and timothy and red top and scarlet fireweed, all mixed with smoke from somebody's supper fire. There was a taste of wildness in the sharp bite of wind, a sense of tension that nobody paid any heed to.

The rugged, twisted plains country rolled out in every direction from Dirty Fork. The town and a few dusty cottonwood trees were tossed down in a basin, a broken place in a savage pattern of sage and withered grassland just greening, unlocking at the touch of spring. The roads and fields and town were dust-gray and winter brown, broken with fences that stretched as far as the eye could see into the sage.

"Old Fondis Estabrook's fences," Moze said in a bitter tone. "And them that ain't Fondis Estabrook's belong to the U.S. Government. And that might as well be Fondis Estabrook, because he practically owns the government."

"I hadn't heard that," Longarm said.

Her voice crackled. "What do you know about it? He owns whatever government there is around here—and that means he controls the land and the grass and the water . . . and the law."

"Like I say, you sure hate good."

"I learned the hard way, mister. If you mean to stay around here long, take my advice and don't go contrary to Mr. Fondis Estabrook. It's downright unhealthy."

Longarm stared at the cloth-and-canvas banner strung across the front of the hotel: NOW. ON OUR STAGE. AMBER AUSTIN.

"Who is Amber Austin?" Longarm inquired.

Moze shrugged. "How do I know? She don't bother me, I don't bother her."

"Sounds like she puts on plays. Don't you ever come into town for plays?"

"Never have. I can tell you, I don't come into this town for any reason at all unless I purely have to."

"Yessir, you really hate good."

Longarm became aware gradually—and then sharply—of a prickly coldness along the short hairs on the nape of his neck, a chill that had nothing to do with this sudden, strange drop in temperature. People stopped whatever they were doing along the street to stare at them as they rode past in the waning sunlight.

"Reckon they never saw a man and a woman ridin' horseback?" Longarm inquired.

Moze's lovely little chin tilted in that defiant way. "It's us. You. Me."

"Us? What's wrong with us?"

"Me, mostly. I can tell you something else about Dirty Fork, Mr. Longarm. It's a town you don't like at first, but then you grow to hate it. These here people, they hate two things more'n polecats. First, they hate strangers like you. And second, they hate me."

Longarm grinned, struck by the hostile silence that greeted them and then followed along after them as they rode in the icy stillness. "I can understand their hating me," he said in a teasing tone. "After all, they don't know me, and lots of people in plenty of places hate anything or anybody they don't know. But why would they hate a lovely little belle like you with flowers in her hair?"

"Just daisies and fireweeds. I picked 'em whilst I sat out there. Nothin' else to do."

"They look mighty fancy."

"They hate me because they hate any Lobatos."

"And you're a Lobatos?"

"That's right, mister." She waited defiantly for his reaction to that name, but when he showed none, she relaxed again slightly, as much as she ever relaxed. She was, to him, somehow like a sad little migrant bird that never really relaxed, even slept and rested on the wind.

He grinned and shook his head, ignoring the malevolent stares of the silent townsfolk. "Mozelle Lobatos. No wonder you grew up so bitter inside. Wonder you ain't turned plumb to vinegar by now. You started out with one hell of a millstone around your neck—a name like Mozelle Lobatos."

"Ain't Mozelle that folks despise, it's Lobatos. You might as well know that, if you don't already. And I warned you, mister, about laughing at me."

"God forbid I should ever laugh at you, Mozelle. Come on, be my friend. I'll buy you a hell of a big steak, at the best eatin' place in town."

She stared at him suspiciously, eyes bleak and sullen. "Why would you do that?"

"Buy you a steak? Because I like you."

"You don't even know me. You don't know nothin' about me."

He shrugged and smiled. "Maybe that's why I like you. Anyway, it's the least I can do. After all, you did save my life, didn't you?"

"You are laughing at me. How'd I save your life?"

"Well, first you shot at me—and missed. Then you led me into Dirty Fork when I was lost. Besides, you got pretty tits."

"That ain't no way to talk to a lady."

"You're right and I apologize."

"It's all right, I ain't no lady. I ain't trying to fool nobody."

"You could have fooled me."

A young man ran suddenly from the bank, yelling Moze's name. His eager voice reverberated in the wind-stunned street. Now people really did stop all other activity to stare. Some of them nodded knowingly at each other.

"Mozelle! Mozelle! Wait up!"

Longarm saw the girl go pale under the dust streaking her face. "Might as well rein in," she said. "He'll chase us down if we don't."

Longarm watched the youth sprint out into the rutted street. He looked to be about twenty, well built and timber-wolf lean, six-feet tall. When he removed his expensive Stetson, he revealed an uncommonly handsome, virile, and yet desperately

42

"You love him so true, why do you lie to him?"

Moze shrugged. "I'll say this much to you. Mr. Kane Estabrook deserves every lie I could possibly tell him. He's earned them all."

Chapter 4

A woman's horrified scream pierced the frigid silence of late afternoon as Longarm and Mozelle Lobatos crossed the hotel veranda.

Longarm stopped, alert, poised on the balls of his feet. For a split second his heart raced as he reacted to that bloodcurdling yell. Then, as his hand reached toward the cross-draw Colt at his hip and under the bulk of the fleece-lined jacket, he looked around warily.

"Came from inside the cafe," Mozelle said.

Longarm nodded and strode forward. Mozelle was just ahead of him. She thrust the door open and they burst into the yellowly lighted room and into a tableau of terror.

Waiters stood with unserved meals or stacks of dirty dishes, as if their shoes had been nailed to the carpeted floor. Most of the cloth-covered tables were occupied. But the people at them sat as if carved from stone, not even looking at the woman and her tormentor.

Longarm stared at the woman, standing where she'd knocked over her chair at a table near the center of the room. In less than the space of a breath, too hasty to be a thought, it flashed through Longarm's mind that this was one of the loveliest females he'd ever encountered in his misspent life. Mozelle Lobatos was a pretty girl, but this woman was magnificent, fragilely and stunningly gorgeous, from her high-piled, red-gold hair to the tips of her slippers showing at the hem of her surah-and-crepe dress. This outfit, skirt of cream-colored surah trimmed at the full bottom with pleating and a surmounting puffing in layered silk over her elegant hips, was of the latest high fashion, he was certain, though he knew absolutely nothing of such matters. Her smooth golden com-

46

plexion caught and reflected the wan lamplight of the room. Her frightened eyes seemed enormous under soft, upcurled lashes. Her features were almost perfectly classical, but just sharp enough to be human and appealing. God knew, she was appealing.

He forced his gaze away from her low-cut bodice, from her trim waist and flaring hips, to the man pawing at her. This creature was an unprepossessing range maverick, the like of which one encountered in every saloon west of St. Louis— thin, bewhiskered, armed, and sotted with whiskey. This coy-ote wore a planter's black hat secured by leather thongs under his chin. The hat was back off his sweating face and he was grinning fatuously and reassuringly at the furious young woman while he continued to reach for her.

The woman retreated from his grimy hands and moist mouth, from the smell of his clothes, in shock at this public attack.

The beautiful young woman may as well have been alone in an alley with her attacker. No one in that cafe offered to assist her. In fact they withdrew, as if denying the ugliness might cause the whole unpleasant situation to go away.

Moze whispered across her shoulder. "That's Cody Boyle. Everybody in this town is scairt of Cody Boyle—ceptin' me and my pa."

Reaching for the young woman again, Cody Boyle knocked over the woman's cup of coffee. The brown liquid erupted over the tablecloth and ran down the pleats toward the carpeting. Cody laughed again and ignored the upset china. "Ain't goin' to hurt you, honey," Cody said to the woman. He licked his mouth and nodded. "Ain't gonna hurt you none at all."

Frantic, the young woman clutched a butterknife and held it poised and trembling over her head. The ineffectuality of this weapon amused Cody Boyle and he roared with laughter. He caught the girl's slender wrist, twisting just enough to force her to drop the silver knife. The small piece clattered to the table.

"You asked about Amber Austin the actress," Mozelle whispered over her shoulder. "That's her, puttin' on her 'terrified virgin' act."

Longarm said, "Excuse me, Moze." He stepped around her

and went to the table where Cody continued to twist Amber Austin's wrist, forcing her forward toward him.

Longarm paused just behind Cody Boyle. He tapped the drunken man on the shoulder. Cody's attention was riveted on the actress; he was totally unaware of Longarm at his heels or of the punch of Longarm's extended fingers.

Amber stared at Longarm across Cody's shoulder. This was the drunk's first clue that they were less than totally alone. And Longarm extended his fingers again, but this time he drove them into the small of Cody's back, sending his message via the man's kidney.

Cody got the message. He grunted and heeled around, swinging.

Longarm caught Cody Boyle's right wrist and jerked it upward, high above the man's head.

Cody stared at him, didn't recognize him, and then raged aloud, "What you want, hombre?"

Longarm kept his viselike grip on Cody's extended wrist. "What I want is not important, pardner. What do *you* want?"

"You back out of here and I'll forget you butted in."

"Oh, I wouldn't want you to forget that, Cody."

"If you know I'm Cody Boyle, stranger, then you also know I ain't no joker for you to fool around with. I'd as soon put a slug between your eyes as look at you. No, I make an exception of you, pilgrim. I'd *rather*."

"What you'd like to do to me ain't our problem, Cody. You're annoying this young lady, and that's impolite as hell."

Cody jerked his wrist free. His body quivered and his face flushed red. He peered up at Longarm, his moist mouth trembling. He drew the back of his hand across his whiskered lips.

"Get away from here. This here is between Amber and me. She's no *lady* for you to worry about. Hell, she's just a stage actress. You know what kinda sluts them women are. She's just a whore, just like all the rest of 'em."

"Don't look like she wants to have any truck with you, Cody."

"I tol' you, fellow. Butt out. This here whore has been leadin' me on ever since she got here into town. I seen her up on that stage, lookin' out right into my eyes...."

"I can't even see anybody over those footlights," Amber Austin whispered in a voice that was like violins.

"She's lyin'. The whore's been leadin' me on. Then when I come up to her, she gits coy. Hell, I ain't gonna hurt her. Whore or not, I'm mad in love with her. I got a terrible ache for her."

Longarm said, "Oh. Hell, if aching is what you want, pard-ner, I'll be right pleased to oblige you."

Moving swiftly, long before Cody Boyle's besotted mind could react, Longarm grabbed Boyle by the shoulders. He yanked the drunk toward him, and as Cody fought for balance, spreading his legs, Longarm brought his knee upward, driving it into Boyle's crotch.

Retching, Boyle first straightened to his fullest height, going up on his toes. Then he buckled in the middle, clutching at the agony racing outward from his loins. The sounds of pain that emanated from him were almost subhuman, growls and whim-pers and snarls.

Boyle toppled hard to the floor, on his side. He writhed there, his face ashen, his eyes glittering with pain. His face contorted out of shape, he stared up at Longarm and then crawled away like a sidewinder between the tables, gasping and muttering.

For a few long moments, nobody in the room moved. They formed a tableau, gazes fixed in sick fascination to the man wriggling along the floor like a smashed cockroach.

Cody managed to drag himself to a wall, where he lay with his back pressed against it, balled up, gasping for breath and sobbing with the sudden and overwhelming flashes of pain that flared from his scrotum to the crown of his head. He kept his fists knotted against his belly.

Longarm waited, but neither the proprietor of the restaurant nor his waiters made any move to clear Cody Boyle from the premises, or to send for the local law to do it for them. Longarm didn't really question this inertia on the part of the law-abiding citizens. Each of them knew Cody Boyle—by reputation at least. They knew Cody would not forget a wrong. They did not want to be involved. In fact most of them wished devoutly that they were almost anywhere else at the moment. It could be fatal if Cody Boyle even connected them vaguely in his

49

vengeful mind with this moment of terrible humiliation and unutterable agony. Somebody was going to pay, and any of them who could do so wanted to stay out of it, well out of it.

But Longarm had no intention of letting them off so easily. His voice rattled dishes on the tables. "Aren't you going to send for the sheriff?"

"You, Bower," Mozelle said to a stout, balding man in white shirt and soiled apron behind the counter near the front door. "Go get the sheriff."

"Yes. Please." Amber Austin's voice would break your heart in its resonance and appeal. "Please. Send for Sheriff Carr."

Bower jerked his head toward one of the waiters. This man, thin and narrow-faced, his hair stringy across his freckled forehead, nodded. He put a tray of soiled dishes down on an unoccupied table and hurried out, wiping his hands on his apron. His footsteps resounded as he crossed the veranda and went down the plank steps to the boardwalk. A sigh of relief rolled across the room.

Moze gazed up at Longarm admiringly. "You tricky bastard," she said.

Longarm grinned down at her. "There are all kinds of ways to slow down a stud."

"You just happened to choose the quickest."

"Old Cody won't be chasing ladies for a few days, that's for sure."

Mozelle shrugged. "Anyway, his heart won't be in it. Let's eat. I've worked up one hell of an appetite watching you play the hero."

Amber Austin smiled wanly at Longarm as he knelt and righted her upset chair. She supported herself with her fragile, golden hand upon its backrest.

"I can never thank you enough, sir," she said. "Never repay you for your bravery . . . your gallantry . . ."

Mozelle's voice cut between them abrasively. "Why, Miss Austin. Mr. Long would do as much for any woman with a set of tits like yours."

Amber Austin flushed, winced, retreated half a step, one hand still at her bosom. Then she decided to ignore Mozelle.

"Please accept my deepest appreciation, sir," she said to Longarm, her smile still pale and lopsided.

Longarm was unable to take his gaze from Amber Austin's incredibly lovely face. He began to appreciate, if not to sympathize with, Cody Boyle's unreasoning fascination with the beautiful actress. At his side, Mozelle elbowed him in the ribs. "Let's eat," Moze said again.

Amber Austin extended her hand toward Longarm. "Won't you join me? I'd feel so honored—and so much safer—if you did eat with me. Both of you are my guests."

"We can't intrude, Miss Austin," Longarm began, but Moze's jeering tone raked him like cruel spurs.

"Oh, hell, Longarm. You know wild horses couldn't drag you away from this here table. You know you're going to eat with her. And she's offered to pay for it. Sit down."

Mozelle pulled out a chair across the table from Amber's and flopped down into it. She glanced over her shoulder and called, "Hey, Charley? This your table? Over here."

A waiter, hobbling on sore feet, smiled and nodded, hurrying toward them. "Yes, ma'am, Miss Lobatos."

Longarm grinned. He held the chair for Amber Austin, who smiled her thanks up at him as she sat down and replaced her fallen napkin across her lap.

Longarm removed his greatcoat. Charley the waiter grabbed it from him, bowing obsequiously. "I'll just hang it on the coatrack by the door for you, sir."

Longarm managed to pull his gaze from Amber Austin's lovely face long enough to thank the waiter, then his eyes returned, as iron filings leap to a magnet.

As he pulled out a chair between Moze's and Amber Austin's, Longarm was struck hard in the side. Mozelle sprang up from her chair and lunged against him, knocking him off balance. He staggered, catching at the table to support himself.

As he fell, he was aware of Mozelle's hands grabbing at him. Before his mind cleared, he saw her come up with his Colt in both her hands. She crouched for a moment like a puma beside Amber Austin's table and pressed the trigger.

The gunfire exploded deafeningly in the cafe, rattling and reverberating and bringing screams from the women.

Realizing in that instant that he had come damned near dying because he'd totally let his guard down, Longarm jerked his head around as the gun detonated.

Cody Boyle was braced up on one knee against the wall. He was bringing up his sixgun when Mozelle shot the weapon from his fist.

The gun leaped away, struck the wall, and clattered to the floor a few feet from Cody, but Boyle had no interest in it. His gunhand suddenly blossomed bloody red. He stared at the shattered member and screamed in agony.

Longarm stared at Mozelle. He managed to keep his voice light. "Well, you've saved my life again."

But he wasn't thinking about Cody Boyle, or even about Amber Austin's unearthly beauty. He was remembering this afternoon, when Moze had shot at him from that grassy mound. He knew now that she could have put a bullet between his eyes as easily as she had missed him. All he didn't know yet was why she had chosen to shoot past him.

Moze shrugged. "It was nothing. I'd do it for anybody with a body like yours, old fellow."

"No," he persisted. "It was *something*. I thought you said you couldn't shoot a gun."

"I reckon I can shoot a little."

"And you said you were shooting at a scarecrow."

She shrugged. "Well, I lie pretty good too."

"I reckon everything you've told me so far is a lie, isn't it?"

She moved those slender shoulders in that ragged sweater again. "I don't know. I didn't keep count."

"You'll make Kane Estabrook one hell of a wife, won't you?"

Her mouth twisted and her eyes glittered. "No. I won't. Kane's father won't ever let Kane marry me...even if Kane wanted to."

The cafe door was thrown open. The waiter entered, followed by a young deputy sheriff and a handsome man in frock coat, lace-front shirt, and black, pointed-toed shoes. The deputy and the waiter went directly to where Cody Boyle moaned and writhed against the wall. They hauled Boyle to his feet. The waiter retrieved Boyle's gun and handed it to the deputy, who

52

shoved the gun in his belt. Boyle was crying out in pain and supporting his right arm in his left hand. Blood pulsed and ran in strings along Boyle's arm.

By now, crowds had gathered on the hotel veranda. They pressed against the windows and at the open doorway. Others had gathered in the double doors to the hotel lobby. They stared intently, chattering at each other. The whispered name "Cody Boyle" raced through the crowd. A few of them crossed themselves and others stared in satisfaction at the gunslick's shattered right hand. A lot of people would breathe easier tonight, Longarm thought.

"I want a doctor," Boyle growled.

The deputy led him toward the outer door. "You want horns, Boyle, but you're gonna die butt-headed."

Longarm reached out and retrieved his gun from Moze. She watched with a twisted smile as he replaced the weapon in its cross-draw holster.

The handsome young dandy who'd arrived with the deputy came directly to the table. Slender and almost six feet tall, the fashionably attired dude was incredibly good looking, almost pretty, as a matter of fact. His features were finely chiseled, his red lips petulant, his black mustache closely cropped, his eyes a fragile china blue, his thick blond hair carefully trimmed in waves and curls from forehead to neckline.

His beautiful young face was contorted with concern. He knelt beside Amber Austin's table, searching her face for any signs of harm. Finding none, he exhaled and managed to smile. "My darling," he said in a deeply cultivated voice, "are you all right?"

Amber smiled and touched his unlined cheek with her golden fingers. "Yes, darling. Thanks to these good people, I am all right."

He glanced toward Longarm and Mozelle briefly, then quickly brought his gaze back to Amber. "I should never have let you out of my sight. It's all my fault."

"I told you, darling. I'm all right." She laughed again and gestured toward Mozelle and Longarm. "This is Miss Lobatos and Mr. Long. I am eternally in their debt. Mr. Long, Miss Lobatos, this is my husband, Elliot."

Longarm extended his hand. "Good to meet you, Mr. Austin."

The young man contemplated Longarm's callused hand without any real enthusiasm. Then his face reddened. He stood up, bowed at the waist. "I am most grateful for all you have done for my wife, sir. But my name is not Austin. My name is Elliot Brockbank."

"Elliot's a truly accomplished actor," Amber Austin said hastily. "Always excellently received. He's only accepted second billing to me on this tour because he loves me."

"Of course I do, my darling." Elliot took her hand in his and kissed it, aware that everybody in the cafe was staring at him as if great lights played on him alone.

"Could we order?" Moze said. "I'm starved."

She ordered a steak, with fried potatoes. Longarm said, "I'll take the same, Charley. Make mine medium."

"They just throw 'em on the fire back there, mister," Charley said. "No matter what I tell 'em. No matter how many times I tell 'em." He turned and walked wearily away toward the kitchen.

Longarm was aware that Mozelle Lobatos had caught her breath and was holding it. Going tense because he'd already come near to tragedy by letting his guard down, he turned his head quickly.

Kane Estabrook pushed his way through the crowd still blocking the doorway. His Stetson in his hand, he crossed the room, unaware of anyone in it except Moze.

He came directly to her, eyes troubled. "Are you all right?"

Moze shrugged. "Sure. Why wouldn't I be all right?"

Amber Austin smiled up at Kane. "We are just going to have dinner, Mr. Estabrook. Won't you join us? Then you must all see our show tonight at the Silver Palace . . . as my guests, of course."

"Oh, by all means," Elliot Brockbank said without much enthusiasm.

Mozelle shook her head. Longarm saw that though Amber Austin captured all the light in the room, she seemed not to exist as far as young Estabrook was concerned. He had not taken his gaze from Mozelle's smeared young face.

Mozelle said regretfully, "I'd truly admire seeing your playacting, Miss Austin. And yours too, Mr. Brockbank. I ain't never seen a real actual stage play. And I know yours would be truly beautiful. But if I stayed out that late, my pa'd take a lightered knot to me. I got to git on out home, soon's I eat."

"Why, you can't ride out in that prairie country alone at night," Longarm said, tongue in cheek.

Mozelle laughed back at him. "What makes you think I'll be alone, Mr. Long? I just know Mr. Kane Estabrook's pantin' to tie my pony to the back of his runabout so's he can drive me out to Screamin' Springs, cozy under blankets and all. Ain't that right, Kane?"

His face flushed red, and Kane nodded. His belief in a kindly God had just been extraordinarily reinforced, but Mozelle couldn't let him off that easily. "Or do you have to get permission from old Fondis, Kane?"

Sitting between Amber Austin and Mozelle Lobatos, Longarm was amazed at the differences between the two young women. Amber ate sparingly, daintily, holding her fork with pinky tilted and bent slightly. Between bites she chewed quietly and unobtrusively, dabbing at her exquisite lips with her napkin.

On the other side of him, Moze Lobatos attacked her sirloin steak with vigor and intensity. She ate as if she'd been starving for a week, chewing loudly, her lips pulled back in a grin of sheer animal delight with the taste of the meat. She jabbed her fork into the slab of steak, carried the meat to her face and bit off a large hunk, letting the remainder of the steak and her fork clatter to her plate as she chewed.

Longarm glanced toward Kane, eating nothing on the other side of Moze. Kane seemed unmoved by the savagery with which Moze assaulted the food on her plate; on the other hand he did not notice or applaud Amber's daintiness.

A stir at the veranda door attracted all eyes except young Estabrook's; Kane went on watching Moze covertly, warmly.

Longarm stared across the cafe as the sheriff arrived. Though he had never seen Lawson Carr before, no one had to tell Longarm this was the local lawman. There was an air of quiet authority about him. He moved the remnants of the crowd from the veranda without lifting his voice. He strode into the cafe as if he owned the land upon which he walked.

Carr removed his dark planter's hat and came directly toward the table where Longarm sat. Carr seemed aware of the others in the room and at the table, but his steel-gray eyes were fixed on Amber Austin's face. Longarm saw Elliot Brockbank go tense, his pretty face tightening, his weak mouth suddenly more petulant than ever.

Carr's hair was almost white—prematurely—with a few dark streaks running through it. His eyebrows were black and arched, his mustache salt-and-pepper, his cheekbones high and his thin jaw squared. Tall, thin, he walked erect but stiffly, favoring his right knee, which had carried a minie ball since Antietam. He wore plain black boots, black wool trousers, a pristinely white shirt, and a black string tie secured at his starched collar—he changed collars three of four times a day, Longarm had no doubt. He buckled his gunbelt under his frock coat at his waist, but wore the holster low on his right side, thonged down. He prided himself on his prowess with a pistol, boasting in his soft, magnolia-and-grits Southern voice that he was slow, deliberate—and still alive. He was thirty-nine years old, and ever since he'd entered the Virginia Volunteers at Richmond in 1861, he'd lived by the gun.

Gazing at Amber Austin now, Carr smiled. His face was smooth, with small lines only at the corners of his haunted eyes. His was a severe and somber face, hewn from personal agony that showed in the pallor underlying the worn leather brown of his wind-singed flesh. One thing that was immediately obvious about Lawson Carr, and remarkable, was that his arms were uncommonly long, his big hand unconsciously bumping against his holster as he walked.

Carr went directly to Amber Austin and bent over her, as courtly as though they were in some Virginia cotillion. "I came as quickly as I could, ma'am," he said.

"It's all right, Carr," Elliot Brockbank said, his voice rasping and losing its cultured roundness. "Amber is quite all right. You needn't have worried."

"Miss Amber knows how much I worry about her," Carr said in that soft voice, still speaking directly to the actress, as though her husband were not even there. "I'm sure she knows how much her safety means to me. How much *she* means to me."

"I'm certain the whole town is quite aware of your *concern* for my wife by now, Sheriff Lawson," Elliot Brockbank said.

Chapter 5

Longarm pulled down the window of his second-floor hotel room. The cold-crisped curtains sagged brittlely against the framing. It was as if he'd shut a ravening animal outside that glass pane. The street below was almost deserted, nearly totally dark.

He turned away from the window, shuddering with cold in the chilled room. He undressed quickly, aware of the stitch of pain in the slow-healing bullet wound in his side. He forced himself to wash at the earthenware commode in the icy water from the large old white pitcher. His teeth were chattering by the time he got into bed, wearing his stockings and balbriggan longjohns against the still cold. To his surprise, he found the lightweight goosedown spread as warm as a toaster, and he sighed expansively. He was exhausted, and as soon as he was warm, he'd fall asleep.

He lay in the darkness, curled under the spread. Faint, remote, and subdued noises reached at him from inside the hotel and from the street. It was hellish strange weather, and Dirty Fork promised to be a hellish strange town.

He had finished dinner in the awkward silence silence caused by the tensions between Elliot Brockbank and Sheriff Carr over the lovely actress Amber Austin.

He grinned faintly, remembering. Carr had managed to pull his gaze from Amber long enough to glance fleetingly toward Longarm. Carr had quickly sized him up, neither impressed nor very interested. He did say, "Oh yes. Custis Long. Fellow from Denver. Why don't you come in to see me tomorrow?" Carr didn't wait for an answer, but turned back at once to Amber.

Little Mozelle Lobatos had finished wolfing down her steak

and potatoes and had gone away, with Kane Estabrook following at her heels almost as slavishly as her mustang pony.

Finally, Longarm excused himself. Only Amber Austin seemed aware that he was departing. She said, "I'm leaving a ticket at the Silver Palace box office for you, Mr. Long. I'll be bitterly disappointed if you miss my show."

Longarm smiled down at her full breasts, glowing and pulsing at the bodice of her dress. "I wouldn't miss your show for anything, Mrs. Brockbank."

He had used her married name in order to needle Sheriff Carr. But he may as well have saved his breath. The Virginian had already forgotten his existence.

Longarm walked out of the restaurant into the early night darkness. Wind rolled tumbleweeds and bits of debris along the wide, shadowed street. He asked directions to the town livery stable and then walked his borrowed roan down there.

A single lantern glowed outside the stables. The large barn was closed as securely as it could be against the cold. Longarm's hands burned with the chill. Inside, a couple of Indians slept under tattered blankets. Three white men sat over a makeshift table, playing poker. An Indian sat silently inside the ring of lantern light, watching the game.

Longarm led the horse inside the livery. One of the men looked up and yelled. "For God's sake, man, hurry and close that door."

Longarm secured the door behind him. He walked the roan toward the light. None of the players looked up. The solitary Indian watched him intently, but without great interest.

"Hellish funny weather, ain't it?" Longarm said.

One of the white men grunted and shrugged. The others stared at their cards and did not speak.

"Wolf wind," said the indian. He nodded and spoke the words again. "Wolf wind."

Finally a thin man in a straw hat and thick coat looked up from his cards. The lantern light glittered in his eyes and deepened the crags in his cheeks. He didn't bother to smile. "You can put your horse in any empty stall back there, mister. Water and hay and one feedbag of mixed grain included in the fee for the night. Four bits. You can pay me now."

Longarm placed the money on the side of the table. The

thin hostler immediately shoved it into the pot. "See you and call you," he said to the man across the table.

Longarm led the roan deeper into the shadowed stable. He removed the bridle, saddle, saddlebags, and blanket while the horse drank. He found a feedbag and filled it with grain from the hampers. He threw a few forkfuls of hay into the stable trough along with the grain. Using the saddle blanket, he rubbed the roan down, then threw the blanket out over the stall rails.

Carrying his rifle, he returned to the front of the stable, where the men bent over cards around the lantern. He said good night, but none answered. The Indian looked up and shook his head and said, "Wolf wind."

Longarm returned along the street, finding it lined with wagons and carriages and saddle horses outside the Silver Palace. He rented a room, left his possibles on the bed, and walked over to the big saloon, which had been turned into a theater, with a stage at one end and chairs set up in front of the long mahogany bar.

The show was a sellout. There was little entertainment offered in towns like Dirty Fork. Most people rode all the way to Denver, or they didn't see a stage performance from one year's end to the next. An air of expectancy charged the atmosphere in the brilliantly illumined Silver Palace.

Longarm found much to entertain him in the theater, though the play was far from the best he'd ever seen. It was professionally done, there was no doubt about that; the costuming was excellent, the staging was thoughtful, the direction far better than the script deserved. Called *The Missing Rose*, the play took place in an English hunting lodge where members of a peerage family are gathered for a party. An evil mystic holds several people under his power. The heroine, Phyllis, played by Amber Austin, has ability as a ventriloquist. Her voice, in any accent, tonal quality or range could seem to come from anywhere, though she sits quietly, barely moving her lips. The mystic forces Phyllis to use her voice to deceive and terrorize his victims into doing his rotten bidding. Of course, the mystic is after the fortune left in escrow for a second cousin missing since babyhood. The money will go—on this night— to the young lord, unless the legal claimant arrives. This is hardly likely, since she was stolen in infancy. The young hero,

Lord Horatio, is played by Elliot Brockbank. Of course, by the time the curtain had been up for four minutes, the audience saw that Phyllis had fallen desperately in love with Lord Horatio, who is so far above her as to be beyond any hope. She does not want to proceed with the mystic's infamous scheme to part Lord Horatio from the huge inheritance. She tries to get free, but the mystic threatens to tell Lord Horatio about her past—that she is not the gentle person she pretends, but is rather a foundling and former London street girl who would this moment be in the gutter but for the mystic's kindness to her. Among the guests at the lodge is the family barrister, who controls the huge estate in trust. The barrister believes the lost girl might be alive, that she was stolen by gypsies, but he is ready to turn over the money to Lord Horatio, who badly needs it, because all attempts to find the stolen child have been fruitless these twenty years. The mystic forces the street girl to be the missing heiress's disembodied voice. But she, in the crisis, using her power of ventriloquism in a terrible, booming, offstage voice, denounces the mystic as a charlatan and a fraud. She, of course, loves young Lord Horatio too deeply and too purely ever to steal from him. The mystic goes berserk. He tears off the girl's bodice before Lord Horatio overcomes him and thrashes him badly. (Even with the bodice off, Phyllis is better clothed than most women in the audience.) The aged barrister stares at her shoulder and cries out. The rose mark on Phyllis's bared shoulder is the birthmark of the heiress!

The audience loved it. They wept and applauded and laughed in all the right places. Elliot Brockbank's unearthly and idealized beauty turned the women to putty. The men already were mesmerized by Amber Austin's gorgeous hair, face, and body. Her helplessness against the evil mystic made the spectators tremble and rage and hiss.

Strangely enough, Brockbank was an excellent actor, giving his shallow role far more than it called for. Longarm could believe that the fellow had truly forsaken what must have been a brilliant career in New York for this fearful travel through the sticks, as second lead to Amber Austin, because of love. But somehow this didn't make sense. The actors he had known were far too self-centered for any such sacrifice. But for whatever reason, he *was* here, and he added a great deal to the show.

Amber's abilities didn't quite measure up to her beauty. But perhaps, as lovely as she was, to expect outstanding acting skills would be too much. She brought in the audiences. A man could live out his lifetime and never see anything as lovely again.

Another thing that struck Longarm forcibly before the play ended was Amber Austin's trick of playing directly to the eyes and faces of certain men in the audience. She did stare across those footlights, just as the drunken Cody Boyle had accused her. She had protested that she could not even see faces across those footlights. But the fact was, she certainly did look long and hungrily into certain faces in an upsetting way. About that, Cody Boyle had not lied.

For Longarm, however, the most intriguing part of the evening was not what went on up on the stage of the Silver Palace, or even the enchanted reception it received from the audience. He found himself watching Sheriff Lawson Carr almost as intently as he watched the melodrama unfold beyond the footlights.

Carr entered the converted theater just in the last moment before the house lights were dimmed and doused. A chair had been reserved for him and he proceeded directly to it. He walked with that slight limp, looking neither left nor right, his black planter's hat in his large hand at his side. The lights glowed in his prematurely gray hair and glittered in the steel of his eyes. He was austere and unsmiling.

Carr sat alone, watching the stage. He did not laugh or applaud. Once Amber Austin entered, he did not take his eyes from her. There was in Carr's face, even in the dim light reflected from the stage apron, a look of anguish and hunger that was either comical or tragic. He gazed at Amber as though she were some remote star, fixed in the impossible distance. One almost believed he saw in her the beauty and gentility forever lost to Carr in the destruction of the Confederacy. He was almost like a lovestruck youth, except that he remained grim and cold and unbending, his gaze fixed on the golden girl gracing the brilliantly illumined stage.

Longarm grinned faintly. It was not hard to see that Lawson Carr could not work up much interest in cutting barbed-wire fences, or even in his own reelection as sheriff in the coming primary. He was like a man lost, a hopeless alcoholic, a drug addict. There was only one thing on his mind.

When the play ended and the actors had taken a dozen curtain calls, Longarm left the theater in the chattering crowd and drifted alone to the hotel.

The streets emptied quickly. People hurried to escape the frigid winds. The temperature seemed to have plunged incredibly since sunset.

Longarm paused for a moment on the darkened veranda of the hotel. The night sky was coldly, crisply clear and cloudless. Surprisingly, there was no sign of the thunderheads he'd seen boiling along the horizon just at dusk.

Stars blazed like fiery lamps in the night sky. They hung still, huge, and unwinking. Stars were always startlingly bright on the High Plains, but this was remarkable—and somehow, in this strange cold, disturbing.

At last, coiled under the goosedown comforter in his hotel bed, he felt the warmth as his blood circulated. His eyes grew heavy. He remembered Bonnie and her hips and her thighs and he wondered vaguely, *Why in hell am I here*? The last thing he heard was the lulling rattle of the window in the night wind. It seemed far removed, like chilled talons reaching for him and unable to find him. He sighed contentedly and sank into sleep.

The rattling sound grew louder. At first, rising slowly from sleep, he decided the wind was just shaking the window harder in its sill. But then the sound stopped, and just as he dozed off again, it was repeated.

Longarm came fully awake. He heard the rattling again, subdued and yet persistent in the darkness. The room was as cold as a cell. Alert at last, he realized someone was rapping lightly at his door. It stopped, and then he heard it again.

Shivering, biting down hard to keep his teeth from rattling with cold, Longarm got up and padded in his stocking feet to the door. "Who is it?" he said.

A voice whispered, "Could I talk to you? Please?"

Longarm unlocked the door and opened it far enough to peer out into the hall, which was dimly lighted by small lamps at each end. His mouth sagged open.

At first he thought he was still asleep under his comforter

and dreaming. Amber Austin stood there. Her face looked younger and lovelier and fresher than ever, with the heavy stage makeup scrupulously scrubbed away with creams. She wore a knitted shawl over her head and about her shoulders.

She smiled as sweetly and pleasantly as though it were midday and he weren't standing there in his longjohns, his hair sticking out wildly on each side of his head.

"I hope I'm not disturbing you," Amber said.

"What time is it?" Longarm stifled a helpless yawn.

"Oh. You were asleep. This is unforgiveable . . . I'm sorry. You see, I am a night person . . . I sleep until almost four every afternoon. I forget that other people don't keep such weird hours."

"What can I do for you?"

"Oh, nothing. Really. You go back to bed. I'm sorry I disturbed you. I hope you can forgive me."

"I can forgive you, but only if you tell me what you want."

"I found that you had the room just down the hall from me. I'd just made a pot of tea . . . an English habit I picked up from dear Elliot. I just hoped you might have a cup of tea with me."

"A cup of tea?"

"A cup of tea. Please forgive me, and go back to bed."

"No. No. A cup of hot tea is just what I need in this cold."

"I promise you, it will be hot," Amber said.

"Let me put on some clothes."

Amber smiled. "It will be most informal, I promise you."

"I'll dress informal. And fast," he said.

"I'll leave my door ajar. It's just down the corridor there."

Longarm grinned faintly and closed the door. He dressed in the darkness, struggling into his trousers and shirt, pulling on his boots. He ran his hands through his hair and washed his mouth out with a swig of rye. He started to spit it into the commode, but changed his mind and swallowed it.

He checked his watch and found that it was ten after one. Tea? In her hotel room? At ten after one? And her husband? Where was Elliot? Somehow the tone of her invitation had not included her husband.

He let himself out of his room and went quickly along the vaguely illumined corridor to the door Amber had left ajar for him. He rapped once on its facing, stepped inside, and closed it behind him.

He stood just inside the brilliantly lighted room and gazed around, awed. Clothing, dresses, underthings, gowns, and shoes were hung or stacked everywhere. There was a strong, almost overwhelmingly sweet scent in this room—the smell of Amber Austin. It was in everything she wore, in the room she slept in, the bed covers and sheets and even the curtains at the closed window and the drawn drapes.

She had removed the shawl, but was as formally attired as she had been when she wakened him. She had set a small table with small sweet cakes and biscuits. A teapot sweated and steamed in the center of the condiments and silverware.

She was serious! She meant to serve him hot tea at one in the morning. Stunned, he stood unmoving, incredulous, disbelieving.

Amber Austin gestured toward a straight chair before the small table. "Please sit down, Mr. Long. I'll pour our tea."

Longarm perched his large frame as delicately as possible on the small chair and took the small cup of steaming tea, which looked like a thimble in his big hand. She told him something about the tea: it was a brand that Elliot ordered from London; it had a special bouquet. . . . He barely listened.

He sipped the hot liquid and watched Amber over the cup. She said, "I felt I owed it to you to invite you here, where I could properly thank you for what you did for me. I can tell you, that horrible man terrorized me. And I could see no one meant to help me—until you came along."

"I'm a lawman, Miss Austin . . . or Mrs. Brockbank—"

"Amber." She smiled gently over her teacup.

"Amber. Most ordinary people know they can get killed when they interfere with men like Cody Boyle. Maybe you shouldn't have flirted with him across those footlights."

Her face flushed brightly. He saw that she was going to deny it, but then she changed her mind. She chewed at her underlip and sighed. "It's only a little game I play."

"To you it's a game. To a man like Cody Boyle, who never saw anyone like you before, and probably never will again, it could be something pretty serious. He's a man ridin' loose-cinched as it is."

"I know." She shuddered. "He's crazy. Insane. I could see it in his eyes."

He tried to smile. "You must see that light in the eyes of plenty of men."

She shook her head. "No. I've worked hard. All my life. Would you believe I've been an actress, on the stage professionally, since I was eleven years old?"

Longarm grinned inwardly. He coughed and studied his tea. If she meant did he believe she'd become proficient in her craft in a life devoted to a career, the answer was no. But he merely shook his head. "I guess it's not an easy life," he managed to say.

"It's one of the most difficult of lives," she said. "It's a lonely and very disciplined life. You're studying or working all the time—or you'd better be! You're without friends, except those you make as you travel—one night here and gone tomorrow. How lonely it is, Mr. Long. And people think acting is so glamorous. I can tell you, there is no glamour—except during the play itself, when you're in front of those footlights."

"Is that why you flirt across the footlights?"

She winced faintly, but nodded finally. "I can't really recognize a face across the footlights. But I can tell if it is a man or a woman. Mostly, the face is a blur, except for the eyes. I play to those eyes."

"For God's sake, why?"

She shivered suddenly. "I may as well admit the truth to you, Mr. Long, though I've never told anyone else, not even Elliot. Oh, Elliot wouldn't understand at all! But I believe you will. I have never had . . . a life . . . the kind of life I read about in books. I have heard about the terrible excitement that can happen between men and women . . . but I've never had it. Never. Except in my dreams. Sometimes I am ill with desire for a man . . . like that. I have to hide it, but I cannot escape it. So I play my little game . . . with strange men in my audiences. I pretend one of them is the one who will . . . ravish me. I know I sound like a fool, a silly school girl. But maybe I am retarded . . . in my love life."

"Married to Elliot Brockbank? There wasn't a woman in that audience tonight who wouldn't have gladly changed places with you."

She exhaled heavily. "That's because they don't know Elliot as I do. Elliot married me so he would have a leading lady for his plays. And that is the only reason."

He stared at her. "I can't believe that."

She shrugged. "Well, it's true, Mr. Long. I assure you it's the truth. Since I'm playing truth-or-consequences with you, I may as well tell you the whole truth. Do you think Elliot shares this bed—or this room—with me?"

He looked around, but found no sign of the actor. "Unless he's crazy, he does."

"Oh, I assure you, Elliot isn't crazy. It's just that . . . he doesn't want me. Not like that, anyway. Elliot doesn't want *any* woman. His room is there, Mr. Long. Next door."

"Won't he . . . dislike our keeping him awake?"

"Oh, he isn't there, Mr. Long. He won't be there until the bar or the poker tables close down at the Silver Palace. Whichever comes first. Elliot's first love is liquor. His second love is gambling. His third love is money. His fourth love is acting. And then, somewhere down the line, is whatever Elliot feels for me."

Longarm listened to Amber's unhappy words, and to all the reasons why she had invited him here, but his gaze was fixed only on her body. "I find that hard to believe," he said.

Her smile was cold. "You can believe it, Mr. Long. I didn't know there were men like Elliot, until I married him. There is no reason for jealousy or anything like that. He wants no woman. But that's not very reassuring to me. He doesn't want me, either."

He scowled and took another sip of tea. He looked uncomfortable and then Amber smiled. "You're wondering if Elliot . . . wants other men? No . . . he's neuter, I guess."

Longarm tried to laugh, to lighten the moment. He said, "I've seen mules that can't reproduce, but Elliot doesn't look like a mule."

"He drinks. He gambles. Maybe he drinks because he's dead inside, and doesn't want to be. He drank until he was fired from all the decent theaters in London. Then New York put up with his drinking and gambling debts as long as it could. All he has now is this show . . . and me to keep it together for him. It's not a very exciting or glamorous life, Mr. Long."

He sighed. Her body was silhouetted against the glow of her bedlamp. Her breasts strained tautly at the low-cut bodice of her dress. The saffron-tinted lamplight cast a faint aura around her slender body. But suddenly he saw the truth. Amber Austin was starving. He managed to grin. "No wonder you flirt across the footlights."

For a moment there was silence in the sweet-scented stillness of Amber Austin's room. The wind shook the window impotently. Suddenly, Longarm caught the sound of muted footsteps at the door. He jerked his head around and saw the doorknob turn. Then the door was flung open.

Amber cried out and leaped to her feet. She dropped her cup of tea and its saucer. She stood as though stricken, staring toward that doorway.

Longarm reached for his Colt, suddenly feeling naked without it. Both of his handguns, as well as his rifle, reposed down the hall in his own room.

Elliot Brockbank stood wavering like a reed in the lighted doorway to the corridor. He held a small nickel-plated gun tightly in his fist.

That gun was fixed on Longarm's navel.

Chapter 6

Elliot Brockbank staggered into the room, leaving the door standing ajar. He waved the small gun in his unsteady fist. He was drunk, perspiring, outraged.

Before the handsome young actor could pull the trigger, Longarm spoke in a cold, warning tone. "Just be sure that first shot gets me, fellow. Or I'll take you apart and make you eat that nickel-plated toy."

Amber spoke across Longarm's shoulder. "Elliot! What are you doing? What crazy thing are you doing now? Put that stupid gun away."

"Don't tell me what to do!" Elliot raged. His voice carried, as it did from the stage. His shirt was open at the collar. He'd never looked more handsome, or more impotent, waving that gun he was obviously afraid to use even when he caught another man with his wife.

"Put that gun away, I tell you." Amber said.

"You ought to listen to her," Longarm said. "You could get hurt."

"Hurt? Hurt, do you say, sir?" Elliot's voice rang almost as if he were reciting lines he'd learned for a part. "How can I be hurt more than I am at this moment?"

"Try a bullet in your gut," Longarm said.

"No bullet has the power to destroy as I am destroyed here tonight, by you, you foul interloper," Elliot declaimed.

"Stop being a fool, Elliot," Amber said. "And close that door. Do you want to wake up the town?"

Elliot kicked out and slammed the door behind him with the heel of his continental boot. He stared at Amber, his eyes glittering with tears.

"It's not what you think, Elliot," Amber said in a calmer tone.

"I don't have to think. I see," Elliot raged. His jaw quivered. "I see a man . . . here in your room. Somebody told me there was a man up here with you."

He waved the gun again.

"If that thing goes off accidentally," Longarm said, "anybody could be wounded. Even you."

Elliot waved the gun back and forth again. "I want to hear nothing from you, sir."

Amber's voice lashed out at Elliot. "You're drunk."

Elliot's head jerked up and he gazed at his lovely wife. "Is that so new, Amber? My being drunk—because of you?"

"Don't blame your drinking on me," she said. "Drinking has cost you almost everything you ever had."

Elliot drew his hand across his eyes. "Don't try to change the subject!" he raged. "I hurt no one if I take a drink or two. But I can tell you, madam, I won't have this . . . your carrying on like a common whore with strange men. My God. My God. A scandal could ruin us."

"If your drinking and gambling doesn't ruin us, Elliot," Amber said, "nothing will."

"I won't have it," he said. "What will people think? We are the perfect couple. That's what they call us. The most beautiful couple in the world. I won't have you spoiling that. I won't have people laughing at us."

"Or are you afraid they might laugh at *you*, Elliot?"

Longarm watched them with some fascination. They threw lines at each other as if their heartbreak were not even real, as if they were onstage.

Maybe, under the circumstances, this was not too strange. Maybe all they truly knew of emotions was in their acting. Maybe the only reality for them was in a performance on a stage. It was as if they acted out their agony now for him.

Elliot cried out as if Amber had clawed his face. "Laugh at me? I won't have it, Amber! I swear. I'll kill you first. I'll kill both of you."

Suddenly, Longarm clasped Elliot's wrist in his fist and twisted it. The beautiful young actor cried out in pain. He dropped the gun. Longarm retrieved it from the carpeting and placed it behind him on Amber's littered vanity. "Like your wife said, Elliot. It's not what you think. She invited me down here for tea. And that's what we had. Tea."

Elliot stood, his slender shoulders sagging. He massaged at his wrist. Tears welled in his eyes and ran along his sharply hewn cheeks. "I don't know what to believe," he whispered in agony. "They told me—"

"You better believe what you see," Longarm said.

Amber stepped forward and placed her hand on Elliot's arm. "Of course he does. Please, Mr. Long, Elliot meant no harm. Unfortunately, a few weeks ago in a town in Kansas, a man broke into my room . . . and tried to rape me. He knocked Elliot down when he came running in from his room. The man got away, though my screams brought help before anything more happened. Elliot bought the pistol then, to guard me."

Elliot nodded. He looked around, his gaze taking in the tea table, the teapot, the cakes, the cups, and the fact that both his wife and Longarm were fully and impeccably dressed. He winced. "I guess I went off half-cocked," he apologized.

"Of course you did. I asked Mr. Long here to thank him properly for all he did for me tonight in that restaurant."

"The middle of the night," Elliot protested. "You know what people in a town like this will think."

Amber's embittered tone sharpened and raked him cruelly. "They wouldn't have thought anything, if you hadn't made such an evil scene."

Elliot winced and retreated, as though Amber had struck him across the face. Longarm felt sorry for the young actor. He said, "You're right, Elliot. Middle of the night. I shouldn't have come here."

"No." Amber's voice struck between them. Longarm thought that if she acted as well on the stage, she would be sensational. "Elliot knows better. He knows I don't live like other people. He knows the middle of the night is the middle of the day for me. He knows that, don't you, Elliot?" The young actor nodded, but before he could speak, Amber ripped at him again. "He just got drunk and listened to some fool, even though he knew better."

Elliot seemed to shrink inside his own handsome skin. "I

71

didn't know what to think," he whispered. "Maybe I *was* drunk. I was afraid . . . you were being hurt. All I could think was to kill—"

Longarm said, "You didn't ask my opinion, Mr. Brockbank, but maybe you better take my advice. When you charge into a room with a little gun like that, you better use it, and keep firing until whatever you're shooting at is dead. It's not very accurate, and unless it's a direct hit, it's not lethal. It's a lot easier to get yourself killed shooting at somebody with a gun like that than it is to kill somebody else."

Brockbank looked sick to his stomach. "I apologize, Mr. Long. I have made a fool of myself. All I can say is—and say it before Amber does—it is not the first time."

"A man has got every right to protect his wife, Mr. Brockbank," Longarm said. "I regret this whole misunderstanding. If you folks will excuse me, I'll get on back to my room down the hall."

Amber caught his arm. "Why, you'll do no such thing. You came here as my guest. You came for tea. We shall have our tea."

"Some other time, ma'am," Longarm said. "Maybe when Mr. Brockbank is free to join us."

"No." There was a ring of determination in Amber's voice now. For the first time, Longarm saw that he and Elliot were dealing with a determined, willful young woman. No wonder she was a successful actress. No wonder she kept this traveling company together despite all odds and Elliot's weaknesses; she had a will of iron. "Elliot can apologize to you . . . or get out."

"I apologize, old man," Elliot said. "Humbly." He tried to smile. "Please do stay. Have your tea." He grinned faintly, suddenly vulnerable and handsome and likeable. "If you can stomach the taste."

"You may stay if you like, Elliot," Amber said, as a queen might speak to a lowly serf.

Elliot grinned again, lopsidedly. "Anything but tea, my dear. I couldn't take tea. Not at this hour." He checked his watch. "Perhaps I can still get in a couple of hands at the Silver Palace."

* * *

72

The room was deadly quiet when Elliot walked out. Amber and Longarm followed the young actor to the door, but Amber stepped quickly back when she saw that the corridor was lined with curious, sleep-stunned people. They gawked, open-mouthed. "Show's over now," Elliot said in a cavalier tone. "You can all go back to bed now."

Amber closed the door. Longarm said, "I think we ought to have our tea party some other night, Mrs. Brockbank."

"Don't be a fool. You must stay. You would look guilty if you went now, sneaking out. We can't let Elliot behave like this and get away with it. Even if he were more than a husband in name only, he would have no right to make such a vile scene as he has tonight."

The dead silence of deepest night settled heavily in the sweet-scented room. Amber took up the cup and saucer she had dropped, but she did not mention tea again.

"I better go," Longarm said at last.

"No. Please." She tried to smile. "Would you like something to drink? Something a little stronger than tea? I hate for you to go away like this. One drink, Mr. Long, what can it hurt?"

He smiled and shrugged. "Nothing, I guess. Well, one for the road."

He watched her move about the room. She got a bottle and glasses. She poured drinks for them. Looking at the carefully brushed and piled and lacquered blond hair, he could think only one thing: Amber Austin truly was the loveliest woman he'd ever encountered, even at two in the morning.

Everything about her glowed. Despite her studied manner and her carefully schooled way of speaking, there was nothing contrived about the sharp lines of her beautiful jaw and long throat, or the Grecian elegance of her profile. Her complexion, shining warmly like ripe peaches in the lampglow, was the result of good health, enforced virtue, correct diet, and constant attention. Her beauty was her most important asset; it was the product she and her husband merchandised in their traveling shows. Longarm gave her credit. She was the best of the beautiful, she was the ultimate beauty to this moment in nature's unceasing struggle toward perfection, or whatever in hell nature was struggling toward.

He took the drink from her and tried to remember to sip it.

He gazed over his glass at her, entranced even by the faint sadness in her eyes. He supposed this sadness was something she had learned, something taught her by Elliot, along with his instruction in acting, walking, dancing, smiling, crying. . . .

"I don't feel real," she said. "Even with you, here like this."

"What do you mean?" He took a long drink despite his best efforts to relax. "You look real to me."

"But I don't *feel* real. Like a real woman. I guess I'm not real. Not really. I've never been . . . truly alive . . . except up on a stage somewhere. And that's all playacting."

"Trust me." He grinned. "You're real."

"I want to be a real woman, with a real woman's emotions. I want to be awakened . . . as a real woman is."

He swallowed hard. He had to admit to himself that he understood what she was saying, and what she was leaving unsaid, and what her invitation was. He also had to admit that he had a hard-on, just hearing those words, just looking at her enchanting body. But he also had to admit that although he had a hard-on and he wanted her desperately, this was not really very unusual. Wanting her made him no different than any other man who looked at her and wanted her, except that it made a difference to him. He had to get out of here now, or he had to have her. It was that simple and that real to him.

"I'm like a virgin," he heard her saying. "No. I really am. I'm almost untouched." Her face colored.

"That doesn't sound believable."

"Believe it. I work hard. I spend most of my time traveling or studying or acting on a stage. I have my fantasies, but I've almost given them up. . . . Or I had, until I saw you tonight."

"We haven't any right to do this to your husband. He *was* upset and miserable."

"If you take . . . my body . . . you won't be taking anything from Elliot. He doesn't want it, except as a mannequin on his stages."

Longarm finished off his drink and set his glass aside. His face felt hot, and sweat prickled his chest. "I better get out of here," he said.

"Are you afraid of me?"

"In a way. You could get us killed."

She shrugged. "Elliot won't be back. He won't come in this

room again tonight, unless I invite him in. He can't. The door is locked."

He went on standing there. She finished off her drink. They listened to the wind crying at the window, at the silence inside the room, hammering at them. She said, "Maybe you don't want me."

"You know better."

"No. I don't. I probably won't be any good. You've had many women. I'm . . . without experience."

Longarm smiled. "It's not that hard to learn."

She took a step toward him. "Tell me. What do you think of me? Right now?"

"Right now? I think you're a bubbling volcano that's about to erupt. But I know a volcano can destroy everything it touches. Even itself."

"And I'm not worth it?"

"I didn't say that. I think you're one hellish lovely woman. I feel like a wild stallion right now. God knows, right now I think you're the loveliest woman I ever met. And that's why I came in here at this ungodly hour, to drink tea with you."

Amber smiled faintly, as if she were sleepy, but she wasn't sleepy, she was intoxicated with desire. She went on staring at him, dropping away the last vestiges of her normal outward air of reserve. He was seeing her as her audiences—and maybe even her own husband—never saw her, with her guard down.

Longarm's gaze struck against Amber's, and her eyes wavered under his. A look of fright flushed across her face. She was suddenly young and unsure of herself. He grinned inwardly. It was as if she'd led him on and suddenly found herself without weapons in a cage with a tiger. She was trapped and she knew it. She had only fantasies about what might happen to her in the arms of a virile and hotly aroused man. She trembled visibly under the boldness and heat she saw in him.

She wavered forward reluctantly, and yet without the will to stop herself. Whatever restrictions had stopped her before, she had gone beyond those controls now. She wanted to plunge ahead, but it was a strange, frightening experience and she was suddenly timid.

She leaned toward him. The second her body touched his, it was as if their heated bodies coming in contact ignited a flame inside her and burned away her last defenses, her last reluctance.

She uttered a little cry and pressed closer, moving so her belly pressed against the rigidity of his crotch. He felt her part her legs slightly so the perfect fit of their bodies was even more thrilling.

Longarm's arms went around her, his hands sliding along the curve of her spine to the rise of her rounded hips. He smiled, exultant. She wore no girdle; there were no stays or thick fabrics between his hands and her pliant flesh. His fingers closed tightly on her youthful, compact, pliable firmness, and he lifted her so she rested upon his throbbing hardness, her toes barely reaching the floor. She clung there, breathing raggedly through parted lips.

His head bent down and he covered her mouth with his, opening his lips, tasting the sweetness of her mouth, suffocating her, crushing her, and kissing her until she whimpered helplessly. Gasping for breath, she struggled like a trout on a hook, but all the time she stretched upward to meet his kiss and put her head back to receive the thrusting of his tongue.

Finally she broke away from him, panting raggedly, her eyes wide and wild, her porcelain cheeks flushed and her blond hair toppling loosely about her shoulders. This gave her a young, vulnerable, and at the same time, hellishly wanton look.

No matter what, he knew they could not turn back now.

"Oh God," she whispered. "I never felt like this before. We mustn't do this . . . I'm afraid."

He lifted her again, upon his hardness. She sighed and sagged there upon him, her thighs working involuntarily. "It's too late to be afraid, Amber," he whispered against her face. "You know it is."

She only closed her eyes and nodded. She let her head sink back and her mouth parted for him.

Longarm swung her up into his arms and carried her to her sweet-scented bed. He laid her down and bent over her. He kissed her and sank down, lying on top of her. He opened her mouth, forcing her lips wide with the pressure of his tongue. He felt her go limp under him, and after a moment she began to nurse furiously at his probing tongue.

When he released her for a moment, she gasped. "It makes

me all weak...down there. I never knew it would be like that."

"It will be," Longarm said. "I promise you, it will be. You'll take it and you'll love it."

"I never have," she said. "I don't know."

"I know," he said.

He kissed her again, and then knelt on the bed beside her and traced his hands over every inch of her body, the way an Apache gentled and soothed and tamed a frightened pony. She whimpered, twisting, her hips rising and falling in an uncontrollable rhythm, trying to hurry him, but he would not be hurried.

When he closed his palms over her fevered breasts, she cried out, pleading. "Oh God! If only you would hurry...just a little. Hurry."

"Do it my way," was all he said.

"I can't stand it."

"You'll stand it."

When he had carefully and slowly outlined her whole body with his hands, caressing and loving her, he slipped off her shoes. As he tossed them carelessly aside, it occured to him that those slippers had probably cost her more than he made in a week as a lawman. It didn't matter. For this moment, this night, she was his.

He rolled her pure silk stockings down along the sensitive white flesh of her legs. As his hands drew the stockings downward, he left a trail of goosepimples in their wake.

He held her dainty foot in his palm and kissed her toes, her instep, drawing his lips upward to her trim ankles and along her calves to the hot undersides of her knees.

"Oh dear God, what kind of devil are you?" Amber whimpered. But she no longer protested, only lay still, enjoying the thrills that radiated from her body every time he touched her.

He turned her easily on the bed so she lay facedown. Then he slipped her dress over her head and tossed it over his shoulder to the floor. When she was naked, he turned her again, forcing her to lie across the mattress, her lovely legs parted slightly.

Her bared breasts pointed upward, their nipples pink and rigid. Her pubic mound was faintly feathered with dark blond hair, and he sank his fingers into its moistness, working them until she closed her legs spasmodically on his hand.

"God knows, you are lovely," he whispered. "I'll bet you don't even know how lovely you are."

"Then why do you make me wait?" she begged.

She trembled under his hand, waves of pleasure quivering through her. His hands caressed the upthrust breasts, and then his mouth closed on her nipples, suckling them. He nursed so fiercely that she cried out in delicious pain. She clutched the back of his head and held him to her breasts with all her strength. She put her head back, sobbing in ecstasy. They would hear her all through the hotel, but she did not care.

He stopped nursing at her, then removed his hand from the heated liquidity of her thighs. Her eyes flew open and she stared up at him, troubled and chilled. "What's the matter?" she whispered.

"I've got something for you," he said.

Holding her breath, Amber watched him jerk loose the buttons of his fly. When his staff hove into view, quivering and taut, she cried out in delight. Involuntarily she clutched the rod in both her hands and fell upon it, breathless and panting.

He let her love him with her mouth for a few moments, he let her live out her wildest fantasies. Sometimes sucking it for a moment like that insulated it and made it last longer when he mounted her. God knew, at this moment he didn't care how long they lasted.

He pushed her legs apart and poised himself above her. Her hands clutched him and he let her guide him into her fiery wet orifice.

He clamped his hand over her mouth to keep her from screaming out her frenzied pleasure at the top of her lungs. He carried her up past sanity, reason, resistance, and resolve. Unable to endure the frantic delight, she exploded. Sobbing, she chewed on the palm of his hand.

They sagged upon the bed, spent, but Amber kept her legs locked about his waist and would not release him. "You are a devil," she whispered at last.

"Then you're the devil's woman."

"God knows, I hope so."

He sighed and sank his nose into the heat and exotic fragrance of her rich, thick blond hair. She clung to him, exploring, touching, driven compulsively to praise him with her hands and mouth.

Her unrestrained explorations with lips and tongue and fingers excited him when he'd thought he was finished. He felt his staff engorge with blood, pulsing with desire, and he began to ride her again, savagely.

She exhaled, submitting and thrusting herself up to his punishment. Her head sank back, her hair golden against the white of the bed, her eyes shimmering with unshed tears, her cheeks soft and flushed and bruised. She went wild, loving him frantically.

She was asleep when he drew the covers over her and crept silently from the room, fixing his clothing as well as he could.

He was almost to his room when a whisper of sound along the corridor brought him up, tense. He stopped, legs braced apart, staring.

Sheriff Lawson Carr stood, cold and unmoving, watching him from the deepest shadows of the hallway....

Chapter 7

Longarm awoke just after sunup. He stretched under the goose-down comforter, wincing slightly at the pain in his side, but he felt good, relaxed, satisfied. He grinned and threw off the covers in the withering cold of the hotel room.

Teeth rattling, he used the chamber pot and washed up as much as he could endure with the icy water. Then he walked to the window and stared down at the main street of Dirty Fork. A strange gray rime frosted the world beyond his dusty pane as far as he could see. A benumbed and chilling stillness held the world in thrall. Even the sunlight was pale with cold, and he turned away from the window, shuddering involuntarily.

He dressed quickly, thinking about Amber to keep his blood stirring. He even thought about walking four doors down the corridor and climbing in her bed again. He knew better. There was trouble in Dirty Fork, and he was on the taxpayers' time.

He went downstairs to the hotel restaurant. The room was almost empty and the strange morning chill pervaded the place. People huddled over their tables, wearing greatcoats as they ate.

"Funny weather," Longarm said to a man seated at a nearby table.

The farmer nodded, shivering. His voice was heavily accented. "Aye. I keep looking for the blizzard, you know. But no sign. Never saw nothing like this, not even up in Minnesota."

"Maybe it's too cold to blow in a blizzard," Longarm said.

"Never saw nothing like this."

"You live around here?"

"Aye. Homestead. Out on the fenced ranges. Put in my crops. Got a hellish feeling I'm going to be wiped out again this year. We already had a spring greenup. Looks like a man could count on it being spring. Our cow had dropped her calf. A freeze right now would kill the calf for sure, and maybe the cow. In town to talk to Banker Estabrook. I'm scairt, I can tell you that. Even if the cold holds off, we got no guarantee no more that them Texans won't cut government fences and tromp our gardens to dust." The man tried to laugh. "A man has got to be three-quarters fool to try to farm in Colorado."

Longarm nodded, silently agreeing. He ordered eggs and sirloin, spending his daily breakfast and lunch allowance. A man needed his strength.

Though it was bitterly cold, dry, and still, Longarm decided to take a stroll around the town. He hesitated on the hotel veranda, looking both ways along the nearly deserted street. A few election signs decorated storefronts and poles and up-rights: "*Reelect Lawson Carr. Your Sheriff. He Saved Your Town. He's Earned Your Trust.*" Three or four other men were opposing Carr for the office. Among the challengers was a nester named Haswell Nunn. He admitted no law experience, but his pitch was that he would truly represent the people.

Longarm bit the end off a cheroot, fired up a match, and breathed deeply of the warm smoke. It clouded for a moment across his face. He buttoned his fleece-lined jacket to the throat and turned up its shaggy collar. Smoking, he strode out on the boardwalk, thankful for the woolly chaps. Only his feet were cold as he tramped along Main Street.

Longarm met only a few people on his stroll around the town. Whenever he did meet another soul brave enough to be abroad in the strange and pinching chill, he tried to take a sampling of opinion on the coming election, on the average citizen's feelings about the way government fence and government graze were being destroyed. He could find no agreement among the citizenry. Most of them were too involved in the daily business of staying alive to care about what happened to government property. As far as they were concerned, the government was a pack of dishonest bureaucrats in Denver and Washington, and they were lucky that the rascals were kept together as much as possible. He found that most people thought Lawson Carr was a great sheriff and had done a lot for this town when it was wild and dangerous. But he also got the feeling that Carr wasn't widely loved. Admired and feared, yes, and respected, but not totally trusted. People were hesitant to say anything against Sheriff Carr, but those who did gather up their courage suggested that as far as they could see, Lawson Carr served the interests of Mr. Fondis Estabrook and not those of the ordinary people of Dirty Fork.

As to the cut fences, most of the people couldn't have cared less. One man at the general store said, "This here town was a trail town. That there was its only excuse for being. By all rights, Dirty Fork ought to be dead and deserted, like a lot of other ghost towns 'twixt Austin and Cheyenne. It's a dying town. I don't reckon it matters much what happens to it now, one way or the other."

Another man said, "We ought to do all we can to encourage them Texas drovers to run their herds through here. Hell, let 'em cut all the fence they need, eat all the grass their cows can stomach. If it wasn't for them drovers, we'd have no money coming in at all. We'd be dead then, all right."

"The hell! I say fine them Texas bastids ten bucks a head for every cut fence 'twixt here and the state line. The government set that good land apart for us farmers to homestead. It's homesteadin' land, not graze country, and us farmers is got a right to expect to be protected from cattlemen and their herds."

Dirty Fork's county building was one of the only two red brick structures inside settlement limits. The single-floored, oblong building crouched a couple of blocks from the Silver Palace, which seemed to mark the center of town, in an otherwise empty square. A gallows stood beside the sheriff's office like some grim monument to swift and unyielding justice.

Longarm walked along the silent street in the wan midmorning sunlight. Though the sun rose, it did not heat; yet it grew no colder, either. The weather held, nothing changed from the day before. It was puzzling weather, that was all that was certain about it. Longarm, range-wise and experienced as he was in the open country, had never encountered anything to match it, because though storms, cyclones, tornadoes, or snows seemed to threaten, nothing happened. Everything seemed suspended, waiting, breathless. The sky shone sharply clear and vacant and cloudless. As the sun rose, the wind stilled, and yet to add to the confusion and sense of wrong, there was almost a hum of expectancy in the static atmosphere. Something was about to happen. Only God knew what.

It was a little after ten in the morning when Longarm reached the sheriff's office in the county building. He paused on the stoop, finishing off his cheroot and tossing it toward the street, where a couple of horses shuddered at the hitch rail, heads drooping in the chilled sunlight.

Voices spilled through the doorway: one savage, yet soft and controlled, the other whining and complaining. The discussion ended suddenly and the outer door, marked SHERIFF, opened and Elliot Brockbank came through it.

Both Longarm and the blond young actor stopped dead in their tracks, shocked and discomfited at this meeting. Longarm admitted to himself that though his loins felt good, his conscience bothered him. He had come from the heated bed of this man's wife. Brockbank looked as if he had woes enough without some stranger putting the spurs to his woman.

Longarm stared, stunned at the besotted man. If he had not seen Elliot drunk last night in Amber's bedroom, he would not have recognized this derelict as the same idealized male beauty who'd enchanted the women from the Silver Palace stage.

Elliot Brockbank shivered in the anguished depths of a hangover. Maybe he had lived through many of them, but he'd never learned to live *with* them. He looked haggard, beaten, destroyed. His pale beard smeared his smooth cheeks like patches of dirt. His purple-encircled eyes squinted, red-lined and bitter, against the light of day and the grim prospect of his own future. His curly hair matted his forehead, sweat ran along his face, and his clothes were sweated and sour.

Elliot clutched a few greenbacks in his trembling fingers. The instant he recognized Longarm, he tried to conceal the rumpled paper money in his fist. He hid it not because he feared it might be stolen from him, but because his conscience clawed at him. Obviously this was money he'd cadged inside that office. From Sheriff Lawson?

Longarm winced, pitying the fellow. He wore a frock coat, but no overcoat. He seemed unaware of the freezing chill; he was begging for pneumonia.

"Hellish day," Longarm said.

Brockbank nodded, though he was still oblivious to the cold.

Brockbank attempted a smile, a caricature that twisted his face out of shape. "I meant to look you up this morning, Mr. Long."

"Oh? What for?"

Brockbank's face twisted again. He looked as if he might weep. But his beautifully modulated voice remained painfully controlled. "Apology, sir."

"Apology? For what?"

"The way I behaved last night. There was no excuse for it. I went out of my head."

"It's all right. I told you then, a man has every right to protect his wife—"

"But he can't, can he?" Elliot said, voice quavering. "Not really. There's nothing he can do, is there?"

Longarm exhaled. "Standing out in this cold won't help you solve anything, Elliot. I'm sorry for the misunderstanding. Why don't you get on to the hotel and get out of this cold?"

Elliot gazed at him a moment, eyes anguished. "I appreciate your concern, Mr. Long . . . I really do . . . I would have sworn you . . . didn't give a damn."

He peered into Longarm's face for the space of a long breath, and then he staggered past him, half toppling down the steps and listing along the boardwalk toward the hotel.

"Damn," Longarm said under his breath. "Damn. Damn. Damn."

The sheriff's office utilized every inch of the building space allotted to it. Four desks, gun racks, filing cases, chairs, and other equipment crowded the area. Behind it were the cells of the county jail.

Two deputies lounged at desks pushed back against a wall. Both got to their feet and departed at a curt nod of Lawson Carr's graying head.

"No sense burdening them with anything we have to say to each other," Carr said. He gazed up at Longarm, and tension crackled in the charged atmosphere of the room.

"Oh? Do we have anything to say to each other that doesn't come under the heading of official business?" Longarm inquired.

Lawson Carr remained chilled. "That's up to you, Long."

Longarm said, "I'm here for one reason, Sheriff. Just one. Government property is being destroyed in your jurisdiction. Only nobody's doing anything about it. That's the only reason I'm here."

"I see." Lawson Carr fingered a couple of rifle bullets on his desk. His reserved manner returned, and he wore it like a mask.

"You people bringing some kind of charges?" he inquired.

"What's that supposed to mean?"

"Politics, Long. I'm the opposition party, as far as you people in Denver—and Washington—are concerned. I reckon a good way to get rid of me would be to bring some trumped-up charges of dereliction of duty right here at election time."

"Nobody mentioned your politics. They told me that fences are being cut on government graze across the Arkansas Divide—"

"Bobwire fence is hellish unpopular, Long. It's being cut just about anywhere it's being strung."

"That don't make cuttin' it legal. Whether fences are right or wrong has nothing to do with it as far as I'm concerned. I'm as blind as that lady justice is supposed to be."

"You mean that naked whore crooked judges keep on their desks?"

"That's the lady. Somebody else makes the laws and we enforce 'em."

"Oh, I enforce the law, Long. Even that one. I see somebody cuttin' bobwire, I arrest him. Somebody brings in charges against a wire-cutter, I bring him in and indict him. But do you mean do I go out of my way to check on government-graze bobwire? No, I don't. And I don't need you coming in here telling me how to do my job."

Longarm drew a deep breath. In spite of his anger against this snobbish Southern son of a bitch, he felt a stirring of pity for him. In his mind he saw Carr as the sheriff had looked, rooted to the floor in the darkness, staring at Amber Austin's bedroom door, knowing a man was in there with her, and powerless to do anything about it. The conflict between him and Carr over the cut wire was just the coverup for what was really sticking in the sheriff's craw. Plainly, Carr wanted to kill him, but he needed an excuse that had nothing to do with Amber Austin and what had happened in her bedroom last night.

Longarm kept his voice level. "I'm not going to try to tell you how to do your job, you know that. But I may have to do it for you."

"I won't have you coming in here throwing your weight around in my jurisdiction," Carr said in that soft Virginia accent that concealed his hatred under a thin crust.

Longarm shrugged. "Either you and I work together, or we work at odds, Sheriff. That's up to you. That's your decision. My orders say that this cutting of government fence has got to stop, one way or the other. You and I stop it, working together, or we work against each other. But I'm here until it stops."

"Long, you know damned well you can't stop Texas drovers from cutting that wire, working with me or against me. You want to stop wire-cutting, you bring in the fucking cavalry and station a man every hundred yards." Carr grinned coldly. "That might do it."

"I don't reckon it needs to come to that, Sheriff. "Longarm said. "We are willing to repair a few cuts the drovers make in passing through here on the Goodnight-Loving-Trail north. It would stir up another Civil War if we tried to stop them, or if we imposed fines. We hear that locals are cutting that wire. That's the shit I'm here to stop."

Carr stared at him coldly for a long breath. Then he grinned tautly, the smile pulling painfully at the corners of his wide mouth. The sickness swirled deeply in his gray eyes, but he managed to keep his handsome face smiling. "I think maybe you need to know more about Dirty Fork and what goes on here, Long. I'm going to do you a friendly act. I'm going to help you find out—before you start something you can't undo."

Longarm and Sheriff Carr walked shoulder-to-shoulder along the boardwalk. Longarm was aware that people paused in whatever they were doing to gaze at them in overt admiration. It occurred to him that he and Lawson Carr did make a formidable duo—two big, experienced lawmen walking side by side.

Longarm grinned inwardly. If only those townspeople knew

the truth, they wouldn't feel so elated and warm and secure. Carr hated his guts. It had nothing to do with their job, but Lawson Carr would see him dead before he lifted a finger to help him—and that had to make one hell of a difference in how the law was enforced around Dirty Fork in the immediate future.

Longarm sighed. It was too bad. Carr was one hell of a lawdog, but it was as if Amber Austin strode between them on that walk, as if she built a wall between them, a wall that would come down in one way—blasted to pieces by gunfire.

Lawson Carr paused outside the second red brick building in Dirty Fork—its bank. The sheriff glanced at Longarm and limped ahead of him, holding open the thick front door. He ushered Longarm into the lobby ahead of him.

The bank was small; a safe was set against a rear wall, there were latticed windows for deposits and withdrawals, and an area of desks stood near the safe, the heart of the institution where its officers congregated.

Carr limped ahead of Longarm toward the officer's region, which was cut off from the rest of the bank by a mahogany railing. Carr stood tall and reserved until the aging man at the largest desk looked up and recognized him.

This man was engaged in a violent but subdued quarrel with young Kane Estabrook. When the older man recognized Sheriff Carr, he ended the raging dialogue abruptly and jerked his head, ordering Kane out of the area.

Kane's face was gray, set, his eyes bleak. He managed to nod toward Longarm and Sheriff Carr, but was unable to smile.

Fondis Estabrook was not what Longarm had expected him to be. The bank was not large, but even if it had been, its interior would have been dwarfed by the older Estabrook's dominating presence.

Estabrook got up from his desk and strode to the mahogany railing, hand extended. "Sheriff Carr. Good to see you. Come in. Come on in."

Estabrook's voice was deep and powerful. Though he was confined by the demands of commerce to this desk in the bank for at least part of each day, Estabrook spoke as if he were shouting orders on wind-riven ranges, in tones the wind had never diluted or torn apart. It was obvious his orders were always heard and always obeyed.

Underlings jumped to bring chairs for Estabrook's guests even before the bank officer ordered it done. Estabrook didn't bother to thank them, or even to acknowledge their presence. He shook hands with Longarm and said he had been expecting him. "We can use help down here, Mr. Long. If the fucking government is the only place we can get it, that's where we'll take it. Am I right, Lawson?"

Carr smiled in that reserved way of his. His soft voice taunted the older man. "You never got where you are by being wrong, Fondis."

"That's the God's truth," Estabrook agreed. He was just under six-feet tall, his keglike legs supporting a barrel-heavy body that didn't look fat in rich whipcord trousers, frock coat, and white linen shirt. Estabrook was big, but not obese. He was in his early fifties, but he was still rough and hard and muscular. His hair was graying and his jowls were thickening; he looked as if he had devoured too many of his home-grown steaks along with potatoes smothered in butter-rich gravy.

He was the kind of man who seemed to look down on others in a way that had nothing to do with physical size. He gazed along his nose, sneering slightly, even when he smiled—a man used to giving orders and not even looking to see if they were obeyed, because he was too busy counting his money. He had wielded power all of his adult life; he dominated everything and everybody around him. As far as he was concerned, this was the correct order of things in this world where might made right. In this world he was always right because he was richer and stronger and more powerful than anyone else.

Fondis Estabrook looked perfectly at ease at his banking desk. The only false note was the gun strapped and tied down low on his hip. He looked as if he were ready to use that gun anytime his smiling and his money and his demanding didn't get him what he wanted, the moment he wanted it. He'd live and let live, or he'd kill—as long as he got his way.

Longarm had the sudden feeling that he was wedged in between these two ruthless and powerful men, without room to breathe unless he played their game, their way.

He wished now that when he'd first been alone with Lawson

Carr, he had given the sheriff the chance to speak up about last night, to get that business about Amber off his chest. The wrong between them was bad, and it was festering. Outwardly, Lawson Carr was all business, the able lawman, but there was tension in the way he sat there, as if braced against Longarm, seething with hatred, even while he smiled and spoke in that gentle voice that sounded like it was strained through a washpot of grits.

"My job down here is real simple, Mr. Estabrook," Longarm said. "They sent me here to stop whoever is cutting government fences. If you and Sheriff Carr can help me, I'll deeply appreciate it."

"Oh, we can help you, all right. Ain't that the truth, Lawson?" Fondis Estabrook said. Sheriff Carr smiled and nodded. Estabrook said, "Nobody is ever going to stop them Texans from cutting wire when they take their herds north."

"The Interior Department understands that," Longarm said. "That random cutting and the once-in-a-while grazing of passing cows is something they expect to have to live with. But this cutting is bigger than that, more persistent, and downright everlasting. Somebody don't want those fences. Unfortunately, the government does want them up—and uncut."

"Very good, Mr. Long." Estabrook nodded decisively. "If that there is all you want, get your warrant spelt out, and I can tell you where to serve it—because I know for a by-damned fact who is cutting that fence. He's done it before and by damn he's still doing it. He's a criminal and a vulture and a known rustler, and his name is Flagg Lobatos."

"Flagg Lobatos," Longarm said. "I will certainly investigate the gentleman—"

"The vermin," Estabrook said. "The scum of the earth, him and his brood and his running iron."

Longarm kept his voice low. "Still, I don't want to go off on some wild-goose chase. You can see that. I ain't here to settle any personal hashes—"

"What in hell are you daring to say to Mr. Estabrook?" Carr said in that gentle, steel-ribbed voice.

"What in hell do you mean, sir?" Estabrook said, face flushed.

"I mean what must be clear to both of you. You sound like

89

you carry a powerful deep hate for this Flagg Lobatos. If you got evidence against him, that's one thing, but if you want to destroy him, for personal or business or private reasons, that can only be between you and the sheriff and Mr. Lobatos. The U.S. Government doesn't like us marshals to get involved in local squabbles."

Estabrook controlled himself with almost visible effort. A blue vein appeared in relief along his forehead, and tendons stood in his neck. But he managed to keep his voice controlled. "Well, sir, you come in here asking for my help. I offered it to you. And it seems to me you're downright insulting."

"I don't mean to be. But I can't pretend to be ignorant of the fact that your son Kane is in love with Flagg Lobatos' daughter, and that you oppose the union, or match, or romance, or whatever in hell it is."

"You bet your goddamn bottom dollar I do, sir. My son Kane is not in love with that Lobatos bitch. He's got the scent, that's all. When he comes to his senses, he'll know I'm right. He'll thank me. But I'm not talking personal affairs with you. You asked me who was cutting your goddamn bobwire and I told you—and suddenly you're making me the villain of the piece and I can tell you goddamn square out, I don't appreciate that none."

"I don't mean to upset you or to antagonize you."

"You're doing a pretty fair goddamn job, without trying."

"I apologize, Mr. Estabrook. Let's start over. Maybe you'd like to give me some evidence—the kind I can use in a court-room against Flagg Lobatos."

"All right, Mr. Government Marshal, I'll do that. First, I'm a local rancher. I been here in this country since the early sixties. That's a long time. I've seen this here country grow. I've seen it become lawless in many ways—more so than when the ranges were open and a few of us run our cows free on them. I know times do change, and I change with them. I've made big investments in this here region, in this town. I own this bank. I own the saloon-theater, the Silver Palace. I own the hotel, though most folks don't know that I had to take it on a bad mortgage. People say this here town is dying. Well, maybe. And maybe it would be dead if it wasn't for what life me and my money has pumped into it."

"That's the truth," Lawson Carr stated.

"I don't doubt a word so far," Longarm said. "But that still don't give me what I need from you—evidence against Mr. Flagg Lobatos."

"I'm coming to that. I'm just trying to show you that I got the good of this here Divide country in my heart. I have! By God I have."

"Nobody denies that, Fondis," Carr said in a soothing tone.

"Well, sir, here I am with my investments and my blood and energy in this range. You know what a vaquero is—or was, Mr. Long?" Longarm nodded, but Estabrook went on in his outraged, booming voice. "Vaqueros, as they called them down on the border—they've been around as long as us honest ranchers have, even though we've done all we could to stamp them out. They're wandering cow-herders. They have no ranch, no home base, nothing but a running iron and brass guts. They rounded up and branded half-wild cattle, fed them as best they could, and then sold them off wherever they could. And the profit—except for sweat and labor—was one hundred percent because they had no expenses, no ranch, no workers except their family. They were rustlers because they preyed on the spreads of honest ranchers. Ranchers are businessmen with a home base and big expenses. A rancher is a businessman that raises his cows on his own or permitted ranges. That's what I've always done and that's what I still do. I pay my two bits a head for any Flying F cattle that eat on government graze.

"Well, the open range has shrunk, and most of the vaqueros have died off or been killed or jailed. Flagg Lobatos is one of them herders. He's the plumb last of the breed. He's got no ranch. He still wanders—or did—from place to place, using his running iron to brand his Wolfhead—a triangle with two ears—on wild or loose cattle.

"But now, for some reason, he's settled on land that had always been considered mine, up at Screaming Springs. But in order to feed his cattle, he's got to cut bobwire, and he's got to steal water and grass. His cattle spread hoof-and-mouth disease and anything else they can pick up and transmit, them half-starving critters he calls cows. There you are, sir. There's your goddamn evidence against Flagg Lobatos. Squatting on my land. Cutting bobwire. Stealing grass and water I pay for, and leting my cows break free through the fence the son of bitch cuts."

Longarm nodded. "Sounds pretty firm, your evidence. I'll ride out to Screaming Springs and talk to Lobatos."

The two men stared at him. The contempt in Lawson Carr's face was almost tangible. Estabrook burst out laughing. "You just going to ride up there alone, eh?"

"If I have to."

Estabrook threw his head back, roaring with savage, raking laughter. "Then you take my advice, sir, and make up your will before you go—because you ain't coming back alive."

"Why not?" Cold with rage, Longarm moved his gaze from Estabrook's flushed face to Carr's unsmiling features.

"Because since Flagg staked his claim up at Screaming Springs, he keeps his three sons and reprobate daughter on guard, watching for strangers who come too close. They got Flagg's orders—shoot to warn, and if that don't work, shoot to kill."

Longarm exhaled heavily. "I got off my trail yesterday coming in here. Mozelle Lobatos said she shot at me accidentally."

Carr's voice showed his contempt. "I can tell you, sir, if Mozelle had shot at you, even accidentally, she'd have got you. She can handle a gun better than any man I know."

Longarm nodded. "I know that now, but why would she say it was accidental?"

Carr shrugged. "Because you hung around—but evidently didn't try to go on up to Screaming Springs. When she shot at you, she didn't expect to have to talk to you. Most people the Lobatoses shoot at take off running with their tails between their legs. The next time you go, you'll turn back or they'll bring you out with your toes turned up. They don't shoot to miss, not twice."

"Still, I mean to talk to Flagg Lobatos. How do I get word to him?"

Fondis Estabrook's voice shook with hatred for Lobatos and his family and for the misery they'd brought him. "Let my son Kane take your message up there. Then Lobatos can decide if he'll come out to see you. My son Kane has the honor of being one of the only outsiders the Lobatoses will allow up at Screaming Springs."

Chapter 8

Dirty Fork showed a bit more life around noon, when Longarm left Fondis Estabrook's office at the bank. Warming sun and abating wind had brought in some of the sod farmers and cowhands from nearby ranches, as well as restless Indians from the nearest reservation. They shivered against the cold and begged money for drinks. The poor bastards bore no resemblance to their forefathers. Most wore run-over moccasins made for them by their women, and cast-off Levi's from some church rummage sale or spasmodic Christian relief package. Their denim shirts were open at the chest, and any jackets or sweaters they wore were ragged or threadbare.

Longarm walked down to the livery stable, where he rented a single-seat buggy and carriage horse for the afternoon. The Indian who had named the gale "wolf wind" last night was tossing hay and shoveling manure. He gave Longarm a brief nod of recognition.

Longarm grinned at him. "Figured out this weather yet?"

"I told you, mister, last night. Wolf wind." The Indian shrugged. "I tell all these people. For what? Nobody listens."

"You mean you're telling them to run for the cyclone cellars?"

The Indian nodded. "Or to the saloon. You got to be safe or drunk when the wolf wind strikes. I have seen it."

"You're not running for a hideout."

The Indian shrugged again. "Maybe I make enough money to get drunk. Who knows, eh?" He pitched another forkful of hay.

Longarm laughed, liking the young redskin. "What's your name?"

"Sam Brown."

"One hell of an Indian name."

The Indian shrugged. "I get by."

Longarm watched him. "What do you think of being out on the open plains this afternoon in a one-horse rig?"

"I try not to think about that at all."

"You wouldn't do it, huh?"

"Not if I had good sense."

"Maybe you'd like to hire out to show me the way over to Sun Patch and back?"

"You mean you'll pay me?"

"Won't do you much good if the wolf wind gets you."

The Indian tossed aside the hay fork. "You ready to go now?"

"I thought you were scared of the wolf wind."

"I ain't scared of it. Wolf wind can't do much to me, now that the white brother has worked me over. Maybe I die in the wolf wind. That's not the worst way to die. Anyhow, none of us ever pick where we die, mister."

Sun Patch was a clean little settlement ten miles along the south trail from Dirty Fork. Like Dirty Fork, Sun Patch was set down in the bare prairie, without much reason or design. But the town looked alive, though it too was stunned by the cold. Trees had been planted across the north and west town limits as windbreaks, and other trees grew dusty and frail in yards and along the main street. Some of the buildings had been recently painted. Longarm nodded his satisfaction. He was impressed with Sun Patch. He wouldn't want to live there, but it was a village its people cared about.

He bought Sam Brown a beer and a cheese sandwich, and left the youth sitting wrapped in a horse blanket in the runabout while he talked with merchants and clerks in the stores along Main Street. Sun Patch was little concerned with the cutting of government barbed wire. Tempers didn't run high here. When the Texas herds came through, folks battened down and collected what they could for food, water, and whiskey. Otherwise the countryside was quiet, with more and more dirt farmers moving in, so the area was less and less dependent on the trail herders. They considered Sun Patch a farming community, but they had learned to live with the herders, as they lived with the blizzards and the months of drought and the deerflies and all the other delights of High Plains living.

With a horse blanket over his knees, Longarm went west off the trail on the return to Dirty Fork. He had gone about five miles when he found signs of snipped barbed wire, and other places where the wire had been restrung and cut again. The grass east of the fence was trampled and shorn to dusty stubs. West of the wire, the first greening of spring showed. The reason why the fence was cut was clear: that grass on the other side was a temptation too great to resist. Longarm could recall Amber Austin lying naked on her bed last night and understand exactly how cattlemen felt about that grass and that barbed wire.

He sighed heavily and glanced at Sam Brown. The young Indian was scowling, studying the horizon and the cloudless sky through troubled, squinting eyes. "What do you see, Sam Brown?"

"Nothing. That's what scares me good."

It was after four o'clock when Longarm returned the horse and rig to the livery stable. The owner taunted the Indian. "Never expected to see you alive again, Sam Brown. What happened to your wolf wind?"

The Indian shrugged. "It's out there, all right. Wolf skulks, but when he howls, it's already too late to run for cover."

The livery stable owner laughed and shook his head, amused and exasperated with the red man. "Indians are sure hell funny," the stable owner said. "Sam Brown is the best of the lot, and he ain't much."

Longarm paid Sam Brown two dollars for guiding him. The stable owner protested. "My God, man, what you trying to do? Ruin him? He'll stay drunk a week now. Maybe end up with pneumonia."

Longarm grinned and clapped Sam Brown on the shoulder. "Just giving Sam a weapon against the wolf."

"May the full moon light your night path," Sam Brown said. He kissed the money and laughed. "Let the old wolf howl, huh?"

Longarm had a single straight rye at the Silver Palace. He stood at the bar and tossed off the drink against the dust of the road.

Shivering in the plunging cold, he went along the vacated boardwalk to the hotel.

As he entered the lobby, the clerk looked up, his face troubled. "Someone to see you. Up in your room, Mr. Long. I didn't know what to do. . . ."

Longarm shrugged and strode past the clerk. He went up the stairwell to the second floor. The hallway was like an icy corridor with the wind blasting through it.

He saw his door standing open and he hesitated, loosening the lower buttons on his fleece-lined greatcoat and slapping the flap back from his cross-draw Colt. Flagg Lobatos? Could the herder have come in this quickly?

He paused at the doorway. Then he saw Amber Austin standing across the room at the closed window. Her back was to him, but she looked better going away than most women did full on. She was incredibly lovely, even with her slender shoulders rounded wearily.

When Amber heard his steps at the door, she wheeled around. "Oh, Custis! I've waited so long."

Longarm took a couple of long steps into the room and then stopped, staring at Amber. The lovely face was battered, bruised, and swollen. Her shapely mouth was cut. "Holy Moses, what's happened to you?"

"Elliot," she said.

"He did that to you?"

She sighed. "It was much worse. He only stopped when he thought I was unconscious. But please, never mind that. I . . . I'm in terrible trouble."

Longarm touched her arms, found her trembling. He narrowed his eyes, gazing into her face. "What happened?"

"Elliot," she said again. She had difficulty speaking through the broken lip. "I left him in the dressing room . . . a long time ago. I think I killed him . . . I ran away . . . I had nowhere else to go . . . I came here . . . oh, I've been waiting so long."

"Maybe you better tell me what happened."

She nodded, then hesitated, pale and uncertain. "It all started this morning. Elliot came to my room. He looked terrible, and smelled like an old bar rag. I told him to get out. He said something I didn't understand then—he said he could pay for it if he had to.

"Then he seemed to calm down. He said he had met you outside the Sheriff's office, and that he had apologized to you for the way he had acted. He said it was not until later that he found out that you'd spent the rest of the night in my room with me . . . and he didn't apologize to you for being angry about that."

"He didn't mention it."

"That was it. He was very strange. Cold and withdrawn. It was as if all the rage and hurt and violence were pushed down inside him, and he was holding it in with some super-human effort and that really he didn't mean to speak of it to me.

"At last he went away, into his own room. The last thing he said was that I had missed a dozen cues last night in the play and that we had to rehearse as soon as I'd had breakfast. I agreed. He went to the barbershop, where he had a hot bath and a shave and a manicure. When he changed his clothing, he looked like his old self. All signs of the hangover were gone—except for his eyes. They seemed to burn murderously."

"Why didn't you stay away from him?"

"Because I've never been afraid of Elliot before. I've never had any reason to fear him. He's never struck me in anger before. Never."

"Well, he's sure as hell made up for it now."

"That's it. It's something else. He's never been jealous. I've had my friends and he has his—and his pals were other men, and sometimes they spent the night with him in his bed-room. I would hear them laughing and drinking and talking. I never protested. But now it's almost as if this were a scene from *Othello*—as if poor Elliot's jealousy was being fed to him by someone else. As if it were liquor—the more he gets, the drunker and more insane he becomes. Just when he would quiet down, it would flare up again."

Longarm took a long breath. He said, "Your friend and suitor, Lawson Carr, was standing in the hall out there when I came out of your room. He may have passed on the word to Elliot."

She shuddered. "Lawson acts as if he owns me. I've never let him touch me. But he doesn't act as if he wants to, the way you did. It's as if he put me on a pedestal, as if I were a statue, and not real at all."

Longarm nodded. "It's the way those plantation cavaliers treated all their 'good' women. No wonder so many Confederate belles went crazy, or hid in closets with house servants. A 'good' woman is untouchable. I'm sure Sheriff Carr would tell you that."

She winced. "He has told me that. But I only laughed at him. I didn't realize he was serious. Surely he wouldn't tell Elliot—"

"Somebody did. Why don't you tell me the rest of it?"

Amber nodded. "We—Elliot and I—went down to the Silver Palace and backstage to our dressing room. He started finding fault with my performance in *The Missing Rose*. And suddenly he was screaming at me, and he began beating me. I tried to get away, but I couldn't. He knocked me down and I lay still. He bent over me, crying and saying he was sorry. He thought I was unconscious. I let him think I was terribly hurt. He stood up and got a bottle of whiskey. I watched him take a drink and then I was more afraid of him than ever. I tried to crawl to the door, but he heard me and grabbed me. He yelled something about my trying to sneak out to one of my rutting lovers, but he wasn't going to let me. I fought free. I grabbed up the whiskey bottle and hit him with it on the head as hard as I could."

She sank against him, shuddering and crying. Longarm held her without speaking for a moment, then said, "What happened next?"

"Nothing. He staggered and fell to the floor. He didn't move. I was in terror. I was afraid I had killed him. All I could think was that I had to get to you, you could help me. You were the only one who could help me. I came back here to the hotel. I asked for you, but they said you were out. They let me stay in your room. I've been half out of my mind."

"And you haven't heard any more from Elliot?"

Her teeth chattered. She cried out. "Didn't you hear me? I told you. I think I killed him."

Longarm smiled and kissed her cheek gently, trying to reassure her. "I know. You told me. But sometimes men aren't that easy to kill. Even actors. Why don't you wait here? I'll go down and see if he's all right. Then I'll come back here. When you know he's all right, you'll feel better."

"I'll never feel better. I feel like my life is over."

The wind had ebbed slightly as the sun set beyond the distant Ramparts. Longarm walked swiftly across the wide, wheel-ribbed street to the Sliver Palace. The first person he saw when he entered the saloon was Sheriff Lawson Carr. The lawman sat alone. Longarm forced himself to slow his pace. He went to the bar, ordered a beer, and then carried it to a table against a far wall, near the doorway to the backstage area.

He drank, taking his time until two men came in. Though it was obvious Carr hadn't invited them, they sat with him, talking coldly, quietly, and steadily. Silently, Longarm thanked them for the diversion. He finished off the beer and sidled through the door to the silent backstage area.

He didn't have to look far for the dressing room Elliot and Amber shared. A gold-tinsel star decorated the door. He rapped on the facing. There was no response from within. Faintly troubled, Longarm turned the knob. The door was unlocked. He stepped inside and closed the door behind him.

He exhaled a long sigh, not realizing that he had been holding his breath. The room was in disarray. There was no doubt that Elliot and Amber had fought in here earlier. Their vanity mirrors reflected the disorder, overturned straight chairs, clothing strewn about.

In the middle of the dishevelment, Elliot sprawled in a club chair.

Longarm crossed to where Elliot lay, with his handsome head back. Elliot was unconscious, but he was alive. A small goose-egg on his forehead was the discolored souvenir of his battle with Amber. She had hit him all right. But it was the whiskey inside the bottle that had finished Elliot off. He smelled like liquor. He was totally sotted. Longarm wondered how many performances this impossibly beautiful young actor had missed like this, and for this reason.

Elliot breathed softly, contentedly blowing little bubbles between his blood-red, shapely lips.

"You poor, miserable little son of a bitch," Longarm said.

He glanced around, found nothing else of interest, and went

out of the room. He closed the door behind him, hoping Elliot could sleep it off before the eight o'clock curtain.

He was almost back to the door to the saloon when he remembered that Lawson Carr was sitting out there. He didn't want to talk to the sheriff just now. The hell with him. As far as he was concerned, Carr had poisoned Elliot's mind against Amber, had continued to pressure the drunken actor, had likely challenged the poor little bastard's manhood, practically demanding that Elliot take the kind of action any wronged husband would have to take to protect his home and his honor. Carr had never left Virginia; he had brought the Confederacy west with him, along with the minie ball in his knee.

Longarm let himself out a rear door into the alley. It was abruptly dark with the sun gone. A few lights glowed yellowly along the street. He hunched up his shoulders against the cold and hurried toward the hotel.

All he could think was that he had good news and bad news for Amber. The good news was that Elliot was alive; she had not killed him. The bad news was that she had to somehow go on living with him. . . .

When Longarm let himself into his room at the hotel, Amber was sprawled facedown across his bed. She was fully clothed and she had pulled the goosedown comforter haphazardly across her shoulders. Longarm felt a rush of pity for her. She was beaten, emotionally exhausted, deathly afraid.

He sat down on the bed beside her. She turned over and gazed up at him, her battered face taut, eyes swirling with terror. "How bad is it?" she whispered. "Is . . . he dead, Custis? Tell me."

"Elliot's as alive as you are, and a hell of a lot happier."

"Happier?"

"He's passed out. Dead drunk. That's where he looks for his happiness, ain't it? You put a goose-egg bump on his head, but you didn't really hurt him. He'll be as pretty and as good as new tomorrow. Unfortunately, you won't. He did a more thorough job on you."

She clung to him, trembling. "I don't care what I look like, just so he is alive. Did he say anything to you?"

"He's sleeping it off. I don't know if you have enough

100

makeup to cover that purple shiner Elliot gave you, but if he has learned quick recovery, the curtain will likely go up tonight at eight o'clock—as usual."

But she was not relieved. She pressed closer, her arms under Longarm's, her hands digging into his shoulders fiercely. "I don't care about the show. I don't care about anything. I don't see how I can go on with Elliot now, after this."

"Every family has its knock-down fights, Amber. Once you get away from here, you'll forget all about it."

She shook her head. "No. I'll never forget. Any of it. The way he beat me, the terrible names he called me, the vicious things he said to me. It was like somebody else's words spewing from Elliot's mouth. I'll never forget any of this." She shuddered and pressed closer. "Just as I'll never forget you . . . and last night . . . and what you taught me."

Longarm felt the heat flush upward along his throat. Now that Amber was reassured about Elliot, she had forgotten him. Her hands moved, unbuttoning Longarm's greatcoat and peeling it from his shoulders.

"I don't think we ought to do this," he said. "Not now. Not here."

She smiled and kissed his lips gently and cautiously with her broken mouth. "I think we ought to. I think we must. In fact, I think I've earned it."

"You're only asking for more trouble with Elliot."

"I don't care about Elliot right now. I don't know how I can go on living with him or working with him. It's not only that I'm desperately afraid of his violence now. I don't want to be cheated—as he has cheated me—all these years. Please do it, Longarm. Take me. Make me forget all that ugliness. Help me forget Elliot and what he did to me. Only you can do that."

"You've got more than Elliot to be afraid of right now," Longarm said in a low tone, aware that Amber had loosened the tiny buttons at her bodice and had lifted her full breasts, baring them to tempt him. He tried, for the moment at least, to keep his gaze from the exposed beauty.

"All I'm afraid of is that you won't love me, that you won't give me that wonderful rod—that staff that comforts me." She smiled, though it plainly hurt her ruptured lip.

"You've got not only Elliot to worry about, Amber. As long as you're in this town, I can tell you that Lawson Carr will be watching you."

"I don't belong to him," she cried out. "He has no right. Ever since I've met Lawson, he's . . . acted as if Elliot doesn't even exist."

Longarm sighed, puzzled and troubled. He could not forget the murderous silence in the way Lawson Carr had stood outside that door last night, the way the tensions stretched him taut today, the rage that ate at him and colored everything that happened between them. He said, "I don't know what Lawson Carr has in mind for you, but I know he doesn't want you here, like this, in bed with me. I think he pushed Elliot into trying to stop you. I think if he can't get Elliot to stop you, he might well do it himself. You've got to understand about a Southern gentleman and his honor."

"I don't care about Lawson Carr," she whispered, her breath hot against him. "Are you afraid of him?"

"I'm afraid of anybody that's sane on most subjects and loco as hell on others. And that's Lawson Carr. Maybe you haven't given him any reason to think he owns you, but I can tell you that's exactly what he does think."

She shivered. "He's crazy. I've never even been alone with him. I've done nothing—"

"You did nothing with Cody Boyle, either."

"Oh, don't talk about them, Custis. I'm so . . . so hot down there. I'm on fire. I am. Touch me and see. Touch me down there, and if I'm not bubbling hot, I'll get up and I'll go away and I'll leave you alone."

"It's you I'm scared for," Longarm protested, feeling his flesh weakening as it hardened.

"Taste my breast," she whispered against his face. "Suck my breast, Custis. If you're still scared, we won't do it." She cupped her hand under her breast, lifting its taut pink nipple toward his mouth.

The knock on the facing of the hall door sounded like a rifle shot in the silent room. Longarm caught his breath and lunged upward, like a schoolboy caught behind the barn, his hand going for the gun at his hip.

Longarm plodded across the room as if he walked in ankle-deep mud. He opened the door slowly, keeping his hand on the chilled butt of his Colt.

Lawson Carr stood there, looking for all the world like the avenging angel of God. His austere face was coldly grim. He stared at Longarm and was about to speak when he discovered Amber behind him on the bed. Without looking, Longarm knew Amber was frantically trying to conceal her bared breasts.

Carr staggered slightly, as if he'd been struck suddenly and viciously in the solar plexus. He looked as if he might vomit. Then that old austerity returned, and his face became a chilled mask again. Only his gray eyes betrayed his roiling inner agonies. He said, "Mrs. Brockbank, I didn't expect to find you here. I was on my way to your room—with bad news, I'm afraid. I stopped here only to be sure Long had not skipped town."

"Why would I do that, Sheriff Carr? You ought to know damn well you're not going to get rid of me that easy," Longarm replied angrily.

Carr shrugged. "I think I am rid of you, Long. U.S. Marshal or no. You can be arrested—and possibly executed—for civil crimes."

"What civil crime is that, Sheriff?"

Again, the sheriff's eyes looked at Amber on the bed, the softly accented voice reached for her as Carr bowed slightly at the waist. "I'm sorry to break the news this way." His mouth twisted and he looked as if he might weep. "Perhaps I shouldn't have been so concerned. Perhaps you don't give a damn, ma'am, but I have the sad duty to inform you that your husband has been found dead . . . brutally murdered in his dressing room at the Silver Palace."

Chapter 9

"I'll just take your gun, Long," Sheriff Carr said. The gray-haired lawman stood unmoving as if inwardly begging Longarm to cross him.

"That's what you'll have to do—take it," Longarm began. Then he saw the unswerving snout of the sheriff's gun fixed on his belly. The callused hand gripping that gun didn't waver. Those gray eyes remained fixed on him.

"You'll make me kill you, Long, I'll be pleased to oblige you."

"You're too damned anxious, Carr. I'd say you hold aces. You're in a position to request and receive my gun. I want you to know, I'm offering no resistance. You can have it." Longarm handed over the Colt, butt first.

Carr didn't relax. He remained taut, watchful, wary. He nodded and said, "The hideout too, Long."

Longarm's eyes widened. He loosened the clip on his derringer, palmed it, and handed it to the lawman. "No secrets from the sheriff, eh?"

"No matter what you think about me, Long. No matter what else I may not be, I am a good law official. I know my job . . . As I know tricky bastards like you."

Longarm sighed, letting that pass. He kept his voice low, conversational. "So what's your charge?"

"I think you know the charge, Long. I believe you killed Elliot Brockbank."

"You mind saying how it was done?"

"I'll tell you what you need to know, Long. Nothing more. Just don't say too much. It can—and will—all be used against you."

"The first moment I met you, Carr, I thought you were a

son of a bitch. But I didn't think you were a *stupid* son of a bitch. You've been able to change my mind about that."

"What murderers think about me doesn't touch me, Long."

"Murder? Elliot Brockbank?" Longarm shook his head. "You're trying too hard, Carr. You're letting your rage blind you. You'll never make a damfool charge like that stick."

"Won't I? You were committing adultery with his wife. He came into the room. He caught you. He threatened you. You went to his dressing room. Why? You were there. People saw you go into the rear of the theater from the saloon. I saw you. But you didn't come back into the saloon, did you? You sneaked out through the alley. I believe I have a case that will stand up in court—and will see you hang."

Amber spoke from the bed. "Custis couldn't have killed Elliot," she said. Eyes red and stricken, she got up, patting at her skirts and straightening her dress. She shook her head, walking toward them.

Carr caught his breath. "Name of God, Amber! What happened to you? Did Long do this?"

"Don't be a fool, Lawson," she said. "Elliot did it."

Carr hesitated, then nodded. "So that's your motive. You saw what Brockbank had done to his wife and went down to the theater—"

"Sure. And stopped and had a beer on the way."

"I know why you had the beer, Long. You rightfully suspected that I was watching you."

"Seems like every time I look up, you're watching me, Carr."

"Well, you won't have to worry about that now, will you? We have a nice cell for you, where I can see every move you make."

Amber cried out, "Oh, Lawson, stop being a fool. I don't know why you are doing this. Maybe because you're jealous—"

"I'm a lawman, ma'am, doing my duty. I arrest men where I have to, when I have to. Thank God it wasn't you last seen with your husband down at that theater. I'd be sick, but I'd be arresting you. I've got the right man, all right."

"Custis couldn't have done it. Elliot was alive when Custis left him."

"Oh?" Carr's left brow tilted slightly in the grim, dark face. "How do you know that, ma'am?"

Amber exhaled heavily. "He told me. I was worried sick. Custis went down to that theater because I sent him—because I was worried about Elliot. He came right back—and Elliot was alive."

"I see. Well, ma'am, I know you're overcome with grief, out of your head with shock and sadness. Any good woman would be. But don't put your trust in the wrong man, Mrs. Brockbank. I'm afraid the testimony of a trusting young woman won't do Long much good in a court of law. He could have washed the blood off of his hands and told you anything."

"He could have," Amber cried out, "but he didn't. You know he didn't. Maybe my testimony won't help Custis, but no one will believe the word of a sheriff out of his mind with jealousy."

"Ma'am, I'm trying to remember that I am a gentleman, but I must tell you, your insults push my patience to the limits."

"That's the way with the truth, Lawson, old son. Nothing hurts like the truth," Longarm said.

Carr rammed the barrel of his gun so hard and so suddenly into Longarm's belly that ceiling and floor changed places. Carr and Amber flew wildly about his head and he swallowed at the bile gorging up in his throat. He staggered and almost fell. He caught himself by sagging against the doorjamb and resting there until the world stopped spinning. His belly felt as if it were on fire. How could Lawson Carr know exactly where his latest gun wound was, and how could he drive that gun into it unerringly? There was something hellishly upsetting in this cold man's hot madness.

"Truth isn't the only thing that hurts, is it, Long, old son?" Carr inquired.

For a long, nightmarish moment, Longarm simply stared through the bars at the empty cells, unable to believe what he was seeing, or more to the point, what he wasn't seeing. Those cells were empty. He peered around the small, crowded office but, as he had known there would not be, there was no other cell, no crib, no door, no place where Cody Boyle could be jailed.

At first his mind refused to credit it. He was aware of Lawson standing behind him, gun fixed on him, of the deputies at their desks, watching in silence. Carr placed Longarm's weapons on a desk, curtly told a deputy to put them away. "This son of a bitch won't be using them for a while," Carr said.

Longarm swung around so catlike on his feet that Carr shuddered, bringing up his gun, and the deputies sprang to attention. Longarm's eyes burned into Carr's. "Where the hell are you keeping Cody Boyle?"

Carr grinned coldly, then shrugged. "I don't have to answer to you, Long, but what the hell, I will. I released him. He sobered up. He barely remembered what he'd done. I let him go."

"How in hell could you do that?"

Carr shrugged again. "Why not? He attacked Mrs. Brockbank. But that lady didn't want to bring charges. After all, she is a public person, appearing on the stage. The publicity would have been detrimental to her. The ugly experience of a courtroom trial would have scarred her. Besides, she is part of a traveling company. She would have had to return here for Boyle's trial. I considered all those things. It's none of your damned business, but I let him go."

"Where is he?"

"I'm afraid I don't know that, Long. He was my prisoner and I let him go. I told you once I wouldn't stand for you interfering in my jurisdiction. Right now you've got your own woes. You don't need to worry about Cody Boyle."

"But I do worry about him. Elliot Brockbank alive wasn't much, but he offered Amber what protection he could. Now she has nothing. Nobody. You got me in jail and that raping bastard wandering around loose."

"You worry too much. Mrs. Brockbank is my jurisdiction. She'll be perfectly safe as long as she is."

"She was in your jurisdiction when Boyle attacked her before."

"Hell, Long. You're facing a murder charge. Stop worrying about things you can't change. I'll announce that there'll be no show tonight. Mrs. Brockbank will be asked to stay here until after the funeral of her husband, and until after your trial.

As painful as it may be, she will undoubtedly be called to testify."

Longarm shook his head pityingly. "You son of a bitch. You've got it all figured out, haven't you? Amber Austin has to stay in your town. How long, Carr? Will she ever leave it, except over your dead body? Is that what you planned all along?"

Carr drew a deep breath. He said. "You better keep your mouth shut, killer. My deputies and I can take turns all night beating the shit out of you and nobody in Denver or Washington will hear your yelling."

Longarm stared at Carr. There was no doubt Carr would pistolwhip him and order it done every hour on the hour. He was dealing with an honorable man who believed his honor besmirched, with a chivalrous knight whose fair lady had been violated, with or without her permission. That part didn't matter, according to Lawson Carr's code. Carr came from that late, lamented land where a true gentleman must take any steps, no matter how heinous, to wipe out a stain on his honor. There was no sense in trying to talk sanely with Carr. Carr's hatred had gone far beyond anything rational. Carr lived only for vengeance against Longarm now, and perhaps Amber herself, who had stumbled from the pedestal where Carr had placed her, destroying his unreasoning vision of her as a saintly, untouchable "good" woman. Amber might be in as much danger as he was, God knew. When the code of the Old South was violated, all hell broke loose.

His cold smile raked at Carr, taunting him. "If you're goin' to start muffling my yells, Sheriff, I reckon I better start yelling right now. I want to send a telegram to Denver. You want to get your ass in a sling, you stiff-necked bastard, you just try to stop me."

Carr stiffened slightly, hesitated. Longarm could almost watch the wheels churning inside that lawman's mind. Carr wanted to refuse, but there were two deputies present. They owed their jobs to Lawson Carr, but if the U.S. Justice Department came down on them, they would be forced to tell the truth, that the sheriff had refused to allow Longarm to get in touch with his chief, the U.S. Marshal in Denver.

Carr shrugged. "I wouldn't do that, killer." Carr forced a

shit-eating grin to match Longarm's and jerked his head toward one of his deputies. "Take down this killer's message—and get it out on the wire immediately. Nobody is ever going to be able to say we didn't go by the book or that we didn't hang this son of a bitch legal down to every dotted 'i' and crossed 't.'"

Longarm laughed at him. "You do that, you bastard, and I'll outlive you."

Carr's intake of breath was the loudest sound in the room. He jerked up the gun he clutched in his fist, ready to bring it down across Longarm's skull. Only the presence of the deputies stopped the sheriff. He exhaled heavily, walked over to his desk, and sank into the swivel chair, fuming.

Longarm dictated his telegram, taking his time, putting in details, taunting Carr until the sheriff said in a sharp, cutting voice that smashed at them. "For God's sake, you writing a book?"

"What the hell do you care, Carr? Uncle Sam's paying for it."

"Get it done. Get it done."

Longarm sat on the corner of a desk as if about to continue with his dictation. Instead he inquired conversationally, "You mind saying where that weapon is that I used to kill Elliot? I'd like to describe it. You know how these bureaucrats are—they like everything detailed in order."

Carr opened opened his mouth to yell out his refusal, but the deputy taking the notes had already pulled open a drawer and brought out a blood-stained bowie knife.

Longarm grimaced at the sight of the outsized weapon. "Are you stupid enough to say I used a knife like that to kill Brockbank?"

Carr had himself under complete cold control again. He shrugged. "That's the weapon found at the scene of the murder. And I believe you used the knife because it was quieter than a gun."

Longarm peered at the sheriff, then shrugged, refusing even to argue anything as unreasonable or unreasoning as this. He finished dictating the telegram, describing the knife and adding, "it's a dull, rusty-looking pigsticker I've never seen before."

"That's your story," Carr remarked in an almost amiable tone.

Longarm matched his calm voice. "Just hope you're not stuck with it, Sheriff."

Longarm prowled the cell, aching with cold. The night deputies stoked up the fire in the iron potbellied woodburner just beyond the cell area. This stove kept the entire structure tolerably warm when it was fired up, but tonight it had been allowed to burn low. Longarm decided there were few things colder than a cold stove. Tonight the patrolling deputies came into the dimly lighted sheriff's office only every three or four hours. Longarm knew they usually came by every hour, but he was sure this new schedule followed Carr's explicit orders. There was no way Carr wanted his guest to be comfortable through the frigid predawn hours. Deadly chill settled like a shroud over the cellblock. Wind crept in through every crack, crevice, and pinhole. A single, scratchy khaki blanket was furnished in each cell. Longarm wrapped it around himself, feeling himself growing cramped and stiff with cold. Only his steadily rising and raging hatred for Lawson Carr kept his blood stirring at all.

He lay down on the straw mattress several times, but was unable to sleep. The cold was like icy lances stabbing at him, twisting his muscles and tendons and rattling his teeth, no matter how tautly he held his jaws clamped shut.

Sometime during the long night, the front door of the sheriff's office was eased open. Standing at the cell bars, Longarm watched one of the young deputies come in, breath steaming.

The deputy carried a yellow telegram in a yellow envelope. Longarm felt his heart pump faster, his spirits rise slightly in his cold-hollowed-chest.

The young deputy glanced up and saw Longarm standing, his fists gripping the cell bars. The deputy grinned slightly and shook his head. "Jesus, it's cold in here."

Longarm said nothing, watching the deputy build a fire from shavings, pine kindling and stovewood. The fire roared at last, and heat emanated from it, spreading as slowly as January molasses toward the cellblock, but Longarm felt better. It was on its way. He said. "What's in the telegram?"

The deputy looked up and shook his head. "Don't know. Didn't read it."

"Well, goddamm it, read it."

"Addressed to the sheriff."

"Well, goddamm it, boy, it's about me."

"Well, hell, Mr. Deputy Marshal, if you already know what's in it, we don't have to read it, do we? I mean, you know what it says, and I don't give a goddamn, and I ain't going to get my ass in a sling reading it."

Longarm did not lie down again. He prowled the cell, always coming back to the bars and staring at that yellow envelope on Carr's desk, a few feet away, an impossible distance, gleaming there like the hope of heaven.

The fire in the stove was almost burned down when the front door was thrown open so fiercely that it struck the wall and rebounded. Lawson Carr, wearing a thick, fleece-lined windbreaker and a beaver hat, strode in. The wind flooded in behind him, raging through in torrents of ice-crusted cold.

Carr slammed the door behind him. For a moment he stood tall, handsome, looking like some rugged Confederate captain on an embattled parapet, his profile hewn from the yellow light and savage dark.

Drawing a deep breath, Carr went to his desk. He turned up the wick on the lamp. Then he took up the yellow envelope, thumbed it open, read the telegram, and dropped the paper on the desk.

He moved more deliberately now. He went to the pot-bellied stove, opened it without using an insulating mat, threw in a couple of half-logs, slammed the door closed with his boot. He did not look toward Longarm in the cell.

He got the envelope that held Longarm's belongings and placed it on his desk along with the Colt .44 and the derringer. Watching him, Longarm felt his spirits rise, his blood move more easily in his chill-cramped body. Carr then got Longarm's chaps and greatcoat and tossed them over a chair near the door.

Longarm watched Carr, somehow feeling a trace of pity for the lawman without knowing why. He still hated him, felt his hatred mounting by the moment, but it was hard to despise a man who looked as vulnerable and lost as Carr did in that unguarded moment.

For a while they remained in silence in the deadly stillness of predawn. Longarm watched Carr's dark face. The lawman looked troubled, deeply preoccupied, lost. He stared at the backs of his hands, at the floor. The loudest sound was the night wind rushing and screaming at the windows.

Longarm didn't know what Carr would say or do, so he was shocked when the Sheriff spoke, because he started talking about his childhood on a plantation in Virginia. He rambled. Longarm wondered if Carr followed his own line of muddled thought. "There was money in my family, Long. From the day I was born. We weren't neighbors of the Jeffersons at Monticello, we lived too far south, but my family's home was built before Jefferson's. Four, five generations. The Carrs were respected, admired because we had everything in the world we could want and our women were true ladies and we were gentlemen.

"We had grace and charm and beauty in our lives. Can you understand that? We were a power in that region, but it was a power we never used wrongly. It was a beautiful world. That's what I grew up in. I had all the money I needed. I married. She was the loveliest lady in a world of lovely ladies. I was twenty-one when I went off to war against the invading Yankee. It was like I walked down into hell, and I never came out. I saw enough murder and carnage and blood and evil and inhumanity to last a hundred men a thousand lifetimes. Only that was nothing. That was barely the first ring of hell. It wasn't until I came back to my home that I learned what hell on this earth can be. She was dead. My wife. Raped and ripped open with Yankee swords, her body robbed after it had been desecrated. Our home was burned to the ground, our animals slaughtered, our people herded away.

"I walked away from that horror, that nameless, useless, senseless crime. But we were less than human beings to the Yankee. We had no rights, we had nothing . . . and they left us nothing. . . ."

He shook his head, staring at Longarm but not really seeing him. "But that was a long time ago. A human being adapts. Or he perishes. He survives. Whether he wants to or not. I survived. I was a good soldier. After my first month in arms, after my first contact with the merciless Yankee, I was a good soldier. I was breveted a captain at Antietam. I survived the hell at Petersburg. I learned to kill, to kill without regret or remorse or even recall. I learned to use guns as few men ever do. I never learned haste, or quick draw, because I knew better. I was slower than most gunmen, but most gunmen who came up against me died. And I lived. I carry a lot of lead, but that goes with the territory. You take a job, you accept its risks. I killed nameless slime and I don't even remember their faces. I learned to live by the gun, and I've lived well . . . but not as well as I plan to live."

Longarm spoke softly. "Nobody ever said life was fair or easy, or that it even had to make sense, Lawson. You want to tell me what's in that telegram?"

Carr's head came up. He stared at Longarm as if only recognizing him at last. "You don't need to read it. I'm trying to tell you something, Long. I'm trying to tell you what kind of man you're up against if you go on trying to fight me, or what I want, or what I believe in."

"I get the picture."

"Do you? I've crossed the paths of a lot of strong men, Long. Men I respected even when I hated their guts. Men that meant to kill me. And tried. I'm still here, Long. They're gone and I'm still here. And I'll be here when you're gone. Do you understand me?"

Longarm shuddered, deep under the heaviness of the sheep-lined jacket. The chill inside him went deeper than even the wind could cut. He walked the false-dawn boardwalk warily, listening in the fading winds for footsteps in the shadows, for whispers of unexplained sound, for telltale movement. He sighed out a long smokey breath. Lawson Carr wanted him dead, out of his way. This didn't necessarily mean that Carr had to remove him personally. He could order it done, hire it done; he wouldn't look back, or care, or remember. Longarm shuddered.

That was the difference between him and Carr. Something had been burned out of Carr's insides, something vital. There was plenty of reason for his feeling as he did, but the fact was he killed easily now, too easily, without thinking about it, then or later. Longarm remembered going up against many men, but the recollection of even the vilest was a hurting cinch in his gut.

Neither the saloon nor the restaurant was open at this hour. A single light burned in the telegraph office at the train depot. Hunched against the cold, Longarm limped across the icy ground to the station. He sent a brief telegram to Billy Vail in Denver: "HOW IS WEATHER NORTH OF DIRTY FORK STOP REPLY SOONEST STOP YRS LONG"

He turned to leave, then changed his mind. He turned back to the desk and showed the operator his deputy marshal's badge. "Could I see the telegram to Sheriff Carr from Marshal Vail in Denver. Came in about four hours ago."

Though Longarm smiled disarmingly, something in his manner made the operator's decision. He thumbed through the copies on his billspike and handed the paper over. Longarm read it, grinning coldly. Then he handed it back across the counter and walked out, shoulders up. It was too early in the morning to whistle, but he whistled anyhow.

When Longarm let himself into the hotel lobby and closed the door behind him, he found the aging building steeped in silence. The lobby was vacant except for the night clerk, asleep with his head on the registry desk. Longarm padded across the carpeting quietly and went up the stairs to the second floor.

As he climbed he thought about Amber, wondered how she was getting along, wanted badly to see her, needed to know she was all right. But all this was erased totally from his mind when he stepped out of the stairwell onto the carpeted, narrow corridor.

At first he thought a shaggy dog was curled asleep against the door. Then he saw that it was a man in tattered range clothing. The thought that it might be the Indian Sam Brown crossed his mind, but at his first step the sleeping man awoke, sat up, braced against the door facing, gun in hand. Longarm stopped cold. He stared at the bewhiskered man. "Who are you?"

"Name's Lobatos. Flagg Lobatos. Somebody said you wanted to talk to me. I been waitin' here for you quite a spell."

Chapter 10

For a moment Longarm stood poised a few feet from his door, where Flagg Lobatos crouched like some shaggy and treacherous animal. Longarm shivered slightly.

Flagg Lobatos was not a man one believed at first sight. He was something ominous from bad dreams, he haunted nightmares; you walked carefully when you met him in a street; his lean, bearded face could freeze a strong man's blood on a clear day. Lobatos looked as tough and taut-stretched, as ready to snap, and as savagely prickly as that barbed wire he hated so obsessively.

Never taking his unblinking gaze off Longarm, Lobatos levered himself to his feet using only the power in the muscles in the backs of his thin, powerful legs. He seemed to slither up the door facing and rest there, the gun unwavering.

Longarm stared at this last of the old-time vaqueros, those free-roaming herders who lived on the ranges much as the Mongols wandered the steppes of Russia.

There wasn't much about the herder to reassure a man. Longarm's stomach tightened and the short hair prickled across the nape of his neck. This man looked as if he would kill you if you spoke the wrong word, or before he gave you a chance to speak, if you moved in a way to disturb his finely balanced reason. Whatever he'd anticipated that Mozelle Lobatos' father would be like, Flagg Lobatos was something else. The range-rover was almost as tall as Longarm, but wiry thin, sunken-chested, flat-bellied, round-shouldered. He moved with the supple litheness of a hungry lynx or a roused sidewinder. But the most remarkable thing about Lobatos was the dirt that covered him from head to foot.

Lobatos wore range dust like an outer skin, thick, cracked,

and mottled. He was no longer even aware of the grit caked in the crowsfeet edging his squinting eyes, blackening the rims of his nostrils, discoloring his mangy clothing. His round-crowned, battered and torn Stetson dripped varicolored sand, and the stuff shimmered on the low-bent brim that shielded his eyes and shadowed his entire visage except the tip of his hawk-like nose. Strands of damp black hair, as dark as an Indian's and as straight, showed about his thick brows. But it was Lobatos' eyes that showed what he was and who he was and where he'd been and what he'd suffered. And they showed, if you looked long enough or deeply enough, how he came to be the mistrustful loner, suspicious, sniffing the air, on guard, wary against the world. His eyes carried old hurts and cold savagery like the dead ashes of old fires. They squinted, habitually narrowed, and, by habit, full of pain and doubt and danger.

A ragged beard, gritty and sweaty, followed the slanting contours of his cheeks and jawline.

His bandanna offered the only color in his attire, a swatch of faded lavender silk, carelessly knotted at the throat of his open khaki shirt. His black vest provided storage for his possibles, extra ammo, matches, and God only knew what odds and ends he'd heedlessly collected. His greasy, streaked Levi's were punched hastily into high-topped, thin-heeled boots. He looked as if he hated walking. He wore a Colt .45 low and tied down on his thigh. It was not a fast-draw arrangement. Lobatos was not a fast draw or even a gunfighter. He carried a bowie knife in a sheath, but it was not handily set for quick access. Neither Lobatos' gun nor his knife made him dangerous. The danger came from his desires and fears and hatreds and mistrusts and memories of old wrongs, all bottled up behind those anguished black eyes.

Peril lurked in those savage eyes, all right. Violence swirled in them, tamped down, ready to erupt. Lobatos was half-wild, part Indian, part Mexican, part Irish; he lived by his animal instincts; he acted on them; he killed on them. One saw in his face how evil Flagg Lobatos' past had been—for himself as much as for his enemies.

"Heard you wanted to talk to me," he said. "My daughter. My daughter's fancy, he said you wanted to see me."

"Why'd you come?"

"Curious, maybe. My daughter said you was a good man. Said you bought her a steak. Said you're from the Justice Dee-partment. I seed damn little justice in my life. Thought I'd like to see what a man from the Justice Dee-partment looked like."

"You want to come in? It ain't much better, but it's a little warmer."

"Gettin' cold, all right. We're in for a heller."

"Wolf wind," Longarm said. Lobatos stepped aside. Long-arm opened the door and pushed it wide.

"After you." Lobatos gestured him into the room with his gun. Longarm entered and lit a lamp, turning up the wick. The room was like an ice chest, or some deep cave. "Leave the door open," Lobatos said.

"Why?"

"I don't like to be penned up nowhere, mister. I never did. We can talk fine with the door open." Lobatos put a straight chair against a wall and sat down in it, holding his gun on his lap. "What you got to say to me?"

"Not much." Longarm sat down, keeping his greatcoat se-cured, his gun out of reach, his hands out where Lobatos could see them. "We get reports of fence being cut down here in the Divide. We figure Texas drovers do some of it. But it's got real plentiful around here and Uncle Sam is pretty damned upset."

"Well, fuck Uncle Sam," Lobatos said.

"I can't, I work for him."

"That's right. That's what I'm saying to you. You work for Uncle Sam. Who the hell is Uncle Sam? The friggin' govern-ment, is that right? Who am I? A citizen. Right? I figure the government ain't some big wonderful somebody that I have to bow down to. I figure the government and the citizen are equal. Not *just about* equal. Equal. Like this. I am as loyal a citizen as you or any other mother-rider working for the government, or out of it. I say the government's got the same rights as a citizen has got in this country. No more, no less. The govern-ment don't need nothing unless I need it, because, Mr. Justice Dee-partment, when you git down to it, I am the government. As much as you, as much as anybody."

"I wouldn't argue with you or Thomas Jefferson about that,

117

Mr. Lobatos. I agree with you. It's something else we're talking about. We're talking about the laws. Nobody makes laws just to put a crimp in a citizen. At least they ought not. Laws are made so people can live together, so we can sleep in bed at night and hope we wake up in the morning. I heard charges that most of the wire-cutting and most of the grass-stealing around Dirty Fork is being done by you and your family, Mr. Lobatos."

Lobatos sat forward. "So I'm guilty, huh? Just like that? Somebody points at me and you come to nail my hide to the barn. Is that it?"

Longarm's voice rasped. "No, goddammit, that ain't it. There have been charges. And they claim they have evidence against you. I want to hear your side of it."

"What for? Why waste your time? You think I don't know who has charged me with stealing and cutting and rustling? Mr. Fondis Estabrook. Mr. Lawson Carr. Some of their toadies. You think anybody in Colorado is going to take my word against them high muckety-mucks?"

"I might."

Lobatos was ready to rage further. He stopped, his head tilted, and gazed unblinking at Longarm. "Why? What sort of thing is this here Justice Dee-partment? Is it something new I ain't heard about?"

"I'm looking for the truth, Lobatos. I don't really give a damn if I learn it from you or Fondis Estabrook or whomsoever, but I will learn it. Now he's told me that you've come in here, squatted on his land, and stolen his cows, grazed grass that he's paid to use, and cut fence so that such of his cows that you don't steal just wander away."

Lobatos' mouth twitched. "Well, hell, looks like you'd have shackles on me by now."

"You got the gun, remember?"

Lobatos almost smiled. "Don't do that, Mr. Justice. I don't want to git to likin' you. Makes me gut-sick to burn down a man I've taken a cotton to. But it won't stop me. What can I say that you're going to believe?"

Longarm considered this for a moment. "I can guarantee you this, Lobatos. I'll give exactly the same amount of belief to what you say as I gave to what Mr. Estabrook said, even if he did smell better than you do. I'll have his story, and I'll have your story. Then I figure I'll find the truth in between somewhere, and I'll make my move from there."

"Sounds fair enough. You're something new in my life, Marshal."

Longarm grinned tautly. "And I can say with the same goddamn amount of truth that you're something new in my life, Lobatos, and I figured I'd been down all the backtrails at least twice."

"I'm what I am," Lobatos said. "I been a free-herder all my life, moving my cows and my family where the grass was and where the market was. Never had no home. Never meant to have one. The life I lived suited me, even when I got three strapping boys and a lovely little girl what's the apple of my eye. I live for that there little honeypot. My life was always hard on my woman, but I figgered Nonnie knowed what she was gittin' herself into when she married me."

Lobatos drew a deep breath. "Then, almost for no good reason, we herded north into the Cut country up here. We found a lot of half-wild cows on the High Plains, seems like they growed like fleas in every draw. Still, I meant to move on. But then my daughter—little Mozelle—that you met, she fell in love."

"With Kane Estabrook."

"A fine boy. I swear he's a fine boy, despite his paw and his family and his raisin'. Tell you true, I never figured to meet any man I'd trust my little girl with, but I trust young Kane. He's got a good heart and he loves Moze with every inch of it.

"So. I'm in trouble. For the first time in twenty-five years Nonnie is talking back to me. She's nagging me when I ain't even talking. Nonnie takes a stand ag'in me for the very first time. She up and de-mands a home for our daughter where Moze could grow up like a real lady."

Recalling the way Mozelle had attacked her steak in the restaurant, Longarm grinned faintly and nodded. "Could help," he said. "Beautiful as she is, with a few nice dresses and some table manners, nobody need ever be ashamed of her."

"No reason for no man to be ashamed of my daughter," Lobatos said edgily.

"Hell, relax, man. No offense. I'm listening to you."

"Just don't gainsay my girl, that's all. Just don't gainsay my girl. I'm trying to be reasonable with you when I got no more goddamn respect for a government man than I have for a government mule."

"So you moved in on Estabrook's land."

Lobatos' thin face pulled into a wry grin. "That's what he says, ain't it? But you check at the land office, Marshal. It's as easy as that. That's government land out there around Screamin' Springs. Land up for homesteadin'."

"Estabrook claims it's always been his."

"Everything 'round here has either always been his, or is just about going to be. You look it up. I filed papers on that land, clear and proper. And I stay on it three years and I improve it, and it's mine. Just like the next section is going to be my son Tom Ed's. Andrew Earl's beyond him. And by God they's even water—drinkin' water!—on the land young J.C. is filed on."

"I won't shit you." Lobatos laughed. "Estabrook never bought up that land or filed on it because he figured it was worthless fault land. Up where we're stayin', in an old summer line shack of his'n, is a double fault where, when the earth was a-tumblin' and twistin', it fell back on itself. That big hump is gradual in the front, but a sheer drop at the back, more'n a hundred feet. No drinkin' water, just that crazy Screamin' Springs that smells like sulfur and tastes like rotten eggs and boils up out'n the ground and runs hot till it spills over the cliff out back." He laughed again. "That's what I got, Marshal. But I filed on it, and by damn I call it home."

"All right, if the land office files back you up, good. What about the cut fence? The stolen cows?"

"What about it? If somebody moved in on land you had been using for fifteen years, and you hated them and wanted them out, what would you do, Mr. Marshal? Just what Estabrook is doing. You'd sic the lawdogs on 'em."

Longarm said, "You mind if I smoke?"

Lobatos shook his head. Longarm reached carefully inside his coat and came up with a pair of two-for-a-nickel cheroots. He glanced questioningly at Lobatos and tossed a cigar toward him. Lobatos let it fall on the floor in front of him, and then he bent down and picked it up, keeping his eye on Longarm.

Longarm bit off the end of his cheroot and grinned. "Know all the tricks, do you?"

Lobatos stuck the cheroot in his mouth and chewed on its end. "Reckon most of 'em been tried on me at least twice—and none of 'em ever worked the *first* time."

"That's because you don't trust anybody."

"No. That's *why* I don't trust nobody, Marshal. Now you talk sweet and you charm my li'l Moze. But that don't mean I'm going to walk in here and trust you, all wide-eyed."

Longarm fired up his cigar, drawing deeply and then exhaling. He watched Lobatos through the swirling smoke. "So you deny any fence-cutting."

"This latest fence-cuttin' I ain't done. My boys ain't done it. I told you I'm livin' here 'cause I want a different kind of life for my li'l girl. Her maw calls it a *better* life. Well, I don't know about that. I'm trying to git along with these people, but they don't want me to. They want my land. They want me and my family out of here."

Longarm stood up slowly. "I'm hungry," he said. "It's been a long cold night. I need a pot of coffee and some griddlecakes. How about having breakfast with me?"

Lobatos stared at him for a long beat, but shook his head. "Thankee, no. Don't feel comfortable 'round too many people. Don't never like to be in a crowd so big I can't eye 'em all."

"Must be a hell of a life," Longarm observed.

Lobatos drew deeply on his cigar and sent the smoke snorting from his nostrils. He grinned faintly and shrugged. "No man can't choose the hand what life deals to him, but he has to play the cards he gits."

Lobatos got up and walked on the balls of his feet, like a panther, toward the door. Longarm said, "I might have to come up to Screamin' Springs to talk to you."

Lobatos paused at the door. He looked back and shrugged. "So come."

"I'd like to think I can come in up there without gettin' bushwhacked."

Lobatos laughed, a weird, chilling sound. "So life ain't all that easy for any of us, is it, Marshall?"

Longarm stood at the closed window. He was gut-cold, hungry, and lightheaded with exhaustion. He was troubled about Amber. But he went on standing there, watching the early-morning street come to life below him.

He drew hard on his cheroot. It didn't make sense but, even talking to Lobatos, he would remember Elliot Brockbank in quick, worrisome flashes. And that was stupid, because if ever two people were totally unlike, it was the range-grimy Lobatos and the effete actor. And yet they remained tied up in Longarm's mind. He could find no logical reason for it, but Brockbank's death seemed somehow tied in with Lobatos and fence-cutting and grass wars. He shook his head, trying to rid himself of the thought, but it buzzed around in his head like a horsefly.

He saw Lobatos come out of the hotel and mount a lean range pony, then ride slowly west along the street, apparently slumped in the saddle but, Longarm knew, watchful and wary. *It must be a hell of a life*, the lawman thought.

He was about to turn away from the window and head down for breakfast when something caught his eye at an angle across the street. He glimpsed a shadowy figure darting from one pit of morning shadows to a corner of the brick bank building and then slithering along it, going out of sight.

Troubled, he pulled his head up and looked for Flagg Lobatos, but the horseman had abruptly disappeared. When he looked back, the alleyway at the bank was silent and still. Yet he remained tense, because something about the man's build, the way that skulking figure moved over there, rang a bell inside Longarm's mind. Even that brief glimpse convinced him he'd seen that man before, and the way he padded through the alley was suspicious as hell.

Yawning helplessly, Longarm turned away from the window. He told himself Amber was all right or she'd be down here looking for him. He was ravenously hungry, but he was even colder and wearier. That goosedown comforter looked tempting, the mattress inviting. Still yawning, he staggered toward the bed.

The sound of gunfire from the street cut his yawn in half. He lunged back around, gripping the sill at the window, staring into the street. A surrey was parked outside the bank. A man who must have been stepping from its tonneau seat was fallen, supporting himself on his knee at the edge of the boardwalk in front of the bank. Staring, Longarm recognized Fondis Estabrook.

Pulling the buttons loose on his greatcoat, Longarm ran out of his room, slamming the door behind him. He was halfway down the stairs before he remembered this was Lawson Carr's bailiwick, and the Virginian wasn't going to appreciate any interference from a federal marshal.

He forced himself to slow down. By the time he came out of the hotel and crossed the veranda to the boardwalk, a noisy crowd had gathered around Estabrook's surrey, parked at a long angle across the street.

Longarm crossed the street. He stood at the rim of the chattering mob because he could easily see over the heads of the tallest people around him. A doctor had already arrived and had removed Fondis Estabrook's frock coat, exposing a shoulder wound beneath a bloody shirt. From where Longarm stood, the wound looked superficial, but it was only inches from vital areas. It was close, a near miss.

Fondis Estabrook was swearing. He kept telling the people to stand back, to get on home, to get about their business. The doctor kept trying to soothe him. "We'll take you inside, Fondis," the medic said. "Have you fixed up in no time."

"You hear that, you people?" Fondis Estabrook spoke through clenched teeth, staring at the faces of the townspeople. "I'm all right. Get on away from here."

But before the doctor and two other men could get the banker-rancher to his feet, the mob sent up another yell and Longarm jerked his head around.

Lawson Carr and a deputy rode on each side of Flagg Lobatos. They had dropped a loop around Flagg's arm and taken a dally welty in it, snugging his arms to his sides. Carr had taken Lobatos' gun, and it was shoved into his belt.

"Here's the son of bitch that shot at you, Fondis," Lawson Carr said. "Larry and me caught him hightailing down an alley out of here."

Estabrook had been coldly in control until this moment. At

the sight of Flagg Lobatos, reason seemed to desert the banker. He shook, trembling, and looked as if he might vomit.

Lobatos didn't even bother answering Eastabrook. His black eyes found Longarm at the rim of the mob. Flagg stared at Longarm, teeth bared in a coyote snarl. "Sure. Son of a bitch. Tricked me into town, did you, so's these vultures could frame me for murder."

Chapter 11

Feeling sick, Longarm turned his head away from the savage hatred contorting Lobatos' bearded features.

As he turned, Longarm's eyes raked across Lawson Carr's face. Something hitched inside Longarm. He caught his breath, and for a long beat his gaze held the sheriff's.

At Carr's bland, smug smile, Longarm felt his heart sink and then pound oddly as if unmoored. Lawson Carr was laughing at him, yet giving him deadly warning at the same time.

In a flash, Longarm saw Lawson Carr as he'd stood, slump-shouldered and grim-faced, in the cellblock before dawn this morning. What had Carr said? *"I'm trying to tell you something, Long,"* Carr had stated in that mellifluous Southern accent. *"I'm trying to tell you what kind of man you're up against if you go on trying to fight me, or what I want, or what I believe in. . . ."*

Longarm felt the prickling of sweat in the nipping chill. As Carr had spoken, Longarm had discounted most of what the Virginian said, putting it down as the mutterings of a man deranged by jealousy. Longarm had thought Carr was talking about Amber Austin, and warning him not to get in his way with the actress.

He no longer believed that's what Carr had meant. He stared at the sheriff sitting lean and cold in that saddle, gun fixed on Flagg Lobatos' spine. What did Carr want? What in hell *did* he believe in? What was he after that he figured Longarm was interfering in? What was he trying to do, that he saw Longarm's very presence as an obstacle not to be tolerated?

Empty-bellied, Longarm stood at the edge of the milling crowd in the biting cold wind. The mob inched forward, yelling, "Hang him! Let's hang the killing son of a bitch! Hang him now!"

Carr sat, as handsome as some figure from a history book, seemingly unaware of the rabble and its raving. Lobatos appeared not even to hear the yells and demands for his scalp. Fondis Estabrook saw the citizenry and heard them, but he gazed through them, his mouth twisted in contempt.

Carr leaned forward slightly in his saddle and spoke to the banker, still half-sprawled at the brink of the boardwalk. "We caught Lobatos racing hell-for-leather down an alley, Mr. Estabrook. Larry and I caught him. We'll take him on over to jail now. He'll be there when you feel like coming over and swearing out a warrant, sir."

"I'll come now," Estabrook said between gritted teeth. His anguished eyes were impaling Lobatos; the pain in his shoulder was forgotten for that moment. "I'll come along with you."

"The hell you will, Fondis," the doctor said. He snagged Estabrook's bicep and nodded to the two men kneeling beside him. "Now you listen to me, Fondis. You let the sheriff handle the killer. You let me tend that wound before tetanus or gangrene or some other rot sets in. You'll have plenty of time to swear charges."

"That's right." Carr nodded, smiling, the idealized knight-errant from the Old South. He touched the brim of his planter's hat in a little salute. "Lobatos will be in jail, Fondis, waiting— no matter how long it takes."

Longarm walked around the rear of the bank. He found the triangle of shadow where he'd first spotted the sneaking man. He studied the ground and found a heelprint, and another, and was able to follow where the man had sidled along the bank almost to the street.

He followed the prints along the building. He found the place where the man had stopped. He picked up the butt of a half-smoked cigarette. He studied it a moment and then dropped it into his greatcoat pocket. He walked in little circles in the alley until he saw a metal cartridge casing winking up at him. He knelt and took up the spent cartridge, and turned it so he was looking down at its dented primer cap. Around the cap were stamped the words ".38 caliber." He tossed it in the air and caught it a couple of times before he dropped it into his pocket along with the cigarette butt.

He studied the alley and found bootprints headed the other direction. He smiled. There was no doubt, it was the heelprint left by the same individual who had crept along the side of the building, fired his gun, ad then run back the way he'd come.

Taking his time, Longarm followed the trail the running man had left for him until it ended in the windblown dust. Ahead of him he saw the livery stable, a small house, and open country beyond.

His greatcoat still loose, the wind knifing through him, Longarm walked across the vacant lot to the livery stable.

The owner was not on the premises, but Sam Brown was there, patiently shoveling horseshit from the stalls.

Longarm let the livery stable door close behind him, shutting out some of the wind. He walked over to the potbellied stove and stood before it, warming his hands.

Sam Brown said, "Morning, Mr. Custis. Come for your horse?"

"No. No fit weather for a horse outside, Sam."

"It's blowing in all the way from the North Pole," Sam said, nodding. "It's taking its time, but it'll get here. You got any more jobs for me, Mr. Custis?"

Longarm shook his head. "Not at the moment, Sam. I been wondering. You seen Cody Boyle around lately?"

Sam Brown stiffened as though he'd been struck suddenly and cruelly in the solar plexus. But he kept his face expressionless, and after a moment he shook his head. "Mr. Cody Boyle, he's in jail, ain't he?" With his eyes shaded under his hat, Sam Brown signaled toward the hayloft behind Longarm.

Longarm shrugged. "I thought he was. But when I went to talk to him, Sheriff Carr said he'd been turned loose. I wanted to talk to him."

"I ain't seen him, Mr. Custis. I sure thought he was still in jail."

"No. He's out. But like the sheriff said, Boyle's likely drifted. I hear he hires on for roundups, and then moves on."

"I sure don't know, Mr. Custis. If I do see Mr. Cody Boyle, I'll sure tell him you're looking for him."

Longarm laughed loudly and rubbed his hands together over

the stove. "No, I wouldn't do that, Sam. I don't believe Mr. Boyle would want to talk to me, and I reckon I got nothing to say to him. I mean, the sheriff did set him free and all."

Outside the the livery stable, Longarm walked toward the main street until he came to the cover afforded by a feed store. He went around this frame structure and, making a wide arc, came in at the rear of the stable.

The hayloft door was closed, but it was locked with a sliding bolt on the outside. A ladder had been nailed for convenience from the height of a haywagon boot to the hayloft.

Moving cautiously, Longarm pressed close to the wood of the stable. He could smell the hay, the ammonia, the leather, and the horse droppings. He pulled himself up to the lowest rung of the ladder, grasped the next one above it, and levered himself upward.

Clinging to the top of the ladder, Longarm felt himself buffeted by the rising gale wind. He gritted his teeth together to keep them from chattering. He reached out slowly and inched the bolt out of its slot. He stopped, hearing the front door of the livery stable open. He held his breath, listening. The stable owner had returned and was talking loudly to Sam Brown.

Thankful for the diversion, Longarm thrust the wooden bolt back. He caught the door and threw it open as hard as he could. In the same movement he lunged into the hayloft, landing on his belly and rolling.

Drawing his gun, he came up. He saw Cody Boyle spring from the concealment of stacked hay bales. Boyle's gun was in his hand, but Longarm's yell stopped him. "Just don't try to pull that trigger, Cody, and you'll be all right."

With Cody Boyle's hands secured at the small of his back with baling wire, Longarm walked him out of the stable. His gun pressed into the cowboy's kidney, Longarm prodded him across the open lot to the main street.

The crowd had grown. There must have been fifty people milling about outside the jail. If there was to be justice, according to them, Lobatos had to hang. If they were going to be safe in their own houses, Lobatos had to hang now, this morning, here, with a fast trial and quick execution.

"Look out, there. Step aside," Longarm ordered. The steel in his voice quieted the mob. Some of them stepped back, crowding their neighbors out of the way.

Longarm jammed his gun hard into Boyle's back. "Move," he ordered.

Cody Boyle sidled through the narrow lane cleared by the people. They stared at Cody, at his hands wired behind his back, at the gun in Longarm's fist.

"It's Cody Boyle," a man said.

"They got Cody Boyle."

"It's that federal marshal fellow."

"He's got Cody Boyle."

Longarm kept his gun pressed tightly in Cody's back. He spoke tautly to his prisoner. "You got any friends in this mob, warn them off, Cody. Any trouble, any shooting, just remember this gun of mine's a double-action."

Cody Boyle shook his head but did not speak.

With Boyle ahead of him, Longarm went up the stone steps to the narrow stoop outside the sheriff's office door. Longarm banged on the door facing. For some moments nothing happened. Longarm kept pounding.

A deputy sheriff unlocked the door, held it slightly ajar. His eyes widened. He gazed at the gun in Longarm's hand. He stepped back and held the door wide enough for Longarm and his prisoner to enter.

The sheriff's office was crowded. Lawson Carr sat at his desk. Another deputy leaned against the bars that separated the cell area from the office. Beyond the bars, Flagg Lobatos paced like a trapped fox. In the office, Fondis Estabrook sat at one of the deputies' desks. His face was ashen; he'd lost a lot of blood, but the doctor had patched his arm and put it in a sling and Estabrook had draped his frock coat over it. The doctor stood worriedly at Estabrook's side.

The deputy closed the door behind Longarm and Boyle.

Carr came up from his desk, his swivel chair squealing like a tomcat. The blood rushed from Carr's sun-leathered face, leaving it as pale and drawn as Estabrook's. Shadows whirled and wheeled in Carr's gray eyes. He stood braced, legs apart, fists clenched at his sides.

It took the space of three long breaths, but Sheriff Carr got himself under control. No one else inside the office spoke. In the rear cell, Flagg Lobatos had gripped the bars in his fists and stood staring through them.

Carr's low voice lashed at Longarm. "Marshal, you mind saying what the hell you're doing here?"

Longarm jabbed Cody Boyle in the back. "I brought you the man who took a shot at Fondis Estabrook outside the bank this morning."

Silence shrouded the room. The loudest sounds were the shouting of the mob from the street, the icy wind battering fierce fists against the windows, the futile roaring of flames in the potbellied stove.

Carr kept his voice level. "Marshal, I thought I warned you about interfering in my jurisdiction."

"You want the man who shot at Estabrook?"

"We got him," Estabrook said. "We got the son of a bitch behind bars. Only thing we're palavering about is whether to hold him for trial or turn him over to the decent citizens of this town to hang him."

"Unless you people want trouble with the whole law enforcement in the First District of Colorado, you better slow down and walk easy," Longarm said.

"We don't need you federal people marching in here, telling us how to run our affairs," Estabrook said.

"Whether you want it or not, that's sure as hell what you'll get if you don't ease off. Now." Longarm's voice matched Estabrook's for savagery and determination.

"The sheriff caught that son of a bitch Lobatos riding away fast. Lobatos hates me, everybody knows that. We got the guilty man."

Longarm lowered his voice, but it remained chilled and relentless. "I don't reckon you have."

Lawson Carr stepped forward, taking charge. His voice was soft but unyielding. "All right, Long. What is this?"

Longarm glanced at Carr. "Did you ask Lobatos *why* he was ridin' hell-for-leather out of town, Sheriff?"

"We knew why. We heard the shot. We saw Lobatos wheel his horse down an alley and run for it. We were able to cut him off, Long. We didn't have to ask him."

Longarm remained unmoved. "Why don't you ask him now?"

"Why ask that son of a bitch anything?" Estabrook raged. "He knows he's going to hang. You ever heard a polecat tell the truth when a lie was easier?"

"Ask him anyway," Longarm said.

Lobatos' voice taunted them from the barred cell. "I heard that shot. I saw Estabrook knocked from the step of his fine carriage. I knew I didn't want to be within ten miles of that bank. I tried to get away as fast as I could. These toadies of Estabrook's was waitin' for me. They cut me off. They said they was goin' to kill me 'less I come quiet."

"We have the guilty man," Carr said. "And that settles it."

"Did you check his gun? Was it fired?"

"It had been fired."

"I shot at a coyote on my way into town last night, just didn't bother reloading," Lobatos said.

"Hell," Estabrook raged. "Why listen to him? Lobatos will have a lie for every charge. Any of us that knows him at all knows that. He's guilty, and ain't you or nobody else gettin' him out of this jail alive."

Longarm kept his voice low. "I know you're upset. I know you've been shot, Mr. Estabrook. But I reckon you'd best eat the old apple one bite at a time."

Estabrook stood up. His voice flared. "And I say we don't need no outsider coming in here telling us how to run our town."

"Just a minute, Fondis. Long is a federal marshal. He's got the U.S. Government behind him. We don't need that kind of trouble. We know we've got the guilty man. But we also want the government—and the world—to know we act legally here. We follow the law. We go by the book. Long says he's got the man who tried to kill you. Let's hear what makes him think so," Carr said.

Cody Boyle writhed, his voice whining. "My wrists are bleeding. Son of a bitch is trying to kill me."

Carr spoke to a deputy. "Cut those wires, Larry." Then he looked at Long and spoke sarcastically. "Or, since Boyle is your prisoner—maybe we better ask your permission."

Longarm merely shrugged. "Just so he stays under guard,

Carr. I want Cody Boyle jailed and held. He's *my* prisoner, Carr, and I hold you responsible for him."

Carr's grin raked his face. "Oh, he'll be here, Long. Anytime you want him."

"See that he is," Longarm said. "I hate to spoil your little case against Lobatos here. I know you people have a powerful craving to see him out of the way."

"Amen," said Estabrook. "And this time we'll put him out of the way."

"That may be, Mr. Estabrook." Longarm gazed at the thickly built rancher. "But maybe you better hear me out first."

"Spit it out, Marshal," Carr said. He sat down at his desk and picked up a rifle bullet, turning it idly between his fingers, as if he'd lost interest in what went on around him.

The deputy, Larry, cut the wires at Boyle's wrists. The prisoner massaged them. He had not lied; the skin was cut and he bled slightly. He stood, slack-shouldered, watching Longarm malevolently.

"I'll begin at the beginning. Tell you what I've got." Longarm spoke to Carr in his swivel chair, but the sheriff watched the rifle bullet slip and turn between his fingers and did not look up. "First, Flagg Lobatos came up to my room at the hotel to talk to me. I stood at my window and watched him ride west out of town. Then something snagged at my eyes and I saw this man Boyle. He was sneaking around behind the bank."

"Does that prove I shot anybody?" Boyle demanded. Carr looked up at him and gestured sharply for him to shut up.

"You'll have your turn, Boyle. We're hearing the marshal now."

"After you fellows arrested Flagg Lobatos, I went around behind the bank. I found Boyle's boot prints—where he had crossed the alley when I first saw him, and where he'd sneaked along the shadow of the bank to where he could get a view of anybody driving up to the front door of the bank."

The room was tensely silent. The crowd shouted from outside. Longarm reached into his greatcoat pocket and brought out the cigarette butt. "I found this. Fresh. Where he'd tossed it when he finished off a smoke while he was waiting. That cigarette butt was new, like the boot prints are new. His boot heels will match those prints over there—"

132

"Hell, I never said I wasn't back there. I just said I ain't shot nobody," Boyle said, massaging frantically at his wrist.

"That cigarette butt is pretty shabby evidence, Long," Carr said in a cold, taunting tone. "You're going to tell us the tobacco will match his sack makings, and the paper will be the same."

"That's right," Longarm said.

Carr gave him a pitying smile. "You're going to sound pretty lame, Long, when you go before a local jury and tell them Cody Boyle's cigarette papers and his makings match. You better ask at the general store and find out how many *kinds* of paper and makings they sell. This ain't Denver, Marshal. Everybody who rolls his own around here smokes the same brand paper and tobacco."

"That's right," Estabrook agreed.

"By itself, maybe the cigarette, and even the footprints, wouldn't mean too much. I guess a sneak like Boyle could just *happen* to be sneaking around at the time of an attempted murder—"

"There's a matter of motive too, Long," Carr suggested mildly.

Longarm nodded. He thrust his hand into his greatcoat pocket again. "I'm coming to that. Like I say, cigarette butt and even footprints don't prove too much. But here's a bullet casing I found in that alley where Cody Boyle just happened to be loitering when somebody shot Fondis Estabrook. Now, I already know the caliber of this bullet matches his gun. And the casing was shot so recent that it still stinks."

Carr turned the bullet more slowly between his fingers. "You've built a pretty fair case of circumstantial evidence, Long."

"No. It is definite evidence. I saw him over there. I found his prints, and proof he was there, and I've got the bullet casing he fired."

Carr's voice was filled with false admiration. "Well, I'm sure the First Judicial District of Colorado is mighty proud of the kind of work you do, Long. There is just one little thing wrong with your case. We happen to know that Lobatos fired *his* gun too. And we all happen to know Lobatos has a motive for killing Fondis Estabrook."

Longarm nodded patiently. "I ain't trying to tell you your business, Carr. That ain't why I'm here. I'm just telling you, a case is built on *one* indisputable fact. Anything matches that fact, you add it. Anything that don't add up with it, you throw away. Leastways, that's the way I work. I got the indisputable fact: Boyle was over there. His footprints are there, his cigarette butt was there, and his spent bullet was there. And as for motive: when I arrested Cody Boyle over at the livery stable, he had a big wad of money in his pocket."

"What goddamn law does that break?" Cody Boyle demanded. He retreated a couple of steps from where Longarm stood.

"Depends," Longarm told him. "If it's fifty bucks or so, it's your pay for working a month on some spread. If it's over a couple hundred, you better be able to prove where you got it, or I say it's a motive for the shot you took at Fondis Estabrook outside that bank this morning." Longarm turned and faced Carr, who'd stood up slowly. "I think we can count that money, and once we know how much it is, I think we can make Mr. Boyle tell us where he got it."

"You ain't searching me!" Boyle yelled. He bolted toward the door, jolting Larry, the deputy sheriff, aside with his shoulder as he went.

Longarm leaped from a standing start. He lunged through the air, tackling Boyle about the waist as the prisoner grabbed at the doorknob. They fell, sprawling on the floor. Growling, crying out, Boyle kicked, gouged, and swung his arms, trying to get free. They wrestled, rolling over and over on the floor.

"Hold it!" Carr yelled.

Longarm hesitated, but Boyle continued to struggle, jerking free. As Longarm wrestled him down, Carr's gun barrel descended like a club. It caught Longarm behind the ear, and he sprawled on the floor, unconscious.

Chapter 12

A soft hand lay gentle on Longarm's forehead. In the warm darkness where he lay, it felt like a woman's hand, only it was large and there was no woman-scent. The light lanced through his eyeballs and exploded at the crown of his skull. He knew he ought to open his eyes; every moment he lay with his eyes closed increased his peril, but for the life of him he couldn't remember why there was peril, what there was to fear. And he didn't want to open his eyes because it was too pleasant in this pool of darkness, the light hurt too much, and he wasn't even sure where he'd find himself when he did fight all the way back up to full consciousness. Recall brought back the painful memory of being struck on the head so sharply and deftly that he'd fallen senseless before he struck the floor. As his senses cleared, a sharp pain flared in his skull, but the worst agony centered in the old bullet wound in his gut, even when that made no sense at all. His belly felt as if it were on fire. The searing pain threatened to knock him out again. He fought against the whirling emptiness that threatened to overwhelm him, even when he hurt so badly he wanted to succumb to it, to say the hell with it, and to plunge deeper into the pit of blackness where forgetfulness waited.

The pain in his side was worse than it had ever been, a gnawing twitching in the pit of his stomach. His hands sweated and he trembled. That gun barrel laid so expertly across his skull had short-circuited the message center of his brain, that was for sure. His nerve ends sent out the old signals of pain, but his mind was unable to localize them; they burned and stung in all the wrong places. When he tried to move, it was worse than ever.

"Take it easy," a man's voice said directly above him.

There were sounds of other men, and movement. He slit his eyes open cautiously. It was hard to tell the time from the sunlight, it was too weak and pale through the window. A faint saffron shaft reached from the closed panes to the desk beside which he lay.

He recognized the doctor bending over him. It was the doctor's hand on his forehead. The medic glanced up and spoke to the other people in the room: "He's coming around now. He's going to be all right. He'll have a headache for a while, that's all."

Sure, Longarm thought, wincing. He'd been through it before; the sensations of pain were nothing new for him. The bullet in his belly was not his first. He recalled the impact of the slug and the fire when it tore through his flesh; he remembered the deadening pain of gun barrel against skull. He always recovered. He was always almost as good as new. Almost. He struggled in agony.

"Thank God he's all right." Longarm recognized Sheriff Lawson Carr's Southern accent. The sound flowed over him like molasses.

He opened his eyes. Close to him, kneeling, was the doctor. At the medic's shoulder stood Carr. Beyond them, distantly to Longarm's battered senses, stood the deputies and Fondis Estabrook.

He struggled to get up. The doctor said, "Lie still for a moment. You got hit pretty good."

Longarm sighed and sank back on the floor. He pulled himself up enough to brace his back against the side of the pinewood desk.

He heard Carr's soft voice. "I'm sorry, Long. Sorry as hell. I never meant to hit you at all."

"You got me pretty damn good—for an accident," Longarm muttered.

"I'm sorry about that too. I know only one way to use a gun to buffalo an opponent. You can't hit a man and let him keep coming at you. You got to stop him cold. You learn the expert way to buffalo troublemakers in a hurry in my trade, Marshal. You can't shoot 'em all, but you sure as hell better be able to stop 'em. You learn just where to strike to put them out—quick and cold."

"I got to compliment you on that, all right," Longarm said.

"I was already bringing the gun down, Marshal, when Cody Boyle wrestled you over. I knew I was wrong, but there was no way to stop. I can't expect you to forgive me, but I hope you can understand."

Longarm straightened a little, fighting against the torrents of hot pain that threatened to swamp him. He moved his head, studying the people in the room and not finding the man he was looking for. "Where is he? Where's Cody Boyle?"

He struggled to get up, but the doctor's restraining hand on his shoulder held him down. The room spun for a moment about Longarm's head. The medic was right—the pain behind his eyes was suddenly intolerable. He exhaled heavily and sagged back. "I asked you, he said, "where's Cody Boyle?"

"Dead," Sheriff Carr said.

Longarm opened his eyes, forgetting the pain, and stared up at Carr. "Dead? He was my witness. My only witness."

"I'm sorry, Long. It all happened fast," Carr said. "We were all stunned when you fell and Cody leaped away, still conscious. Well, in the confusion, Cody grabbed your gun—"

Longarm instinctively touched at his holster; it was empty. Rage flared through him again, at war with the waves of pain.

"He held the gun on us and backed to the door. He got it open, got outside, and ran."

Longarm went on staring at Carr. He was suddenly glad his holster was empty. He would have been tempted to draw on that son of a bitch talking so softly and smoothly in that honey-and-magnolia voice.

"I ran out on the stoop," Carr said. "At first Cody was in the crowd. When he saw me, he tossed off a shot that missed me and struck the wall. I yelled at him to stop. He wheeled and ran. I fired across his head, but he didn't stop. I had to kill him."

"That's the truth, Marshal," Fondis Estabrook said. "We all saw it. It was just like Lawson says. It was regrettable, but it couldn't be avoided."

Longarm swallowed back the acid taste of failure. Then he pushed the doctor's restraining hand away and stood up. He braced himself against the desk.

"Your gun is there, Mr. Long," Larry said. "Right there."

Longarm nodded, thanking him. He took up the Colt, hefted it in his palm, and then dropped it into his holster. "I reckon you did what you had to do," he said at last. "You got all these men to back you up."

"I did what I had to do," Carr said.

Longarm nodded. He turned and stared into the cellblock beyond the bars. The cells were empty. Flagg Lobatos was gone.

"Naturally we had to let Lobatos go," Carr said. "You had strong evidence against Cody Boyle. By the way, he had three hundred dollars in his pocket when we searched him."

"We thought we were right about Flagg Lobatos," Fondis Estabrook said. "We're not evil people here, Marshal. We're trying to live, and to keep our town alive. That's all. No matter what you think, Sheriff Carr has done his best."

"I'm sure he did what he thought he had to," Longarm said. But he did not feel reassured; far from it. In fact, for some reason he could put no name to, he felt more troubled than ever.

Longarm rode his roan up the slight knoll above Dirty Fork to the town graveyard. He swung down and looped his reins over the rail fence that enclosed the cemetery to keep the hogs out.

The temperature had risen slightly in the early afternoon, and a slight drizzle blew in on the cutting wind. The skies were leaden with a high overcast.

He walked through the rows of graves to the open site where the funeral party had gathered for the graveside ceremonies for Elliot Brockbank. The preacher, a slender, bearded man in black named Perkins Forsley, stood at the red mound of earth, a Bible open in his hand. Near him, Amber Austin stood with Lawson Carr close at her side, his hand supporting her elbow, his face set in an appropriately sympathetic expression. It was hard to see how Carr could give a damn that Elliot was dead when, while the young actor lived, all Carr wanted was to get him out of the way. Well, now that Brockbank was dead, Carr could afford to show compassion.

Amber was heavily veiled. Longarm could not see her face, but grief was suggested in the way her shoulders slumped in

138

the dark gray traveling suit she wore. Around her were the four other remaining members of the Austin-Brockbank Acting Company. These people, two men and two women, huddled against the cutting cold mist, against grief, against terror in this wild place.

A dozen or so townspeople were present, most of them there out of curiosity. Kane Estabrook stood to one side, his handsome head bowed.

A soggy tumbleweed rolled across the old graves, struck Longarm's boot, poised there a moment, then fell away, blown along to nowhere. A bedraggled blue jay scolded from the bleak limbs of a dripping cottonwood. The sign on the cedarwood arches at the cemetery entrance whined on rusty hooks.

Longarm stood silently while the preacher droned on about the deceased. One would have thought Elliot was a lifelong resident of Dirty Fork, a close intimate of Preacher Perkins Forsley. Maybe it was good that the poor kid had some kind words said over him at the last.

Longarm's gaze kept going to the other mound, the new grave in which Cody Boyle's body lay, the site unmarked.

Finally the ceremony ended and the spectators drifted away in the cold wind. Longarm waited, but obviously Lawson Carr was not going to release his grip on Amber Austin's elbow. Longarm walked around the graves to where they stood, backed by the silent company of actors.

"Thank you for coming," Amber said through the veil.

"I'm sure Miss Amber appreciates your courtesy," Lawson Carr said in a manner that was a dismissal.

Longarm's mustached upper lip twisted slightly. "I guess we're all saddened now that Elliot is gone. It will be a real loss to you and your company, Amber."

She sobbed suddenly under the veil. "I just don't know what I'm going to do—what any of us will do. Our company is lost without Elliot."

Still crying, she reached forward and gripped Longarm's hands fiercely in hers, breaking away from Carr for the moment. Longarm felt the sheriff stiffen, his face going cold. One thing Elliot's death had not changed; Lawson Carr wanted Brockbank's lovely young wife as relentlessly as he always had.

139

Longarm felt something slipped from Amber's gloved hand into his palm and pressed there. He could not see her face, but she seemed drawn taut.

Longarm palmed the folded paper she had pressed into his hand. He went on holding her hands for a moment longer. Then he murmured a few more condolences and stepped back.

"We'd better get out of this chill, Miss Amber," Lawson Carr said. "You'll catch pneumonia."

"Yes," Amber said. "We'll go now."

Her shoulders had straightened as if suddenly she had found new hope.

Longarm watched the last of the mourners leave, then walked back to where he'd tethered his horse. Kane Estabrook vaulted over the rail fence and stood looking up at Longarm in the icy mists.

"Thanks, Mr. Long," Kane said.

"For what?"

Kane grinned. "For standing against Sheriff Carr—and my old man. They would have let Flagg Lobatos hang, but for you."

Longarm scowled. "Somebody wanted your father dead. They paid Cody Boyle three hundred bucks either to kill him or make a near miss."

Kane shivered. "I don't know anybody that would do that, Mr. Long. It's just hard to believe, even when I know it's true."

"It's true, all right," Longarm said. "How's things with you and little Mozelle?"

"They're going to be all right," Kane said. "Because I'm going to make them all right."

"I don't envy you that little job."

Kane smiled. "No. It won't be easy. But it's got to be done. I can't have it any other way."

The youth gave Longarm a brief salute, another smile of gratitude, then he swung up into his single-seat buggy and rode away down the hill.

Longarm sat astride the roan for a long moment, watching Kane drive away toward Dirty Fork. He sighed and unfolded the small square of notepaper Amber had slipped into his hand.

"Please. Come to see me as soon as you can when Lawson's not there. I'm frightened. Must talk to you. A."

Frowning, Longarm refolded the paper and shoved it into his greatcoat pocket. He sat for a moment longer, then turned the roan's head and heeled the animal around, heading toward the livery stable.

A telegram awaited Longarm at the registry desk in the hotel. He took the yellow envelope and tore it open. Billy Vail's reply to his inquiry about weather conditions north of the Arkansas Divide was curt and to the point. Reading it, Longarm grinned. He could almost see Billy Vail's reddened face, and hear his voice as he raged, dictating his answer:

"BLIZZARDS REPORTED ACROSS FROM IDAHO TO WYOMING STOP BUT WHATS THAT GOT TO DO WITH CUTTING WIRE IN COLORADO QUESTION MARK VAIL"

Longarm folded the envelope and put it in his pocket. He glanced up and grinned at the hotel clerk. "We're in for some hellish weather," he said.

The clerk smiled and shook his head. "I don't think so. Just a little cold spell. It'll blow over. This time of the year and all. First of May. How bad can it get?"

"That's a good question," Longarm said.

Longarm sat in the lobby, reading the weekly *Dirty Fork Tines*, until he saw Lawson Carr come off the stairwell and stride across the carpeting toward the street. Carr glimpsed Longarm in the chair, and hesitated. But Longarm went on reading as if deeply engrossed in the news. Carr stared at Longarm for a moment, then shrugged his coat up on his shoulders and went on out into the street.

Longarm went on sitting in the lobby club chair for five minutes. Then he folded up the newspaper and laid it aside. He got up and walked out onto the hotel veranda. He looked both ways along the street, then he went down the steps and along the boardwalk to the Silver Palace. Inside, he ordered a rye and drank it down, taking his time. Then he left the saloon, crossed the street, going away from the hotel, circled back behind the stores, and entered the old inn from the rear.

The lobby was almost empty. Longarm crossed it and went

up the steps two at a time. He checked both ways along the corridor, then went directly to Amber's room.

He rapped once and the door was opened by the elderly actor who had played the barrister in *The Missing Rose*. "I'm Desmond Bayne, Mr. Long. Part of Amber's acting company. We've got a little problem. We've been awaiting you anxiously."

"I took a little walk," Longarm said. "Came around my elbow to get to my thumb. Thought somebody might be watching." His gaze touched Amber's. "Your note sounded as if you're pretty troubled."

"I am." Amber came to him and took both of his hands. "We are due to appear next week in Denver. But when we try to leave, Lawson finds all kinds of excuses for us to wait. We hoped to leave after the funeral, but now Sheriff Carr says the others can go on, but I must stay behind."

"We're no good without Amber," Bayne said. "She's our attraction, our bread and butter, and our occasional champagne. We'll try to find a new leading man to replace poor Elliot, but without Amber we're dead, the company is finished."

"Out in this wilderness," one of the women said. "I'm in terror."

"It's all right, Ellen," Amber said in a soothing voice. "Custis will help us, won't you?"

Longarm sighed. "I'll do what I can. But I don't want you to think I can do anything superhuman—and that may be what you'll need to break Amber free of Carr."

"He's suffocating me," Amber said. "Since Elliot died, Lawson has not let me out of his sight. He says he's protecting me, but it's more as if he is watching me. I have this terrible feeling he does not intend to let me leave Dirty Fork . . . ever."

"It looks as if that's his intention," Longarm said. "I'm afraid he's fallen in love with you, Amber. But there's nothing ordinary about his fascination for you. The only thing I can think of is that you bring the Old South back to him—and he means to keep you."

"But I'm from Brooklyn," Amber moaned. "He's very nice. Courtly. Lovely manners. Genteel. Gentlemanly. Courteous. And so soft-spoken. Polite and polished and gallant. And everything is as if he is thinking only of my good. And yet I'm in

142

terror. Because it's like he's put a wall up around me and he does not mean to let me out of it."

"We must get away, Marshal," Desmond Bayne said. "Amber is afraid. The only way we can make any money is to honor our play dates. If we don't show up in Denver and they cancel us ... well, financially we're just not prepared for such an eventuality."

"I've got to get away," Amber said. "I'm frightened and I'm suffocated. Sometimes he looks at me so accusingly, as if I've done something that he must somehow forgive ... and yet he finds it hard to do. He doesn't mention your name, Custis, but of course he knows about us. I think he wants to marry me, but he feels the way would be clear only if you were ... eliminated."

"Carr's a strange man," Longarm agreed. "He's been put through hell, and it's left him scarred. I'm sure he doesn't want to hurt you, Amber. He does want to marry you."

She shuddered. "I'd sooner be dead. Marriage to him would be like prison. Living in this ... this godforsaken town ... that would be a living death for me. Oh God, Custis, when I think about it, I'm ill. You must help me."

Longarm drew a deep breath. Then he glanced at the two actors and said, "You own a couple of carriages, right?"

"We must have them," Desmond Bayne said. "We travel in them, and we carry our costumes and makeup."

"I understand. Can either of you handle a team of horses?"

"I have driven one team all along," Bayne said. "But Wilfred here has never handled a team of animals."

Wilfred shook his head. "I've handled horses onstage."

"It's not the same, Wilfred," Desmond Bayne said.

Longarm spread his hands. "Well, I have no real plan. It looks like you could load up, and Amber could tell Lawson Carr goodbye and you could drive away, but I know better."

"We all know better," Bayne said. He shivered slightly. "We've all seen the sheriff with Amber."

One of the women said, "We even saw him before Elliot was killed. I can't understand that. Why would anyone kill poor Elliot? It was not even robbery. He had almost no money on him anyway. He had on a diamond ring, but the killer didn't

143

even take that. I just feel like we'll all die if we don't get away from this terrible place."

"Custis will help us, Ellen," Amber said.

"The only thing I can tell you is to keep yourselves packed up and ready," Longarm said.

"Oh, we're all packed," Desmond Bayne said.

"And God knows we're ready," Ellen said.

"I know an Indian named Sam Brown. He might drive one of your carriages to Denver. Pay him and his expenses—"

"Gladly," Bayne said.

"If there comes a chance when we can pack you up and get you quietly out of Dirty Fork, we'll do it," Longarm said. "Meantime, all I can tell you is to keep rehearsing for your first play in Denver."

"God bless you," Bayne said.

"Don't thank me yet," Longarm cautioned.

"We do thank you," Amber said. She caught Longarm and pulled him to her. She kissed him fiercely. She smelled so good and felt so good that heat stabbed through him, making the bullet wound in his side burn like hell.

All of them clung to his hand as if he were their last hope on earth. He reassured them as best he could and let himself out of the door. He heard Desmond Bayne turn the key in the lock as soon as the door latch clicked into place.

He stood for a moment, leaning against the door. He'd tried to instill hope in the acting troupe, but he could not believe it would be easy to get Amber out of Lawson Carr's reach. The man wanted her. Amber Austin was the first touch of loveliness in Lawson Carr's life since the Yankees had burned his home plantation and raped and murdered his wife.

Longarm exhaled heavily and walked along the corridor toward his own room. He stopped abruptly. Lawson Carr stepped out of a doorway across the hall, his leaden gray eyes fixed on Longarm. "I've warned you, Long, about getting in my way," Carr said.

Longarm smiled crookedly. "You ought to stop hanging around in hotel hallways, Carr. You're liable to hear something you'll wish you hadn't heard."

"Perhaps." Carr's cold eyes glittered. His voice was softer

than ever. "Or perhaps I'll hear something *you'll* wish I hadn't heard."

Longarm shrugged. "Either way, old son, skulking about in hotel hallways is a shabby habit, hardly worthy of a gentleman of the Old South."

Carr bowed slightly. "I learned in the War, Long. You fight evil with evil's own weapons. A thoroughbred can sink to the level of a mongrel, if he's forced to. But a mongrel will die what he is. A mongrel."

"Isn't that strange?" Longarm said. "It sounds like just another tired old saw, but the way you say it, it comes out like a threat."

Carr drew himself tall. "You make out of it what you will . . . mongrel."

Chapter 13

When Longarm walked through the sharp frost to the sheriff's office in the red brick building the next morning, the world was becalmed, as if frozen stuck. There was no sign of snow, almost no wind, and the sky was once more cloudless. Looking around him, puzzled and disquieted, he shivered under his greatcoat.

He paused on the stoop outside the county building office. He drew deeply on his morning cheroot, enjoying the warmth for one last draw before he threw it away. He'd fired up the cigar as he left the hotel restaurant after a breakfast of pancakes, ham, and eggs. He should have felt some sense of satisfaction, but vestiges of a headache pulsed behind his left ear, his side hurt, and troubles gnawed at him from outside. He faced problems with no immediate answers. Like Amber Austin. She and her show people were very much on his mind; he'd even alerted Sam Brown to be ready to leave in a hurry. But minimal surveillance last night had proved to him that Lawson Carr had his deputies watching the hotel. Maybe Lawson himself even lurked somewhere in the shadows. Amber was caught; she'd have to wait, even if she began to think he'd failed her. Hell, maybe he would. He'd never been up against a man quite like Lawson Carr before—a man who once must have been gentle, but was now dead to anything except his own desires and their fulfillment. And, too, the matter of the fences remained on the front burner, and he had no answers there, either, though he meant to make Fondis Estabrook and company believe that he had.

He drew a deep breath, the icy chill burning high into his nostrils. He opened the front door and closed it quietly behind him.

They awaited him. The office was crowded. Lawson Carr looked sleepless, as if he'd spent a wakeful night; Fondis Estabrook still wore his arm in a sling; Kane Estabrook sat quietly to one side. Dave Carmel and Moffatt Pierce were there from the Interior Department. The first thing Fondis Estabrook said was, "My God, it's almost nine o'clock. Middle of the morning. We asked you to meet with us early. Where you been?"

Longarm shrugged. "Maybe you're not as anxious to see me as you think, Estabrook."

Estabrook leaned forward in his chair. "What's that supposed to mean?"

"It means that from all I can learn, you people could stop that fence-cutting any time you wanted to stop it."

"What the hell you talking about?" Moffatt Pierce said.

"I don't find any signs that fences are being cut along the trail maliciously—at least not by rustlers or grass-stealers or even nesters."

Fondis Estabrook stood up. "What kind of accusations are you making, Marshal?"

"None yet. I'm trying to give you people a chance to pull in your horns. Stop this fighting among yourselves."

Fondis Estabrook swore. He paced the office. "I knew damn well that was going to be the answer you'd come up with."

"What other answer is there? You show me. I'm willing to listen."

"That's just what I'm going to do, Marshal. That's the reason I asked Dave Carmel and Moffatt Pierce here from Interior. They are the boys raising hell about the cut fences. Interior. Not me. Not this town. Interior."

"Seems to me they are reacting to pressures they get from you—and people like you, Estabrook," Longarm said. "I'm not saying there ain't cut fences. There are. All I am saying is, it could be stopped by you people."

Lawson Carr's soft voice slashed like a rapier in the room. "You're making slanderous accusations, Long. Why don't you come out and say it? You think I'm working for Fondis Estabrook. You think Estabrook is starting all this trouble just to get rid of Flagg Lobatos and a few cattle-stealing nesters."

Longarm met Carr's deadly gaze levelly. "You said it about as well as I could say it, Sheriff Carr. This fence-cutting battle—with Interior caught in the middle—comes down to a personal range fight between Mr. Estabrook and Flagg Lobatos, with a few nesters adding a little fuel to a big fire. If Mr. Estabrook and Lobatos came to some accommodation, I think the serious wire-cutting would stop."

"You're an insulting young son of a bitch," Estabrook said. "I didn't send for you. Lawson Carr didn't send for you. Interior asked for help. I am a businessman caught in the middle here. I admit I'm getting hurt. I even believe I know who is stealing from me and destroying government property. But I am trying to save this town. I'm trying to save my investment. If that's wrong, ninety-nine percent of the businessmen in this country are wrong. There have been gunfights over that cut fence. Gunfights that neither I nor any of my Flying F men were involved in. But because I'm the one with the biggest stake to lose, you come in here making accusations against me."

"I ain't accusing anybody, because I don't have any proof. I do have circumstantial evidence that you and Carr used the coincidence of Flagg Lobatos coming into Dirty Fork—on his own, to talk to me—to charge him with attempted murder without even asking any questions."

"Dammit," Carr's soft voice slashed at Longarm. "We've apologized. We've released Lobatos. We made a mistake. That doesn't make us criminal."

Longarm grinned coldly. "No. But it gets me to asking myself the same questions over and over, and I keep getting the same answers. You people want the fences and the grass, but you don't want the inconveniences that go with them—the Texas trail drives, the homesteaders, the small ranchers."

Estabrook slashed downward with his hand. "No, Long. We want the trail drives. The town's economy depends on them. We need them. They spend money with us. We need the farmers. What we don't need is land-grabbers and rustlers and fence-cutters."

"You mean Flagg Lobatos?"

"You said the name, Long. I brought these Interior people along today so you'd know how serious this thing is, but you keep coming back to Flagg Lobatos."

"No. I keep hearing charges against Lobatos. But I've seen no proof against Lobatos, just a whole lot of grudge-talk. I saw this town yelling for his blood—and I'll bet more than half of those people had never seen him, didn't know him except for what they heard about him, and read in the local paper about him."

"Our hope, Mr. Long"—Estabrook's voice dripped sarcasm—"was to stop this vandalism one way or the other. What you don't seem to understand, and what we have here, is a little town that is dying. We all know the railroads are putting an end to cattle drives—even the feeders will soon be moved by rails. We hope to survive as a county seat, and a farm-and-ranch community. But we can survive only if the town is tamed, if the wild elements are removed. One way or the other."

"No matter what you start to say, you keep coming back to the battle between you and Lobatos—with some stupid but innocent people caught in the middle."

Estabrook stared at Longarm. "I resent your accusations, sir. Because what you are really saying—in front of these government men from Interior—is that I am fomenting a range war for my own profit."

"No. I'm trying to warn you, Mr. Estabrook. You can overplay your hand."

"Listen to him! He is as much as baldly accusing me of forging evidence against Flagg Lobatos!"

"Let's forget Lobatos for the moment," Longarm suggested. "There is no writing in fire that says Dirty Fork can't just die, just to be allowed to die."

Lawson Carr leaned forward in his squeaking swivel chair. "What kind of threat is this?"

"No threat. It's just that nobody says the government has to let the trail come through Dirty Fork."

"What the hell, it comes through Dirty Fork," Estabrook raged.

Longarm shrugged. "It does now. But I can tell you, if you people don't pull in your horns, the government can cut your balls off." He snapped his fingers. "Just like that. You can wither and die."

"What?" Estabrook was starting to sweat; a thin film of moisture glazed his brow.

"How?" Carr's voice was soft, but unbelieving and unyielding.

"Simple. There's a town that's a hell of a lot more civilized than Dirty Fork, and it's less than a day's ride away."

"Sun Patch?" Estabrook made a curse of the name.

"You got it. A law-abiding town. Modest little place. Would be a good county seat. You people keep cutting fences and battling with guns over them, we'll recommend extending those goddamn drift fences east of here and leave this whole area—including the town of Dirty Fork—cut off in a blind corner behind bobwire fences."

A stunned silence hung for a moment in the office. The loudest sound was the low roar of the potbellied stove. Even young Kane Estabrook stirred uneasily in his chair.

Fondis Estabrook was not going to accept anybody's word on such a serious matter. "Is he telling the truth, Pierce?"

The Interior Department man nodded. "It's up to the government to decide where the drift fences will be stretched, Mr. Estabrook."

"You can't do that. We've got a right to the trail, to our fences and our open country. Dammit, Long, all we wanted from you was to protect our fences."

Longarm's voice raked them. "You want fences, gentlemen? I'll show you fences. You people will learn to live together, or you'll die together. It's up to you."

The doorknob turned and a young Interior Department inspector strode in, breathless, his face ruddy from wind and cold. "Mr. Pierce, we've got a bad cut out on the drift fence—and we've been able to round up the cattle that were driven in on permit grass."

"We'll come right out," Pierce said.

Estabrook stared at Longarm in redfaced triumph. "We'll all go," he said.

Longarm rode on the boot of the Estabrook carriage with the ranch coachman. Lawson Carr and Fondis Estabrook rode in the tonneau under heavy quilts. They did not speak as they left town and they came in silence to the cut in the drift fence.

The young range inspector led the way. He'd traded his exhausted mount for a new horse at the livery. Behind them, young Kane rode with Moffatt Pierce and Dave Carmel. None of them seemed to have anything to say.

The range inspector dismounted at the cut in the barbed wire. The driver pulled Estabrook's coach in close and they all swung down. No physical evidence remained at the scene of the cutting; there were signs where cattle had been driven through, even signs where the cows had raked their hides on the barbs, leaving tufts of hair.

"They headed north across here," the inspector said, "if you folks want to follow me."

He swung back into his saddle and across the plain, head bent, though the trail left by the herd was clear in the trampled grass. Kane Estabrook rode with him, but Carmel and Pierce continued to ride along behind the carriage in the rough grasslands.

Less than two miles inside the cut fence they came upon fifty head of cattle contentedly munching the sweet grass. Two riders from Estabrook's Flying F Ranch rode easy herd on them, letting them graze, but keeping them together.

Longarm could hear the savagery of Fondis Estabrook's breathing even before they reached the outer limits of the outlaw cattle. One of the men rode to the carriage and touched his hatbrim to Estabrook.

"Inspector Powell alerted us, boss. We rode over as fast as we could. Saw two or three men. But they saw us too, and took off. We rounded up the cows and Powell rode into town to report to his bosses."

"Good work, Billings." Estabrook drew a deep breath. "Any brand on them scrawny critters?"

Billings laughed in exasperation. "Looks like they never learn, boss. Same brand as always. The wolfhead."

Fondis Estabrook could barely contain his satisfaction. His mouth twisted, he stared at Longarm. "If you think, sir, that a complete report on your high-handed and insulting attitude won't be sent—with corroborating reports from the sheriff and the two Interior officers—you're goddamn mistaken. You're going to live to regret the day you called me a crook."

Longarm said nothing. Inspector Powell, Dave Carmel, and the range hand called Billings cut a few of the cattle out of the bunch. The ragged brand could not be mistaken. A triangle to represent the head, and two wavy lines off each top angle to stand for ears—the Lobatos brand.

"Looks like you owe Mr. Estabrook an apology," Lawson Carr's soft voice scraped at Longarm.

"You can forget that," Fondis Estabrook said. "No goddamn half-assed apology is going to save your ass, Long. You've made serious accusations against me. Unless you can make them stick, I'm nailing your scroungy hide to the barn wall."

The silence on the return to Dirty Fork inside Estabrook's carriage made the outbound ride seem like a noisy picnic. The driver pulled into the curb before the bank. Estabrook got out. He stood tall on the boardwalk, his shoulders rigid. The morning sun lay livid across his taut face. "Well, this is as far as we go, Long. I may as well tell you, I'm asking for your recall. At once. You'll find I'm not without friends in high places in Colorado."

Longarm swung down from the carriage. His gaze touched at the hatred blazing in Lawson's eyes, the cold fury in Estabrook's. He tried to smile. "I reckon things are working just about according to schedule. They didn't send me here to Dirty Fork to make friends. And so far I'm right on the mark."

Longarm touched the brim of his stetson in a brief salute and left Carr and Estabrook standing outside the bank. He walked down the street, going directly to the Western Union office at the train depot.

He wrote out a telegram to Billy Vail, asking for a rundown on Flagg Lobatos—any wanted fliers in the files, or criminal reports, or jail records, anything.

The sun braved the chill, a faint wan orange ball in a cloudless heaven. Longarm walked in the icy cold to the livery stable. Here he saddled up his horse and rode out the rear door, going at a long angle away from the town.

Before he had ridden five miles, his legs grew numb. He dismounted and, holding the reins in his fist, ran to get the circulation restarted in his calves and thighs. But the pounding of his feet on the hard, cold dobie earth threatened to dislodge his teeth and crack his toes. He swung back up into the saddle, swinging his arms back and forth across his chest and breathing great plumes of gray smoke.

He rode warily as he neared the inclined approach that led between the boulders up to the mesa at Screaming Springs.

He kept waiting for gunfire, for signs of ambushers in the overthrust and tormented country. There was only silence.

He went slowly up the incline between the great boulders, and out into the flat tableland. A bonfire roared beside a single-room line shack. At first Longarm saw only a few animals: hunting dogs, a few hogs, some horses in a lean-to inside a pole corral. Out beyond the corral, the tableland stretched, bare and rocky, to a sheer precipice. Then Longarm saw two people huddled against the brick house supports, near the fire.

The two people got to their feet when they saw Longarm approach. They stood silhouetted at the rim of the blazing fire. They were burning aged wood, bundles of grass, and cow chips, anything that would give off heat.

Longarm swung down from the saddle and walked slowly toward them, leading the roan. He sighed. He'd never seen such signs of poverty. There was an abandoned look about the summer line shack, the yard, the mesa itself.

The boy held a rifle across his chest. He held it easily, but Longarm was not fooled. Both the youth and the older woman were watching him warily, maybe holding their breath without knowing they did it. The boy was a younger, leaner, cleaner copy of Flagg Lobatos. He wore a heavy quilted coat with a fleece collar, a shapeless bonnet with the brim sagging about his face, and a pair of much-washed Levi's. He held the gun, unsmiling, making no move, but waiting.

The woman was an older, wearier version of Mozelle. There was more than a faint resemblance between mother and daughter. The woman looked as if she might have been as pretty as Mozelle once, a long time ago. She was not pretty anymore, but the memory of beauty clung to her like a soft aura in a hard, bitter land, an inner loveliness that shone through run-over shoes, a slatternly dress, and a khaki blanket wrapped about her shoulders, held together in front by her fists.

"Afternoon," Longarm said. "My name is Long. Custis Long. Folks call me Longarm—if they like."

The mother and son stared at him silently. At last the woman nodded. "Folks have spoke of you. Flagg said he owed you. And little Mozelle, she spoke most kindly."

"That was most kind of them," Longarm said.

"We don't cotton much to strangers coming up here." Mrs.

153

Lobatos spoke as if warning him. "Usual, Flagg will have one of the children down at the foot of the incline, keeping watch for strangers or enemies." Her mouth widened in a faint, strange smile. "Strangers and enemies. That's just about ever'body in Flagg's world these days."

The boy laughed. "He ain't never been burdened down with friends."

The mother stopped smiling. "Like Flagg says. A man has a big family, he ain't got no need nor no time for either strangers or friends. I'm Nonnie Lobatos, Mr. Longarm, and this here is my youngest. His name is J.C.; that there stands for John Calhoun. That's a respected name back home in Tennessee, where we come from."

Longarm opened his mouth to answer, but at that moment there came a weird and startling scream, like that of a woman or a puma, from a few yards away in the rocks. Longarm shook all over, not realizing he'd been holding himself so tense. He jerked his head around in time to see a thick cloud of steam spewing upward from the rocks. A hot, overwhelming smell of rotten eggs permeated the air. For a few moments he was unable to draw a breath of fresh air.

"That's Screamin' Springs," J.C. said. "Hit screams like that most every two hours. You git used to it."

"You git used to anything," Nonnie Lobatos agreed. "We'uns lived in a soddy down below on the prairie until spring came. Can't live in this summer line shack in the winter. Not till it's fixed up. Looks like we're goin' to have to move back down to the dirt hut if'n this here cold gits any worse—and Flagg say it's comin' on a killer cold. He knows about these things. And winds kite right through them cracks between them line-shack walls. Yeah, when Flagg comes back, I figger we best move back down to the soddy."

"Flagg's not here?" Longarm said.

"No." J.C. shook his head. "He ain't 'round now."

"Can you say where he is?"

"No, sir, I cain't."

"Do you have any idea when he'll be back?"

"Cain't say that, neither."

Longarm exhaled heavily. "How about Mozelle? Could I talk to her?"

"Moze ain't 'round neither, mister."

"None of the other children ain't here, Mr. Longarm," Nonnie Lobatos said.

"And I guess you don't know where they are?"

"I reckon they're out tending to our cows somewheres."

"I sure would like to talk to Flagg, Mrs. Lobatos. He may be in big trouble. Bad trouble. Only way I know to head it off is to find him and talk to him."

Nonnie Lobatos and her son stared at each other for a long moment. At last, J.C. said, "What they charging Paw with now?"

"I'm afraid it's pretty serious. There's half a dozen witnesses against him or your brothers and sister—or all of them."

"Cut fence?"

"That's right."

"We ain't cut any fence. We keep all out cows up here in the overthrust. They's grass enough. We ain't cut no fences."

Longarm shook his head. "Afraid that won't do this time, J.C. There's more than eyewitnesses against your family this time. They rounded up at least fifty head of cows with your wolfhead brand on them. They're holding those cows too, as evidence." He lowered his voice. "It might be best if you helped me find Flagg as fast as you can."

J.C. and his mother stared at each other again, silently. Then J.C. said, "Paw said you were square with him when they got him in town, and after he cussed you pretty good and all."

"I'm trying to head off bloodshed."

J.C. winced. "Paw left in the last half-hour, Mr. Longarm."

"He couldn't have. I'd have seen him as I came toward the incline."

Again, mother and son exchanged glances. "Paw didn't go out that way," J.C. said.

"I understood that's the only way out, that the drop at the other side of this tabletop is more than a hundred feet."

"More'n a hundred," J.C. agreed. "Straight down."

"Then how did your pa get out of here?"

J.C. drew a deep breath. "Paw is likely going to beat me raw for this. But I'm trusting you, mister. And us Lobatoses ain't lived well by trustin' outsiders none."

155

"We're trustin' you, Mr. Longarm." Nonnie Lobatos' voice matched the withering chill in the atmosphere.

They gestured with their heads for Longarm to follow. They crossed the yard to a place where the strange gray creek ran through the rocks. The smell of rotten eggs intensified. "You don't drink that stuff, do you?" Longarm said.

"Cain't even get the hogs to drink it," J.C. said. "Besides, hit's b'ilin' hot. See, the crick looks like it runs uphill here from the springs in them rocks back there. It don't. Hit cuts its way through the rock so hit falls over the edge of the mesa back here."

They paused at the rim of the rocky edge. The wind battered at them, swirling up the sheer stone face of the tormented overthrust.

"So where is your pa?" Longarm said, staring down at the prairie below the rocky cliff.

"Down there," J.C. said. "Paw found a goat trail down the face of this here wall. None of the rest of us ain't tried hit, but Paw has. Paw likes to have extra ways out of any place. He don't like to be fenced in."

"You could go down the incline and around it," Nonnie suggested.

"If Flagg went down there, he'd have a five-mile start on me."

"If you went down here, you could git kilt," Nonnie said.

"Hit'd be a good way for us to git rid of you," J.C. said. "Maybe Paw ain't really been down that goat trail ... you'd have to trust us."

Longarm gazed at the mother and son for some moments. At last he went to his saddlebag and took out his field glasses. He put them to his eyes and focused on the plains below the sheer cliff. After a moment he located a horseman sauntering away in the buffalo grass. Even at that distance he recognized Flagg's hat and his disreputable clothing. He exhaled heavily. "He's down there, all right."

"You're smart, you'll go out the incline," J.C. said.

"If I'm smart, I lose him."

156

"If you fall a hundred feet straight down, you won't do yourself a lot of good either," J.C. reminded him.

Longarm gazed at them. J.C. and Nonnie were watching him with strange, taunting, challenging grins twisting their faces.

Chapter 14

The cliff itself seemed to vibrate with dizzying motion in the raging wind currents. Gales swirled upward along the face of the broken rocks, a menacing whisper of threatening sound from the mesa above, and he did not even have to step on small rocks to dislodge them; the wind tore them loose and peppered the steep gray walls with them. Mists swirled from the stinking waterfall.

Longarm heard each falling rock. His saddle leather scraped the jutting stones, and each wiry bush grasped at his chaps like living hands to trip him and send him hurtling off the side of the precipice.

The people above him were silent, but he had the sickening sensation that they were laughing at him in his foolhardiness, his readiness to find a trail down the face of this cliff where it was likely none existed.

He paused and stared across the emptiness to the sea of grass far beyond the broken and tormented faults and rifts and canyons. Flagg Lobatos had descended this narrow ledge with his horse. Unless his people lied, there was a goat trail; there was one chance in a thousand that he could find it and trace it to the rock-strewn sump.

The force of the wind plastered him to the side of the sheer rock facing. The sting of fine sand blinded him and stung his face like salt fired from a gun. The wind itself battered at his eyes, forcing him to keep them almost closed. His ears seemed to fill with pressure and pop. For long moments, sounds were lost to him.

He pulled his bandanna up over his nose and keep his head down, searching for the next step on the narrow descending ladder along the edge of the cliff.

The roan whinnied in instinctive terror. They had tied a croker sack over the horse's head. "Better cover his head, mister," J.C. had advised. "If yore pony sees where you tryin' to take him, he'll fight you enough to send both of you into those rocks down there."

The horse strained against the lines wrapped about Longarm's fist. The animal pawed the ledge before it would step forward. When they reached a sudden sharp angle in sheer rock, Longarm had to stand on the brink of the narrow ledge and thrust the horse's head against the facing, inching him around a tight corner.

The down-slanting ledge suddenly narrowed. He studied it carefully, trying to find tracks, if there were any visible. He found nothing. Even if Lobatos had come this way, the driving wind had swept away all memory of his passing.

Longarm straightened against the rough shale, and suddenly he was scared.

He had been a damned fool to follow Lobatos down here. The very fact that Lobatos had made it didn't mean any other man could do it. And he had no proof that Lobatos had come this way. Those people had let him onto their hidden mesa without protest. They had let him find Lobatos in the prairie grass far below, and they had let him believe what he had wanted to believe—that Flagg had found a way down the side of this wind-tortured cliff.

He inched along the narrow jutting of rock. Suddenly the world seemed to fall away below him and he halted his blindfolded horse and braced his back against the rock wall, staring down at the broken shafts and swords and stumps of rocks at the foot of the overthrust. The dim trail, which had been barely wide enough to support him and his horse, led abruptly straight down several feet, and disappeared into a fold of fault rock.

His heart pounded in his chest, but his pumping heart didn't warm his blood; that ran icy in his veins. His hands were numb with cold and his feet burned with the chill. He spent some moments trying to stamp feeling back into them. A misstep could cost him his life.

He glanced upward toward the jutting rim of the mesa and the open, empty sky beyond. He wanted to go back up there, but he knew better; there was no way to get there from here.

He found no alternate tracks; that meant that Lobatos, if he had come this way at all, had braced himself and slid slowly at an oblique angle, taking the horse with him and praying that the forward momentum of the animal didn't carry both of them over the side.

He drew a deep breath. There was nothing to be gained by standing there. There was no sense in studying the options or looking for other tracks, for there were none. He either went down the incline without even broken spikes to clutch, or he turned back.

He crouched slightly and leaned as far backward as he could without falling, bracing himself against his own heels. He no longer believed this was a goat trail down the cliff. No sane goat would place himself in such jeopardy, even if his life depended on it. Suddenly, sliding along the narrow lip of shale, Longarm laughed, a bitter, choked off sound, and asked himself, "Why in hell am I here?"

He found no answer for this either, in the frightful cold and howl of wind. He caught himself at the bottom of the ledge and hung there until his horse skidded down the rock cap to him.

He inched slowly along this rim, looking for the next tier of steps, the path Lobatos must have found for a way down. He kept hoping some fault in the rocks would take them off the very brink of the cliff. But though rocks and boulders jutted outward, what dim lane there was followed the outer ledges.

In places he got down on his knees and crawled along, the horse following at the end of the lines. He was forced to crawl in order to grip rocks and chips in the path to keep from being brushed off the ledge.

In its widest areas, the path or lip was little more than a yard wide. Still, the ledge led tortuously downward, so he followed it because he had no other choice. The trail wound to the very rim of the broken rock formations, and at times it seemed his next step would be into open space.

He rested at a break in the boulders. He took off his hat and mopped at the cold sweat beading his forehead. The path twisted downward along the tattered fringe of the overthrust. One thing was sure. A man was a fool to attempt this trip alone; he was doubly a fool to lead a blindfolded animal. But because there was no return, no alternate route, he skirted the face of the cliff, moving fearfully, slowly downward.

When the narrow ledge reached a broken fault, it abruptly ended. Wind and sand and time had broken away the jutting jowl of the rock.

He stood, weak in the back of his legs, staring downward at the broken bed of rocks yawning below him. He sweated in spite of the cold, trying to decide if there was any way he could turn back. Again, he stared across the broken land below and found the small figure of the horseman riding away from him. He now believed that Flagg Lobatos had come down the cliff, on this trail. There had to be some way and he had to find it.

But he could find nothing promising. He had descended more than halfway down the face of the precipice, but a fall into the rocks below would be fatal. If a man fell this far and didn't die at once, his death would be lonely and painful. He sagged against the cold, wet rock facing, shivering with chill that had nothing to do with the whistling updrafts.

A faint smear of blood glistened on a rock. The mists had not yet washed it away. A man had been here. Flagg Lobatos. He pulled himself up on the bloodied rock and found the way down.

He sagged there, defeated. A small trail, protected by boulders, wound down to the sump of the hill. But in order to reach it, he had to climb over this rock. Somehow he had to force his roan to scramble over it without losing its balance and taking both of them to the broken jumble of sharp crags.

He couldn't leave the horse to plunge from this ledge. If he couldn't get the animal to lunge and fight its way upward, he would have to find some way back up the sheer rock, and this he knew to be impossible.

He climbed to the top of the rock. Gripping the lines with both hands, he tugged. The horse pawed outward, found a wall, and resisted. Before he could force the roan's forepaws up over the head of the rock, he knew why Lobatos had left streaks of his blood behind him.

Squealing, the horse resisted. Finally, when the animal was balanced upon the rock on its chest, Longarm sank into the small depression inside the boulder and simply used brute strength to lever the horse down upon him.

The horse plunged suddenly straight at him and Longarm leaped aside at the last moment. The roan staggered, and at first Longarm was afraid the animal had broken a leg.

He spent a long time soothing the terrified horse and letting his own heart slow down. But after this fearful moment, the rest of the descent was easy. In a few minutes he led the horse out of a narrow rock tunnel, onto level ground.

He removed the croker sack and stuffed it in his saddlebag. The roan was trembling from head to toe. Soothing it, Longarm grinned. "I know just how you feel. You just think you're scared. You should have seen where we've been."

Longarm rode out of the outcropping of broken rocks, into the sea of grass. The sun westered and the wind was colder, with a slicing edge. A strange, brassy light illumined the sky and the prairie.

He pressed his field glasses against his eyes and searched the rolling plain ahead. After a moment he found Lobatos moving unhurriedly through the deep graze. The magnifying glass yanked Lobatos backward, bringing him so close that Longarm felt as if he could smell as well as see him. He focused on the round-crowned hat, the bent brim pulled low, the lavender kerchief, the dark coat on thin shoulders. It was Flagg Lobatos, all right.

He put away the glasses and urged the horse into a lope across the frozen, undulating grass that crackled crisply under the animal's feet.

He crested a small rise, halted, and took up the field glasses again. His heart sank. This time he could not find Lobatos ahead of him in the open plains.

He put away the glasses and swung down from the saddle. He studied the hoofprints left by Lobatos' horse in the muddy places. There was more than one way to follow a man, even a smart and wary critter like Lobatos. If he had to track him, he would. He found the break he needed, a cut in the outer rim of the horse's left rear shoe. Longarm swung back up into the saddle, resuming his steady pursuit.

He picked up the pace a little, using his heels in the roan's flanks. Sometimes he talked to the horse. Mostly he just cursed

Lobatos' tricky ways. Was the bastard sprawled with his prone horse in a draw somewhere now, with his gun fixed on him?

The trail bent to the left and Longarm followed it, riding into the sun. He crested a knoll, pausing to study the land ahead of him. Far below, he glimpsed wisps of smoke rising from clumps of cottonwoods and dwarf willows in the bed of a dry creek.

He slowed, crossing the dried grass that had been just greening with spring and was now burnt and singed with the strange, unseasonal freeze. He found the bed of the dry creek, which cut a shallow, pebbled path between two grassy slopes. He ground-tied his horse and followed the dim, bald creekbed toward the trees in the draw and the faint, rising smoke.

At the rim of the trees, he inched his way into the ground cover.

He grinned coldly and drew his gun, holding it at his side. He saw Lobatos, sitting with his back against an old stump, his hat back, legs and hands stretched toward the fire.

Stealthily, Longarm came around the clump of willows. He held his gun fixed on the figure kneeling before the campfire. He figured ahead, prepared for the possibility that when he spoke, or when Lobatos sensed his presence, the vaquero might swing around firing.

He moved into a clearing in the sump of the dry wash. Bracing himself, he tossed his voice like the loop of a lariat toward the reclining figure. "On your feet, Flagg. Take it slow. Put your arms out wide at your sides and turn around easy. It'll be all right. You just turn around easy."

The figure stood up slowly. But Longarm felt as if the earth itself were suddenly insubstantial beneath his feet. The hat and the clothing belonged to Flagg Lobatos, there was no doubting that. But the person between him and the fire was even slighter than the coyote-thin Lobatos, and much shorter.

Even before Mozelle turned around, Longarm knew he'd been suckered.

She turned slowly as he ordered, with her hands out at her sides.

At the same instant he heard a voice from behind him. "Maybe you're looking for me, Marshal?"

Longarm spun around, bringing his gun up. Lobatos fired. A bullet kicked up clumps of dobie between Longarm's feet.

"Now you just stand easy, Marshal. I can get a bullet closer than that if you make me do it." Lobatos stood, legs apart, angled against the sunlight, his gun steady. In the withering chill of the wind, he wore no hat or coat, but seemed unaware of the cold. His coyote grin didn't waver. "You can't get us both, anyhow. You shoot me, Mozelle will still get you. My little girl won't miss you this time."

Behind him, Mozelle said, "I'm sorry, Marshal Long."

He glanced over his shoulder. She had her gun fixed on him. She didn't look happy, but she looked determined.

Longarm shook his head. "What are you doing here?"

"Kane Estabrook rode out and tol' my girl that you lawdogs was yapping at my heels again. Moze rode out here, and I come down the face of the cliff. Just ahead of you, it looks like." He grinned. "I got some real respect for you, Long. Something I ain't never on this earth felt for a lawman or a government sneak, so I hope you won't try nothin' foolish. Keep in your mind at all times that I could have got you with the first bullet if I'd of wanted to. But I figgered I owed you for what you done for me, bringing in that Cody Boyle when Fondis and Carr meant to string me up. Our slate's clean now, though, so you want to stay healthy, you walk easy between me and my little girl."

"I want to parley," Longarm said.

"No." Lobatos shook his head. "Kane tol' my little girl how snug and neat the frame fits me this time. There ain't nothin' to talk about. The war is broke out between me and Fondis. Him and Carr mean to wipe me out this time, and I don't aim to make it easy for 'em." His voice softened. "Mozelle, honey, would you just walk in there and relieve the marshal of his gun? He don't need it, and havin' it near might give him a temptation that could git him hurt."

"All right, Pa." Mozelle came up behind Longarm, walking with a soft, Indian tread. She took the Colt and returned to the fire.

Longarm said. "The fences were cut, Lobatos—"

"I ain't the only critter in the Divide with wire-cutters, Long."

"Your cows. Fifty of them, driven onto government graze through a cut fence."

"Can't help it. I ain't cut no fences. Once I did. A while back. I might do'er again, if I have to. But not this time. I don't care what you seen, I ain't guilty."

"They're your cattle, Lobotas. I saw the brand."

Lobatos shrugged. "I rounded up my cows out of mesquite flats and draws—arroyos, we call 'em down home. But where I got 'em, anybody else could have done it."

"But why?"

"Hell, man, don't be dense just because you work for the government. You saw 'em try to pin the gunnin' of Fondis on me. They almost had me, but for you. This time they don't mean to let me out of their trap."

"They didn't find the cut fence or the cows, Flagg. Interior Department range inspectors—"

"Oh shit, Long. I hate to think you really are stupid enough to be a government man. My God. You talk plain ignorant."

Longarm sighed, suddenly aware that he had been holding his breath for a long time, seeing things he had not suspected before. He said, "If you didn't cut government fence—this time—and drive those cows onto permit graze land, then you got nothing to fear."

Lobatos laughed. "I got to admire you, Long. You talk like *you* got the gun. You talk like you're doing me some kind of favor. Tellin' me I ain't got nothin' to fear." He hefted his gun. "I say I ain't got nothin' to fear, no way." He gazed beyond Longarm, his eyes warming and his voice softening slightly. "It's gittin' late, Mozelle honey. You best git on back up to Screamin' Springs. Want you to git there 'fore dark. Don't want your maw worried about you. You tell her I'm all right. I might have to kill a couple of knotheads to bring some sense into these people, but I'm all right."

"Please, Paw—"

"Now, honey, don't you argufy against your paw. You know that there is one thing I cain't no way abide—chillern back-talking they elders. You just leave my things there by the fire, and ride on out of here."

They were silent as Mozelle reluctantly removed her father's hat, scarf, and coat. She donned her own greatcoat and hat.

She started to speak, but Lobatos merely shook his head and she fell silent.

She mounted her horse and then hesitated, with the campfire illumining her lovely little face. She said, "Maybe Mr. Long could help you, Paw."

Lobatos smiled indulgently. "You just git on home, girl. I don't need no help. You git men helpin' you, that means you got to trust 'em, and they got to trust you. Gits complicated, honey. People been trying to cut me down all my life, and I'm still here. Just tell your maw don't wait supper, but don't fret none, neither."

Her eyes brimming with tears, Mozelle sank her heels into the flanks of her pony and rode along the creekbed, going out of the clump of trees. Watching her, Longarm sighed. Too bad her old man wasn't as smart as she was.

He turned back toward Lobatos as the rope snaked out and looped over his shoulders. Gasping in surprise, Longarm threw up his arms to break free of the noose, but Lobatos only laughed and yanked downward on the lariat. The loop closed about his ankles. Lobatos ran forward, taking in the slack and yanking upward. Longarm's feet were jerked from under him. He fell heavily, the breath knocked out of him.

By the time he caught his breath, gasping through parted lips, Lobatos had him hogtied, the rope looped about his ankles, snubbing down his wrists at the small of his back and tied off in a slipknot at his throat. When he moved, the rope tightened, cutting his neck and stopping his breath.

Lobatos stood over him. "Reckon you'll figger your way out of this sooner or later, Long. For your own sake, I hope it is later. Maybe you'll have time to think. Maybe you'll see that ol' Fondis and Sheriff Carr is too goddamn smart for government people like you and them Interior range riders. Fondis has likely been gettin' the law to do his dirty work since he first started playin' dirty."

Lobatos caught him casually by the rope at his ankles and dragged him along the creekbed. He positioned him between the small fire and the stump. "You'll keep warm, long as the fire burns, Long. I hope you see that I could of killed you if I'd of wanted to."

Prone on the ground, Longarm stared up at the lean man. "Don't run, Lobatos."

"Why not?"

"I'll have to chase you."

Lobatos stared down at him and then laughed in admiration. "I swear, Long, you're one hell of a pore learner, ain't you?"

"I don't give up easy."

Lobatos hunkered down beside the campfire. He rolled a cigarette and lit it on a greasewood stick, which he tossed back into the small orange-and-blue blaze. He drew deeply on the limp paper and expelled the smoke. Then he glanced toward Longarm. "You ever catch a puma by the tail, Marshal?"

"Not lately."

"You'll think you have if you keep hounding me. Now, you been decent to my daughter, you helped me. But that shit all stops right here. You come after me, I'll have to kill you."

"Still, you're a fugitive. You're now a federal fugitive because you're now running from me. You got more than Fondis Estabrook and his sheriff on your trail. And it don't have to be that way."

"Don't it, Marshal? Seems you talk mighty big, lyin' on yore belly." Lobatos grinned savagely. Idly, he palmed his gun for a moment. The sound of gunfire almost deafened Longarm and a bullet almost grazed his temple, splatting into the hard ground beside his ear.

Longarm struggled in the ropes, raging. "You son of a bitch. You tryin' to dig your own grave? Ain't there charges enough against you? That's assault with a deadly weapon, you stupid mulehead."

Lobatos shrugged. "Just my last friendly little warning to you, Marshal. That there was the very last time I come close; next time I don't miss. You lie here and think about that while I ride away."

Longarm raged. "You can't ever go back home, Lobatos! The sheriff's posse will get you if you do. I'll get you—"

"If I don't git you first." Lobatos grinned bleakly at him.

He started away, but Longarm's savage voice stopped him. He glanced over his shoulder.

"Listen to me, Lobatos." Longarm's voice was hoarse with helpless desperation. "Suppose you do shoot me? You get me, that won't end it. They'll send another federal officer to tail you. Maybe he won't be as friendly as I am. There's a hell of a lot of us federal marshals, Flagg, and we're all mean."

"Law seems to attract mean fellers, like iron to a magnet."

"Maybe people like you, Flagg, make us mean. Now cut me loose. Use your head for a change. We ride into town. I side you all the way. You got my word. We'll make them prove every charge."

"Sure. You'll stand on the gallows, fightin' back your tears whilst they hang ol' Flagg Lobatos. But you'll feel good because you knowed you tried. Well, thanks for your offer, Marshal. But I mean to play this hand my way."

"You can't win, you damned fool. Estabrook and Carr will get you sooner or later. They're on your trail right now."

"Maybe. I'll just tiptoe through that pile of shit when I get to it." Lobatos walked away. He returned with Longarm's horse, leaving the animal ground-tied in a clump of sweet grass. "There you are, Marshal. The last kindness I can do you. You manage to break free, why, leastwise you can git back to Denver without walkin'."

"Damn you. I'm not going back to Denver, Lobatos—not without you."

Lobatos laughed. "Hope you got no children or other dependents, Marshal. They all goin' to have long gray beards before they see your pretty face in Denver again."

He swung up into the saddle and rode slowly away. Longarm struggled to follow his direction as long as he could. All he could tell was that Lobatos had ridden with the creekbed, going away from the overthrust and the mesa at Screaming Springs.

.Chapter 15

Longarm stood wavering with his legs braced apart in the doused, wrecked campfire. He had himself destroyed the fire, writhing agonizingly in it as he fought the fetters Flagg Lobatos had lashed upon him with such fiendish efficiency.

The sky had darkened alarmingly. The sun was lowering, but this wasn't the fading light of ordinary dusk; this darkness was more like the dead, cold end of the world.

The cold felt as if the sun had burned itself out. The wind whistled through the cottonwood trees and whipped the willows wildly.

Distantly, a faint tatting of black edged the northern horizon, looking like the hem of a shroud that was about to be lowered across the face of the earth. The stunning cold burned through him. He stamped his feet and swung his arms and massaged his torn wrists, trying to renew the circulation in them.

He gazed down at the rope cuts in his wrists, the skin raked off the backs of his hands and raw knuckles. He touched gingerly at the necklace of fire those knots had etched in his throat as he fought them loose. Lobatos had strung him up well, arranging the noose on his throat so that he almost choked himself before he could break free.

There was no sense in wasting time standing beside a cold fire, hating Flagg Lobatos. So he wasted no more time. He found his hat, clapped it down low on his head, and strode to where the roan shivered against the chill. At least his horse had enjoyed a nice long rest and plenty of sweet grass.

A silver lining for every dark cloud, he thought savagely. His teeth rattled. The ground was cold and frozen. Every step cut at his feet through the soles of his boots.

He looked about the riverbed for the first time, finding that giveaway hoofprint he meant to follow till hell froze over, which at this moment seemed a likely prospect.

Damn Lobatos. He would catch him. He was no longer sure, though, whether he sought Lobatos to save him or to kill him. Flagg Lobatos was an easy man to hate.

He was hungry. He hadn't eaten since breakfast, and it had been a hellish long day. But he ignored the growling of his stomach because his inner hunger was nothing beside the rage against Lobatos that took double hitches in the taut-stretched nerves at the pit of his stomach.

Taking up the reins, he led the roan slowly along the creekbed, wanting to be sure Lobatos had not turned back on him. His close inspection of the wash paid off. The broken left hind shoe left a clear mark in the rocky sand. The lines were faint, but they were there. Lobatos had headed out, following the course of the dry creek.

As soon as he lost the prints in the sand, he instantly spotted the disturbed place in the grass where Lobatos had climbed up the dobie bank and headed in a wide arc toward the south and west. Longarm pulled his roan up. He had no idea where Lobatos was headed; the man likely knew a score of hiding places in this prairie. Darkness was coming on and Longarm didn't want to lose him. With some fugitives, one could get inside their heads, figure out a destination right along with them. But dealing with Flagg Lobatos was not like that. Flagg was a different kettle of fish.

The wind was not helping any, either. The gale from the North Pole swept down now, with nothing but barbed wire to break its ferocity. The grass was whipped about, making it hard to find any undisturbed sign in it.

He told himself he had one chance. He believed that Lobatos would travel away from the mesa at Screaming Springs. Whatever else you could say about the vaquero—and there was plenty!—he loved his family, and was savagely protective of them.

He found places where the hoofprints were more widely spaced; he decided this meant Lobatos had urged his horse into a gallop. Without looking for any other sign, Longarm swung back into the saddle and headed in the direction Lobatos had sent his running horse.

It was not an easy trail to follow in the wind-whipped prairie, on frozen-hard dobie. But he was lucky. He found places where stalks had been mashed and broken by a running horse. There were no clear prints to be found in the ice-crusted ground. He was stalking that bent shoe, but he was going as much on instinct.

He was pushing the roan hard. He came up the long incline of a rise, and as he topped it, something caught his gaze in the hazy distance.

Longarm reined in the roan, at the same time pulling his field glasses from his saddlebag. He brought the instrument up to his eyes and adjusted the focus—and found Flagg Lobatos in the dead center of it!

He couldn't restrain a short laugh. Lobatos had slowed the horse, likely to spell him before he forced him to gallop again. At the moment this last vaquero was slumped in the saddle, plodding along, hunched up against the cold, but untroubled.

Hell, Lobatos rode as if he hadn't a care in the world, or an enemy, or a hangrope waiting at Dirty Fork.

Deep inside his mind, where his yelling wouldn't alarm or alert Lobatos, Longarm shouted at him. *I'm back here, you son of a bitch. I'm behind you. I'm going to stay behind you all the way to the federal pen in Kansas. Run, Lobatos! Hide, Flagg, old son. It won't buy you anything.*

He urged the roan forward. Still, even as he cursed Lobatos and raged against him, he found himself admiring him—the last of a vanished breed, fighting against a world that not only didn't even understand him, but didn't want to. It was easier to hang him than to try to live with him.

He was still too far away for Lobatos to feel tremors in the ground or to hear his horse's hoof beats in this wild wind, but some instinct alerted Lobatos.

Longarm watched the vaquero hitch slightly in the saddle, turning and staring across his shoulder. Lobatos peered toward him for some moments. Then, with that characteristic calmness, he settled himself in his saddle, shook his rifle free from its scabbard, then booted his horse, sending it racing through the darkening prairie.

Longarm reached down and loosened his own rifle, but left it sheathed. He hated the idea of engaging in a running gun battle with Lobatos. One of them would likely be killed, and nothing settled. Still, he'd tried once to talk with Flagg and had gotten nothing but rope burns for his effort.

Longarm reached inside his greatcoat. He loosened the derringer from its watch chain and dropped it inside his outer side pocket.

We're armed now, Lobatos, he thought coldly. *We can kill each other. All we can't do is reason, talk this out, find some answers if there are any.*

Somebody had lied, that was certain. You could lay bets on that. On the one side a respected cattle rancher, on the other a wandering vaquero. It wasn't easy to know what to do.

Abruptly, up there in the grass, Longarm saw Lobatos yank hard on his reins. Lobatos' lathered horse reared in the grass, pawing at the wind. The man jerked the animal's head around and went racing off at a right angle to the path he'd been following.

Shocked, Longarm saw why. Beyond Lobatos rode at least fifteen or twenty men. They were much nearer to Lobatos than Longarm was. They must have been coming up a concealed incline as Lobatos had raced toward it. He had spotted them and turned, but the horsemen fanned out, riding after him.

Longarm turned his own horse. Inside, he yelled at Lobatos to turn back toward him. *Trust me enough just to stay alive, goddam you,* he raged. *Ride back toward me. Try to get to me before they kill you. I'm your only hope, you wild jackass. At least I have the authority of the U.S. Government behind me. Maybe those men will respect it, Lobatos, even if you don't.*

He felt sick with frustration. There was no way to reach Lobatos, no way to teach him common sense in the little time left to them. The pursuing riders were gaining on Lobatos. He kept turning back toward where Longarm rode, but only at narrow angles. He was still riding away from them, but he was losing ground, every minute.

Lobatos knew this graze country, but so did his pursuers. They had him in their gunsights now. There was no way for him to hide from them. He twisted back slightly the way he'd come, but they curled in on him in a widening snare.

Raging, Longarm saw that Lobatos had no intention of trying to hide, even if he still knew a hiding place in the wild

172

draws and canyons and broken places. Lobatos' motives were clear. He was going to run and fight, fight and run. It was evident in the way he held his rifle as he fled, ready to fire.

Run and fight, you damn fool, Longarm raged inside, *and they'll kill you as they would a rabid wolf. To them that's what you are, a maverick, a mad dog, a wild animal. Looks like you could figure the odds, damn you. They are stacked against you.*

But Longarm could almost read the half-wild man's mind. They might kill him, but Lobatos meant to take with him to hell as many as he could.

The posse rode strung out against the storm-riven sky. These men were a hard breed. They had hunted men and cows and horses many times before. They knew how it was done. And like Longarm, most of them knew in advance how it had to end.

Longarm slumped in his saddle, still too far away to make himself heard, even if any of those bastards would have listened to him. He could almost see Fondis Estabrook's face. The cattleman had his enemy in his gunsights. This was the way he meant for it to end. What the hell, if later it was proved that the wire-cutting was a frameup, he would regret it. Hell, he probably actually would regret it—for five whole minutes. Then he would shrug and forget it.

He watched the posse gain on Lobatos, feeling sick when the riders at the head of the posse fired at Lobatos. Their gunshots must have come close. They turned Lobatos again, angling him back in Longarm's direction.

Longarm saw the posse's muzzle blasts, even when they were too far away for the sound to carry in this howling of the wolf wind.

Goddammit, hold your fire, Longarm raged. *Give him a chance. You can stop him now without killing him. Don't make him kill one of you. Give the stupid son of a bitch a chance, whether he deserves it or not.*

But they were firing all along the strung-out line of riders now.

One rewarding result came from the firing of the posse. They were close enough to alarm the fugitive. Lobatos had kept turning until now he was heading almost directly back toward Longarm. It was clear that Lobatos had figured one set of odds and made his decision. He saw that he had a better chance of riding out of here alive over the body of one pursuer than over twenty.

The posse kept firing, bringing the ends of their wide line closer on the shadowed plain.

Longarm turned his horse so that he rode directly toward Lobatos as fast as his mount could gallop across the flat prairie. Above them the sky darkened and around them the plains grayed out. Beyond them the arc of hard-riding men closed in.

The wind whipped Longarm savagely, cutting at his face like some invisible machete. His roan stretched its head gallantly against the wind, racing. Ahead of him, Lobatos tried to turn again, and found he could not. The horsemen were closing in from all sides. It was almost over.

Without slowing the roan, Longarm took up his rifle and fired it directly into the air above his head three times. Most of the posse riders stopped firing, closing in, but a few kept shooting sporadically at Lobatos. To them he was not a human being, but a quarry, and they closed in for the kill. They could smell blood.

Gradually it all slowed down. Longarm kept his gun fixed toward Lobatos. The herder had sheathed his own rifle. There was no doubt he was willing to kill a couple of pursuers in order to escape, but he had faced the truth. The posse had trapped him.

Lobatos stopped his lathered horse a few yards from where Longarm had reined in and now sat with his rifle across his lap, fixed on the vaquero.

The posse came in cautiously, guns at the ready, watchful and wary.

As the last of the posse closed in, horses sweated and blowing, steaming in the icy air, Longarm saw that he was dealing with twenty nervous men. He grinned tautly. Of all the riders, Lobatos was the calmest. The herder sat in his saddle, his hands loosely holding his reins, waiting. He seemed without a care in the world.

Longarm recognized many of the riders: Pierce, Carmel, and a couple of other range inspectors from Interior, Lawson Carr and three of his deputies, their badges glinting. There may have been a few townsmen and a rancher or two from the smaller spreads. The largest contingent were the Flying F hired hands, led by Fondis Estabrook.

The big rancher sat like something hewn from granite. His cloth sling blew about his shoulder, but he no longer carried his arm inside it. He felt nothing but rage and triumph. He had forgotten any physical pain.

Lawson Carr spoke first. "Get down from your horse, Lobatos. Stand with your arms wide at your sides. You make a tricky move and I promise you one of these boys will put a bullet in your head."

Lobatos didn't answer. His glance toward the sheriff and the owner of the Flying F Ranch consigned them both to the pit beyond hell. He swung slowly down from the saddle and stood, slightly unsteady, in the grass that whipped about his boots.

"We better get one thing straight, Sheriff Carr," Longarm said.

Carr's head jerked up. His eyes glittered and his mouth pulled down. He faced Longarm coldly. "Yes, Marshal? What's that?"

"This man is charged with cutting government fence, stealing permit graze. That makes him my prisoner, not yours."

Estabrook's voice shattered the gale. "You stay out of this, Long."

"Wait a minute, Fondis." Lawson's voice was chilled, but deadly polite and calm. "I figure what Long is talking about is a technicality. He's right about the charges."

"But we run this vermin to earth. He's my prisoner—he's *our* prisoner. I've already warned you, Carr. We finish it off this time. This man Long is not going to stand in my way." Fondis Estabrook's gaze raked from Carr's face to Longarm's, across Lobatos'.

"It doesn't matter, Fondis." The steel ribbing showed under the sheriff's soft tone. "Whether Lobatos here is technically a government prisoner or our prisoner, it doesn't matter. There's just one jail to keep him in. Mine. We don't need to waste time out here arguing about who's got jurisdiction over him."

Estabrook exhaled and nodded, smiling coldly. "All right,

Lawson. I agree. Like you say, Long might have jurisdiction. We got possession." He straightened in the saddle. "I don't give a damn how it's handled. Just so it's handled. Just so this is the end of it."

Carr nodded and gestured with his head toward one of his deputies. "Dumas, disarm the prisoner, and give him a thorough search."

Dumas nodded. He swung down from his saddle and holstered his own gun. He approached Lobatos warily.

Carr spoke to Lobatos. "Put one hand on your horse's shoulder and the other on his flank. Spread your fingers and keep them that way. Put your legs apart."

Lobatos obeyed silently. In his long and checkered career, this was not the first time the herder had suffered this indignity at the hands of men whose faces and names changed, but whose motives never altered—they meant to exterminate a man they considered a plague loose on their ranges.

Longarm sat empty-bellied in his saddle, studying the faces of Fondis Estabrook and the riders backing him. He realized something that Flagg Lobatos probably knew instinctively. This was not a posse of deputies sworn to uphold the law. This was a lynch mob. Only Lawson Carr's presence gave them even the faint coloring of legality.

The first gun Dumas retrieved from Lobatos was Longarm's Colt. Dumas pulled it from under Lobatos' belt and held it up. He moved to toss it to Carr, but Longarm said. "That gun's mine."

Laughter spewed over him, hacking at him, in a savage chorus led by Fondis Estabrook. Even Lawson Carr sat smiling grimly.

Estabrook shouted over the laughter. "Oh, he's your prisoner, all right, Long. If we hadn't of come along, likely he would have killed you with your own goddamn gun."

Longarm bent down from the saddle and took the Colt from the grinning Dumas. He shoved it into his holster. "That changes nothing, Estabrook. I met Lobatos earlier. He got the drop on me. That's the way things go."

"Oh no, mister." Estabrook shook his head. "We ain't pulling your chestnuts out of no fire. This man is our prisoner. You done proved to more than twenty witnesses that you weren't man enough to take Lobatos. If it had been up to you, he'd be ridin' free, rustlin' my cattle and touchin' them up with his running iron. That's all over. He's stolen his last cow from the Flying F. I warn you, don't get in my way." Estabrook looked around and laughed again, the sound like cold spittle in Longarm's face. "You got your gun back now, why don't you ride on out of here?"

When the laughter subsided, Longarm spoke slowly. "I never claimed to be invincible, Estabrook. But I am the law, I represent the U.S. Justice Department here. And my word goes."

"Sure." Estabrook stopped laughing, his voice battering across the howling wind. "Sure, Marshal. Your word goes. Hey, Dumas, give Lobatos his own gun back, and let's see how far Long's word goes."

Longarm urged his horse forward and rode directly toward Estabrook. The rancher straightened in his saddle, his face tightening. Longarm said, "Don't get the idea in your head, Estabrook, that you're in any way above the law. I can arrest you, same as I can Lobatos."

"For what, you big-talking bastard?"

"Who knows, Estabrook? For spittin' in the wind. For hindering me in the performance of my duty. Let me tell you and your laughing hyenas something. Lobatos may be as guilty as you say he is. A trial will prove that, one way or the other. But I can tell you he's something none of you are—he's the toughest hombre I ever met. Tough don't mean guilty, but it don't mean innocent. I don't know what you people got in mind, but I warn you—and if your sheriff is smart, he'll back me up—you better ride easy and let the law handle this."

Fondis Estabrook's savage gaze struck against Longarm's and held for long seconds. Horses pawed nervously, but none of the mén moved, no one spoke.

At last, Lawson Carr gave a soft laugh. "Hell, we're all cold and we're all tired. We can say things here we don't mean. We got what we're after. Why don't we get back into Dirty Fork where we can rest up and get warm?"

The other men muttered their assent. Only Fondis Estabrook remained rigid and unyielding. He was a hard man, hewn from the rough, wild life of the early years in the High Plains, when justice was meted out by the strong, and where there was one definition of justice—might made right. In a way, both Fondis Estabrook and Flagg Lobatos were vanishing breeds. They were on opposite sides, but they belonged to a world that was passing.

Fondis Estabrook shrugged and apparently relaxed. He looked as if he might yield to Longarm's authority. "There's just one thing, Long. And you best hear me too, Carr. Lobatos is not gettin' away this time. I got him. And by God I mean to nail his hide to my barn door."

"Take it easy, Fondis," Carr suggested.

"Oh, I'm taking it easy." Estabrook forced a low, hard laugh. "I just told you fellows how it's going to be. It's going to be my way. I don't give a shit for your legal technicalities. I don't care if Lobatos is your prisoner or Long's. His hide belongs to me. As long as we understand that, we got no problems."

Chapter 16

The blue norther struck the Divide country with terrifying force.

The first snow was driven powder on the wet, cold wind. The posse reached town and Lobatos was placed in the jail cell. He kicked the bars, rattling them, but no one paid any heed to him or the noise he made.

The front door of the sheriff's office swung open and shut continuously. Snow blew in as if to escape the frigid cold of the street. Men slapped the flakes from their greatcoats. They were astounded. A gale-force snowstorm on the first of May? Had the whole damn world gone crazy? It was unheard of.

Fondis Estabrook sank into Carr's swivel chair, his face like granite. He favored the gunshot wound in his shoulder, supporting his left arm with his right palm.

He stared in icy hatred as Lobatos aimed another kick at the cell bars. "Just like any other goddamn wild animal," Estabrook said, jerking his head toward the jailed herder. "Look at him. You ever seen a wild steer batter its head against a rail fence?"

Carr finished his paperwork and glanced at Longarm, slumped in a chair near the wall. "Lobatos is your prisoner, Long. You staying here where you can watch him?"

"That's right," Longarm said. He nodded coldly, speaking more to Fondis Estabrook than to the sheriff.

"I just got one warning for you, Marshal Long." Estabrook leaned forward in the squealing swivel chair.

"What's that, Estabrook?" Longarm inquired. He didn't need to ask, but he wanted all of Estabrook's threats aired, out in the open and on the record.

Estabrook's steely gaze impaled Longarm. He leaned forward and his voice rattled with intensity. "Just don't get any

179

ideas about *your* prisoner. Don't try to take Lobatos away from here. I'm telling you this, Long—that devil's not leaving this town alive."

"Is that a threat, Mr. Estabrook?" Longarm inquired.

"Of course it isn't," Carr interrupted, shaking his head.

"Thanks, Lawson, for trying to protect me from this officious government man. But I want it clearly understood. I'm not saying I'll kill Lobatos personally. But I am saying he won't get out of Dirty Fork alive. Now you make out of that what you will."

"If you won't kill him, who will?"

Estabrook stood up. "The citizens of this town, Long. The aroused citizens who have been harassed and endangered and threatened by that animal behind those bars. I'm just telling you, we've had enough. This town has had enough. Lobatos is going nowhere."

Longarm sat there a moment as if counting up to ten. Then he stood up slowly. His voice lashed out, quieting all the men in the room. "All right, you people. Listen good. You can hear me and you can take the word out to any hotheads outside this room that might have any fancy ideas about what they are going to do tonight. I'm serving notice here and now. I'm doing anything I have to do to protect my prisoner. If that means fighting you people, or arresting you, so be it."

Lawson Carr was the last to leave the office. When the sheriff had gone out, Longarm dropped the two-by-four bolt across the heavy door.

Lobatos watched him idly from the cellblock, his encrusted hands gripping the bars. He said, "That was quite a crock of shit you fed them hombres, Marshal. You think any of them swallowed it?"

Longarm walked to the cot where he would spend the night. He sat down on it. "We'll see," he said.

Lobatos kicked the bars.

Longarm looked up. "What the hell you doing that for, Lobatos?"

"Because it's my life you're puttin' on the line. If some drunken mob breaks in here tonight, it's me they'll skin alive, not you."

"Quit kicking those bars and try to get some rest. Anybody gets at you has to pass me."

"That ain't the most reassurin' thing I ever heard since I left my maw's knee, Marshal."

"Maybe not. But it's the best I can tell you."

Lobatos kicked the bars again. "Maybe. But it ain't good enough. We got to get out of here. We stay here tonight, you know what's going to happen? I can tell you. I seen it too many times. Mob gets drunk at Estabrook's Silver Palace. They come in here and drag me out and hang me. You get killed in the action, and everybody'll cry crocodile tears big as horse turds when they bury us. If you're smart enough to find your way here from Denver, you must have sense enough to know we got one chance—get out of here and get to my people up at Screamin' Springs."

"Sounds like a great idea, Flagg. But you forget one thing."

"Yeah? What's that?"

"I got lost on my way here from Denver."

Boots against the sheriff's door rattled the portal on its brass hinges.

Lawson Carr's voice raged through the thick door. "Open up in there! Goddammit, who barred this front door?"

Longarm got up from the cot and padded across the office. He removed the bar and opened the door.

Carr brushed past him, his shoulder socking Longarm in the chest and brushing him back. Carr's face was gray, his mouth a taut line, and his eyes steel-gray slits. His hands were trembling so badly that he shoved them into his coat pockets to conceal their shaking.

Carr's rage made his voice quiver. "Amber Austin," he managed to say. "Miss Amber and her company. They're gone from the hotel. Their carriages are gone. They've been gone for a couple of hours. I want it straight from you, Long. What do you know about this?"

Longarm shook his head. He heard the howling of the icy wind, saw the snow streaking the windows. Even seasoned travelers would have a hell of a time in this weather. Wherever they were, he hoped Sam Brown was with them, but even so, he gave them small chance of getting very far from Dirty Fork alive.

He shook his head again. "They're gone? In this storm?"

"I reckon maybe it wasn't snowing when they left."

"But—" Longarm stopped. He'd almost named Sam Brown. That could be fatal to the Indian—the sheriff needed a release for his fury. "Anybody who knows anything about storms must have known the snow was coming."

Lawson Carr stared at his shaking hands as if he could barely control his need to throttle Longarm. "They're gone. That's all I know. And I want to know what you know about it."

"I don't know a thing about it. I'm as troubled as you are. If the storm wasn't so bad, I'd say send out a search party."

"I've already thought of that. No sense in it, in this gale, and snow is piling up out there. I got a feeling you're behind this, Long."

"Your head's gone to mush, that's all," Longarm said. "If you had good sense left where Amber is concerned, you'd know damn good and well that even if I hated her, I wouldn't send her out in this storm."

Lawson Carr's rage ebbed slightly. He clenched his trembling fingers into thick fists and stared at them. When he looked up, his gray eyes were rimmed with red and his voice shook. "I tell you this, Long. If anything happens to her, I'm coming for you."

Longarm shrugged. "I'll be here."

Lawson had quieted more now; he was almost rational. He said, "Estabrook didn't lie to you, Long. I didn't realize at the time how right he was. This town is stirred up. There's mob fury in the air. The only hope is that the snowstorm will keep them inside, drinking and yelling."

"I advise you to hold them off."

Carr's head jerked up. "Don't take that tone with me, Marshal. I'm the sheriff here. That's all. I'll do what I can. I'm trying to tell you there's mob madness out there. I'll try to hold them. But that's all I can do. Try."

Longarm simply held Carr's gaze. "That's up to you, Carr. Holding those bloodsuckers at bay, that's your job. You do your job, I'll do mine, and we'll come out of this smelling like roses."

"Too bad we'll all be dead and won't be able to smell them fuckin' roses," Lobatos said as he kicked the cell bars again.

Longarm opened the door and let Sheriff Carr go out of it. He closed and barred it. As he turned around, Lobatos aimed his heel at the bars again.

Longarm walked back to the bars that marked the cellblock. "What the hell you trying to do, break your foot?"

"It's my foot."

"I'm telling you, quit kicking those damn bars. I'm sick of it."

"You don't want me kicking them, Marshal, you come back here and kick 'em for me."

"I don't kick cell bars, Lobatos. I use my head."

"Using your head on bars like this wouldn't do a damn bit of good," Lobatos said.

Longarm laughed in spite of himself. Lobatos laughed too. Then Lobatos kicked the bars again.

Longarm went back to his cot. He turned down the wick on the lamp and lay down fully dressed, except for his boots, and pulled the blanket up over him.

Lobatos rattled the bars. "Hey, Marshal. Put some wood on that fire. It's cold back here."

"You bastard. You could have told me that before I lay down."

Lobatos laughed at him. "You might as well give up any idea you might of had about gettin' any rest tonight, Marshal. Even if I'm willing to let you sleep, them townfolks are going to keep you awake—one way or the other."

Longarm stoked up the stove, then returned to his cot. He sat on the side of it, yawning helplessly. Lobatos said, "Didn't it strike you funny, Marshal, how pleased Carr's deputies all was that you was standing guard here at the jail tonight?"

"I don't give a damn."

"Well, that's where you're wrong, Marshal. You ought to. Two things are bound to happen tonight. Them men are goin' to git likkered up and they're goin' to storm this jail to hang me. Or they know damn well my three sons and daughter are comin' in here to break me free."

"I hope they've got better sense."

"So do I, but I know they ain't. You see, Long, what you don't savvy, you bein' a bachelor and all, my chillern dearly love me. Yeah, they do. My little girl, she dotes on me something fierce, and my boys—they don't even like to think about me here in this lousy cell." He kicked the bars again.

"If they love you so much, and you love them so much, Lobatos, why don't you do them a favor? Why don't you settle down and stop working with a running iron and wirecutters? The day of free ranges and free grass and wild cows to be branded at will where you find 'em, that day is past, Lobatos. In your heart you must know that."

Lobatos shrugged. "My day may be past, Marshal, but I'm still here. Old habits die hard."

"The wandering herder's day is gone. You've got to adjust. You've got to learn to live on a range with other cattlemen. Live and let live. It's the only way to stay alive anymore."

Lobatos spoke softly from the dark cell. "I ain't dead yet."

"You may wish you were before I get you out of Dirty Fork. And when I do, I know you'll wish you were dead when you get inside the federal penitentiary in Kansas."

"Don't lay there countin' your chickens, Marshal. I ain't in Kansas yet."

Longarm shook his head. He stared at the ceiling. He'd never known a man facing so much woe and accepting it so calmly.

A fist battered at the front door, and a voice called out, "Telegram for you, Marshal."

Swearing softly, Longarm got up and called out, "Slide it under the door." He was taking no chances.

The yellow envelope blew in under the door, assisted by a frigid draft that propelled it halfway across the floor. Longarm bent down and scooped it up from the floor, slipped a finger under the flap, and ripped it open. He stood for a moment, reading it.

The voice on the other side of the door asked, "Any answer, Marshal?"

Longarm reached into his pants pocket and pulled out a nickel and slid it under the door. "No, thanks," he said.

He walked back to the cellblock. "Some good news for you, Lobatos," he said. "I wired my office for a rundown on your

184

criminal record. You know what they say? Either they've gone loco, or you ain't *got* a criminal record."

Lobatos snorted. "Shit, I could've told you that."

Longarm shook his head. "It ain't possible. You've been a reprobate outlaw all your worthless life."

Lobatos shrugged. "Don't get your bowels in an uproar, Marshal. I just ain't never been caught."

"Till now."

"Till now."

Longarm went back to his cot. He turned the wick lower and blew out the small flame inside the lamp. The office and cellblock were plunged into blackness. He could hear Lobatos in his cell, humming to himself. Listening, he grinned tautly, exasperated, puzzled, and awed. In all his manhunting years, he'd never come across one quite like Flagg Lobatos.

The night sounds of the town were fragmented and blown away on the gale-force winds. Distantly, a train whistled in the darkness. The wind rattled the windows—and Lobatos hummed to himself in the darkness.

Lying in the stygian blackness, Longarm felt his stomach nerves tighten. The noises outside the windows changed. The wind raged, growing louder. But in the loud darkness, scattered gunshots rang out. Liquored-up men ran up on the stoop and shouted threats, or they threw bricks from across the street. The missiles bounced harmlessly against the walls or rolled from the slanted roofing. None of this was particularly threatening in itself, but it meant the mob was out there. They were tentative now, but they were drinking and they were being spurred on. But for the desperate cold and the howling winds, those hell-raisers would be on the rampage and Longarm and the prisoner would be facing the kind of night Dirty Fork hadn't seen since its wildest years.

The noises increased out there. A hay wagon was set on fire and rolled toward the sheriff's office. The vehicle struck the boardwalk and stopped, burning there. Through cracks in the door and the heavy window shutters, the flames illumined the interior where Longarm lay, though the cellblock remained in cavelike darkness. In the street, men brave enough and strong enough and drunk enough to withstand the blast of snow and wind, milled about, fighting, drinking, yelling, and firing their guns.

Just when Longarm decided the cold would drive the hellions away from outside the jail, they built a bonfire in the middle of the street. They brought logs, furniture, barrels, boxes, anything they could carry, and heaved it upon the flames.

A growling, swelling ululation, like the mindless baying of wolves, rose in the street. Gunfire, spasmodic, but getting nearer with every shot, erupted in the night. Drunken horsemen galloped up and down the length of the main street, hoo-rawing. Kegs of beer were hauled out and set up near the bonfire. They drank and fired guns and yelled threats toward the jail.

Longarm thrust the blankets off and got up in the shimmering, blood-red darkness. He found a match, struck a fire to the lamp, and turned it up.

Lobatos' voice raged at him from the cell. "Turn off that goddamn light."

Longarm laughed coldly. "You're in a hell of a position to be giving orders."

"I got a right to get my sleep."

Longarm laughed again. He got down all the guns he could find and loaded them, checked them, and laid them where they would be handy when he needed them. He spoke over his shoulder. "All of a sudden you're all upset about your own rights. What about the rights of others that you been violating since you left your maw's knee in Tennessee?"

"What about 'em?"

"They do have them. Other people. Same as you, no more, no less. The right to raise cattle or wheat, to build a house and live in it without being afraid of thieves like you."

Lobatos laughed from within the cellblock. "I like you, Long. I really do. You hate good. You're my kind of hater. I like a man with a full-bellied apetite for hatin'." His voice changed abruptly. "Now turn out that goddamn light before I come out there and bust your nose."

Laughing, Longarm blew out the lamp. He lay down on the cot again, with his Colt resting on his belly. Exhausted, he closed his eyes, hearing the cacophony of the mob beyond the

186

closed and shuttered windows. He sagged against the pillow, floating in that space between waking and sleeping.

The sense of terrible wrong and the whisper of sound struck Longarm simultaneously and yanked him out of his half-waking state. He clutched up the Colt on his belly and lunged upward on the cot. He struck a gun snout with his forehead. He hauled up his own gun, but by now he could smell Flagg Lobatos. The herder stood over him with the muzzle of his gun pressed between Longarm's brows.

For a moment Longarm was unable to react, except in disbelief. In amazement, he stared at the barred door of the cell. It hung open. Lobatos had twisted the tongue in the thick lock, enough to release the deadbolt.

"You son of a bitch," Longarm whispered, awed. "I don't believe it."

"You don't have to believe it. You got just a short time to decide whether you want to live or die, Marshal, so you might want to think on somethin' more urgent than how I learned to bend metal. Just believe me. I been in a few jails just like this one. And I got out of most of 'em just the way I got out of this one."

"You ain't out of here yet."

"That's up to you. I can kill you. I got my gun right between your eyes."

"And I've got mine fixed on your belly, Lobatos. You can kill me, but reflex is going to fire my gun—and it'll blow a hole in your belly from here."

Lobatos caught his breath. They heard the mob screaming outside the door, the fire crackling, the horses galloping, the guns firing. At last, Lobatos said, "Looks like we got us a Mexican standoff."

"Looks like it."

"You got any ideas?"

"Give me your gun."

Lobatos laughed. "My God, you just *never* give up, do you? Marshal, I swear it's a pleasure to do business with you. I almost hate to have to kill you. But my folks is out there at Screamin' Springs and they need me. Now."

"Kill me, Flagg. It won't get you to Screamin' Springs. We die together. I guarantee you that."

"Who's that goin' to help? Fondis Estabrook. Lawson Carr. It ain't goin' to help me and my family, but it ain't goin' to do much for you either. You got any better ideas?"

"Like what?"

"Like calling off the dogs. Get Estabrook and them people off my back. You marshals from Denver leave me and my family alone."

"I can't do that until this business is settled."

"Not even in swap for your life? Seems a pretty fair trade to me."

"I ain't the only one dying here tonight."

"Well, we ain't settled that yet. All we settled is that there is damn little profit in either or both of us pullin' the trigger. I can tell you this. I got to get out of here. We're in the middle of a man-killing blue norther. Unless my people got down to the soddy, they're in fierce trouble in that line shack. They need me. Now. I'm on my way there. One way or t'other."

"You let them get through this night—"

"I don't know if they can. They never been out in a blue norther like this."

"You prove your innocence—"

"Don't give me that shit, Marshal. Hang-nooses kill the innocent just as dead as the guilty. Likely just as often. Estabrook means for me to hang tonight. I ain't stayin' here and givin' him that chance."

"How you planning on getting out of here?"

"They're yellin' and snortin' out front, so I'm goin' out the back. Stayin' here won't prove me innocent or guilty. Go with me, I'll prove me innocent."

"My God! Are you suggesting I break out of here with you—and work with you?"

"That's about right. Seems pretty fair to me, a lot easier on your digestion than a bullet betwixt your eyes."

The yelling grew louder, closer. After a moment, Longarm nodded. "Maybe out of here we could settle this thing. Put your gun away."

Lobatos laughed. "Oh no. I don't trust you, lawman. Nothin' personal. I just don't trust no shittin' lawdog. They're all alike. They're all tricky sons of bitches."

"All I want is to stop the fence-cutting. I don't have to see you hung by a vigilante mob to do that. So we work together tonight. Put your guns away. You got to start trusting me—or somebody—and soon."

Lobatos hesitated. Longarm could almost see the wheels churning behind his eyes. Lobatos said, "Any way you figure it, I got the most to lose. You hand over your gun and you got my word—"

"Oh, hell, I can go to any bank with that."

"We'll go together, Marshal. I'd rather have you with me than behind me."

Longarm nodded. He drew a deep breath. "Why don't we both—on the count of three—holster our guns?"

"You got a deal. Start countin'."

Longarm counted slowly. Each of them hesitated, but both slipped their weapons into their holsters. Lobatos nodded. "Now. Come on. Let's get to hell out of here."

Chapter 17

Lobatos tied up the livery stable owner, snugged down his knots, and tossed the man into the hay near the stove. A deadly pall hung over the interior of the stable. Longarm came out of the stalls, leading his saddled roan along with Lobatos' mustang, ready for travel. Lobatos glanced at him, satisfied, and nodded.

Hogtied and gagged, the hostler glared up at Longarm and Lobatos, his anguished eyes promising them retribution to the third generation. Lobatos smiled down at him mildly. "I wouldn't make such ugly faces. Might freeze that way in this cold."

The roar of the mob down the street in front of the jail grew louder. The sounds rocked the night, splattered in the gale winds, promising a new brand of the same old evil that had once made Dirty Fork the worst little town west of Dodge.

"Natives are restless," Lobatos observed, taking the reins of his small horse. His taunting tone crusted over the savage contempt he felt for those yelling men outside the jail.

"They're building up one hell of a head of steam, all right."

Lobatos nodded. "One way or t'other, they mean to hang me."

"One way or another."

Lobatos laughed coldly. "Somebody ought to tell the sheriff. Those fellows are breaking the law."

Longarm exhaled, listening to the ravening cries of the drunken mob at the bonfire. Despite the petrifying cold, the crowd had swelled down there. The word had gone out hours ago that the old town had busted wide open. Men braved the blizzard to ride into town and get part of the action. The smell of blood brought them like wolves to prey. Smoke and flame, fragmented by the wind, rose like winking beacons in the night; in a way, violence was as alluring as any lusty whore. The big fire crackled and called, fed by anything that would burn. Smoke spewed and bent and flattened on the gale, flames leaped, and the updraft carried whorls and sparks of fiery embers. The smell of smoke hung on the driving wind.

Lobatos jerked his head and Longarm followed him to the rear doors of the old barn. Lobatos pushed open the door far enough so they could sidle through. Beyond it there was no familiar form or substance in the night world, only a fearful black fabric of storm, peppered and gusting with snow.

For a moment, Longarm stood shivering under his greatcoat. Lobatos looped his lariat over the pommel of Longarm's saddle and tied the other end of the rope to his own pommel.

Longarm yelled to make himself heard over the wind. "How do you hope to find Screaming Springs in this blizzard?"

Lobatos grinned at him savagely and shouted back. "I know the way. Even I if I don't, my horse does."

"There are no directions out there."

"Just hang on and trust me."

"Is that my only hope to stay alive?"

"You got to start trusting somebody sometime, old son."

Longarm laughed emptily. "Seems to me I've heard that somewhere before."

Lobatos turned and swung up into his saddle, bowing his head before the force of the gale. "Just remember it," he yelled over his shoulder.

Longarm mounted the roan and they rode some moments in silence, the rope slack between the plodding animals. Once, Lobatos yelled something over his shoulder.

"I can't hear you," Longarm yelled. The wind shattered his voice and sent it kiting on the wind.

"Just hang on," Lobatos yelled. "Trust me."

The snow piled higher across the High Plains. It lay all around them in the darkness, blanketing the prairie, muffling all sound. Longarm could hear his own heart beating under his greatcoat, the crackling crust of the snow as his horse minced forward. The roan snuffled and stepped gingerly. The temperature seemed to have fallen thirty degrees since they'd ridden out of the livery stable.

Within minutes they'd been enveloped in stormy blackness. The lights of the town disappeared as if blown away on the wailing winds. How long had they been plodding across the open country? He had no idea. The driving snow was still less than a foot deep, and this was a break for them. At times they dismounted and led the horses.

Lobatos never glanced back. He kept the rope taut between the two animals and plowed forward in the snow like a man obsessed. Longarm sighed, jaw tight. He supposed Lobatos *was* obsessed. The herder meant to get back to his family on that exposed mesa. Cell bars and jails couldn't stop him. This blizzard slowed him and pummeled him and congealed the blood in his arteries, but it didn't stop him, either.

Longarm slumped in the saddle. He lost track of time. After a while he no longer cared. He was too damned cold to care.

The numbness spread upward from his ankles. He began to recall Bonnie, Billy Vail, and a man who owed him five dollars. People in another world, people warm and safe. He became convinced that he and Lobatos were traveling in circles in the blizzard, but he didn't care about that either. He just waited for it to end.

He was aware that they were climbing before he heard Lobatos' yell of triumph.

Longarm brought his head up. The wind had died for a moment and he saw why: they were climbing between the huge boulders that formed the single access to the mesa at Screaming Springs. Ahead of them, at the summit of the tableland, he saw the brilliant crimson glow of a huge fire. The mesa was lighted up as if it were dawn instead of night.

Lobatos waited for Longarm to join him on the incline, taking in the rope and coiling it.

"We made it." Longarm found talking difficult through the ice encrusting his nostrils and mustache and hanging over his lips.

Lobatos glanced at him. "Did you think we wouldn't?"

"The thought may have crossed my mind a couple of times."

The people at the bonfire saw them and came running down the incline. Nonnie Lobatos was the oldest, but she led the others, running like a fleet gazelle, her tattered blanket blowing from her shoulders. Behind her came J.C. and Mozelle and two lean young men in greatcoats, who Longarm figured must be the older boys, Tom Ed and Andrew Earl. They were all laughing and crying at the same time, but the one thing Longarm found missing in this reunion was shock. Not one of these people looked surprised to see Lobatos riding up in the snowstorm. Longarm wondered how many times over the past twenty-five years Nonnie had waited like this and run to meet Flagg like this.

Lobatos leaped from his saddle and ran with arms outstretched. He caught Nonnie, lifting her, swinging her around. They embraced and laughed like young lovers. Mozelle and J.C. stood near them, with Andrew Earl and Tom Ed, grinning and touching at their parents, sharing, but not intruding.

Longarm dismounted and limped on frost-numbed feet. He saw Kane Estabrook run down the incline and join them, close to Mozelle, protective and silent. Kane met Longarm's gaze. No words had to be exchanged. The look on Kane's handsome young face said it clearly: his father had forced a choice and Kane had chosen. He had thrown in his lot with these people of Screaming Springs.

Lobatos was yelling at his family, smiling but raging at the same time. "Why in hell ain't you folks down at the soddy? Don't you know nothin'? Don't you know you're going to freeze your asses off up here?"

"We almost have, Paw," J.C. said.

One of the other boys said, "A little trouble at the soddy, Paw."

"Estabrook's men are holed up at the soddy. With guns."

"Sons of bitches," Lobatos said between his teeth.

"I said the same thing," Mozelle teased. "But it didn't change a thing."

Lobatos laughed, his pride showing. "I don't want you using words like that. Even about Estabrook's gunwaddies." He clapped Kane on the shoulder. "What's the matter, boy, can't you handle this wench?"

"It ain't easy," Kane said.

"Let's get up to the fire, Paw," Nonnie said. She still had her arm around Lobatos.

"Just a minute. First a matter of a little business with Mr. Long here." Lobatos said.

Longarm went tense, staring at Lobatos' unsmiling face.

"What's eating you?" Longarm said.

"Nothin' in this world," Lobatos said, voice bland. "I'll just take your guns 'fore we go on up the hill."

Longarm straightened, then relaxed, seeing that Lobatos' three sons had their guns fixed on him. Some secret signal had passed between father and offspring. Or maybe their years outside the law had made signals or words superfluous. Anyhow, the guns showed, level and unyielding.

Longarm shrugged. He unbuttoned his greatcoat and handed over the Colt. Lobatos nodded, thanking him and shoving the gun under his belt. Then he said in that same mild tone, "I'll just take that little hideout your wear on your vest too, Marshal."

Longarm laughed, shaking his head. He unclipped the small derringer and handed it over. "Whatever happened to all that trust you were talking about?"

Lobatos grinned and shook his head. "No sense running a thing like that into the ground, eh, Marshal? You got nothin' to fear from us. You'll be our honored guest up here."

"As long as you want me to stay?"

"You got it, Marshal."

Leading their horses, they climbed the rest of the way against the blast and gust of the gale to the line shack. The wind whistled, sighed, and roared in chaotic updrafts over the rim of the precipice out back. Longarm saw that the animals were huddled in the lean-to, already nearly frozen.

He hesitated, then stopped dead in his tracks. Pulled up like windbreaks to the north of the fire were the two Austin-Brockbank company coaches. Someone had banked tumbleweeds under the coaches, and the snow had piled up against them, cutting off the wind beneath the carriages.

Forgetting the numbness in his feet, Longarm ran forward. He saw the actors and actresses huddled between the fire and the windbreak afforded by the coaches. Sam Brown crouched against one of the big wheels, under a khaki horse blanket. He gazed forlornly up at Longarm and nodded a greeting without

194

smiling. "Sam," Longarm said. "Why in hell would you start out with them in this storm?"

Sam Brown shrugged. "Lady said she was going anyhow, whether I go or not. I know they will die without me. Now, I figure, they die with me."

Amber Austin got up, shrouded in an ankle-length sealskin coat. Her face was flushed within the thick cowl of the coat. She ran to Longarm and flung herself into his arms. "We had nowhere else to go," she cried. "Kane Estabrook said you were up here early today. I decided my people and I would be safe up here with you."

"We'll do what we can," Longarm said.

"We're going to freeze to death," she whispered.

"We'll see that you don't," Longarm said, but he realized he spoke without a hell of a lot of conviction.

Longarm shoved open the door of the line shack and, holding a lantern, entered ahead of Lobatos.

He stood for a moment, gazing at what had to be misery even in summer weather. A cold woodburning stove. A few cot mattresses, stacked in a corner until they were needed. A pinewood table and shabby chairs. Clothes hung and waving gently on spikes driven into studs. There was no insulating inner wall. The plank outer wall overlapped loosely and wind raged through. It was as cold inside the house as outside. But there was no choice; they had to get in out of the snow, and soon.

"Wind even comes up through the cracks in the flooring," he muttered, mostly to himself.

"This is no good," Lobatos said. "Just like bein' in that lean-to out there. Worse. You can make a windbreak or cave in the snow. You can't stop the drafts in here. You'd freeze, sittin' as close as you could get to the hottest fire you could make in that there stove."

Longarm nodded, agreeing. "We've got to get them inside."

"This ain't inside," Lobatos said. "It's a summer line shack. It's like the outside—only worse in a high wind."

"Still, we're going to have to get them in here. Horses, people, everything."

Tom Ed ran up the plank steps. He said. "Paw. Somebody's comin' up the incline."

Lobatos went out of the shack. Holding the lantern aloft, Longarm followed. A single-seat buggy rolled up the hill and pulled in as close to the bonfire as possible. The driver, bundled in quilts and scarves, was alone.

The man wrapped his lines about the whip socket and climbed stiffly down from the buggy.

"Why, Preacher Forsley," Lobatos said, shaking his head.

"Perkins Forsley," Kane Estabrook said. "Are you lost? What are you doing up here?"

"God's work," Forsley said. "I hope it's God's work. It may cost me my life."

They led the preacher to the bonfire, and he stood rubbing his hands together before it. His body shook with cold. He stood a long time with the firelight leaping on the small area of his face that could be seen peering out from under his wraps. "They sent me up here," he said.

"Estabrook." Lobatos spoke between clenched teeth. "Fondis Estabrook sent you."

The parson nodded. "Mr. Estabrook and the sheriff. It was the sheriff that sent word to you."

"Where are they?" Lobatos said.

"They're down below. They're holed up in the sod hut down there." The preacher shifted his gaze around, touching at all their faces fleetingly. Then, finding he could face none of them squarely, he stared into the fire. "The sheriff sent you an ultamatum. That means it's his final offer."

"Yeah?"

"Yes. They can watch the pass down from here. They won't let anybody out, unless you all come together."

"Is that all?"

The preacher grimaced. "Almost. You are to lay down your guns. The sheriff said you could put all your guns in the back of my buggy and I could come down first. Then, when he saw I had the guns, he would let the rest of you come down—if you come down quietly and surrender to him."

Lobatos' voice was harder than ever. "Is *that* all?"

"Almost. The sheriff said if you lay down your guns, come down quietly, and surrender peacefully, he will let the women

196

go free. He says the male members of the Lobatos family have got to expect to be placed under arrest."

"And if we don't lay down our guns and follow you down out of here, what then?"

The preacher shook his head. "Mr. Fondis Estabrook said to tell you true, you can't stay in this shack overnight in this storm. He said two men did it once, caught in a sudden blizzard. They were found stone-cold dead in the morning."

"Mr. Parson Forsley," Lobatos said in a deadly soft tone. "Can I axt you something?"

"Certainly, sir. Anything."

"Can you see a bit of difference in dying at Fondis Estabrook's hands down there—or at God's hands up here?"

The preacher swallowed hard and twisted his thin neck in his starched collar. "Freezing is one of the worst ways of dying, Mr. Lobatos. I've heard that. You suffer fearful before you die."

"And you recommend hangin over freezin'?"

Forsley gritted his teeth and shook his head. "It don't have to be that way. And anyhow, they said the women can go free. You ought to think about your women, Mr. Lobatos. Freezing is a terrible death."

"I can't speak for my women, Parson. But I got an idea they'd as soon die up here with me as go down there and watch me hang."

"But that's it, Mr. Lobatos. There's no way you can get these people out of here, except through that pass. We all come out together, or nobody leaves alive. They said to tell you that."

"I'll go down and talk some sense into them," Longarm said. "I'll tell them they'll pull out or they'll have murder of innocent people on their hands. I'll tell them Miss Austin and her people are up here. I'll get them to pull out and let you come in to the soddy until morning."

Lobatos laughed at him. "I know you'd like to get away from me, Long. But I can't let you go."

"You going to stay here and let these people freeze?"

Mozelle said, "Maybe they'll listen to Mr. Long, Pa. He is a government man."

"No. He's staying up here. He's all the hostage I've got,"

Lobatos said. "'Cept the preacher and these actor folks. We got them now."

The preacher looked ill. "Sir, you can't do this. I came up here to help you. I came in good faith. I came doing God's work. You've no right to hold me against my will."

"Shit, you're right, preacher. I get sick of listening to you whine. Get in your buggy and get out of here."

The preacher swallowed hard. He dragged his apologetic gaze over the faces of the people around the fire. He nodded, already backing away. Suddenly he heeled around and ran to the buggy. He stumbled, getting into it. He turned the horses in a tight circle and rolled away down the incline. He took up the whip, and cracked it across his team, looking back over his shoulder.

As the preacher went out of sight, Lobatos said, "Long, you had some fool idea of how we could all crowd inside that shack and stay alive?"

"That's right."

"Let's get to doin' it. I can't wait to see old Estabrook's face when he rides in here tomorrow morning expecting to find us all dead. No, sir, I just can't wait."

Rifles cracked at the bottom of the long incline. Lobatos stopped talking, a cold grin pulling at his face. "Just about what I figured. Old Estabrook is a real bastard. He'd even lie to a minister. He never did mean to let a one of us out of here alive."

The others exhaled as if they'd been holding their breaths for a long time. They hunkered down, stunned, staring into the fire. After a moment they heard the pounding of hooves, the squealing of wheels in the high wind.

The preacher rode back into the yard. He looked as pale as death, deadly afraid, and totally disillusioned. "They wouldn't let me out," he said. He kept shaking his head. "They wouldn't let me out."

Lobatos grinned gently, his face a taunting mask. "Why, don't you let it fret you, parson. When a man's doin' God's work, it's hard to tell who his earthly friends really are."

Parson Forsley sobbed once, uncontrollably. "I'll freeze to death up here. We all will."

"Hell, parson," Lobatos taunted him. "You're doing God's

work. You said so yourself. Can you think of a better way to die?"

The minister controlled himself visibly. He gazed around at the faces of the people hunkered before the fire. "He means to let us freeze up here."

"Hell, parson. You see how smart you can get, once you truly see the light?" Lobatos said. "Old Estabrook meant for us to die one way or t'other. We try to leave, he kills us and swears he thought we was attacking him. But if we stay up here like he wants, and we freeze, and he rides in in the mornin' and finds a lot of corpses, he can cry and wail and attend our funeral. And won't nobody be able to charge him with murder."

Chapter 18

The storm howled across the mesa. It struck out of the darkness in a frenzy. The cold was irresistible, nothing repelled or stayed it; it lanced into the body and congealed the blood, weakened the will, dulled the senses.

Longarm scanned his eyes across the faces of the people gathered around the impotent bonfire. Pastor Perkins Forsley had expressed the sense of hopelessness all of them felt. Only Sam Brown huddled under his blanket, willing to allow the storm to cover him with snow and to insulate him against the wind. Wisdom and instinct as old as his people told him that here lay his best chance of survival.

"Estabrook is not going to find us dead in the morning," Longarm said. "He can sit cozy down in that soddy—and think we're going to lie down and die for him. We're going to surprise him come morning."

"That house is no good," Flagg said. "What do you aim to do, lie out here and let the drifts cover us?"

"No. We're going to keep moving. I want everybody who can carry a shovel or a tumbleweed to gather up anything we don't need and bank the airspace under the shack."

He demonstrated what he meant by gathering tumbleweeds that had snagged in a corner of the lean-to, and shoving them under the low edge of the flooring. Almost immediately, snow began to settle and drift against it.

Inspired, the others got to their feet and began gathering odds and ends, shocks of brittle grass and broken dobie, and banking the airspace under the hut. "The way the wind cuts through them loose side walls," Lobatos protested, "what good's that goin' to do?"

"It's already done its good," Longarm said. "In two ways,

old son. It's keeping their blood circulating and it's given them hope."

"We're going to need a better windbreak than hope," Lobatos answered, but he gave Longarm a look that almost had a tinge of grudging respect in it.

As the running people began to win against the wind, Longarm said, "Sam, you and Flagg's boys, get all the horses and hitch them along the north and east walls inside the house."

Sam Brown nodded. He and the three Lobatos boys ran toward the lean-to, where the horses blew and stomped and trembled in the half-open stalls. Sam carried armloads of hay as he led the horses across the yard and through the door into the shack. The Lobatos boys imitated the Indian.

"You're sure as hell full of bright ideas, all right," Lobatos said. "You expect us humans to share that hut with them horses?"

"Body heat is body heat."

"Horseshit don't figure to make it all that pleasant."

Longarm grinned. "There's heat, Lobatos, even in horseshit. In this below-zero cold, horseshit will congeal and harden fast, and it'll burn if it has to."

When the sides of the old shack were banked and the horses had been secured to pegs and boards along the walls, Longarm carried in wood and built a fire in the woodstove. Flagg helped him now, reluctantly, but he had to protest because he considered himself as range-wise as any man. He'd seen these blue northers—sudden cold that laid down rime frost even south of the Rio Grande. "You know, don't you, Marshal, you can freeze to death a few feet from a stove like that—even if it's red-hot?"

"We'll tiptoe across that pile of shit when we get to it," Longarm said. "People who die like that don't keep water or something cooking on the stove."

"You got all the answers, huh?"

Longarm shook his head. "I don't have all the answers, but I mean to stay alive as long as I can . . . and to keep all these people alive, if I can."

Lobatos hesitated a moment, then he said, "Long?"

"Yeah?"

"You want your guns back?"

Longarm laughed and took them. By now the hogs had burrowed under the shack, the dogs had curled up behind the crackling potbellied stove, and most of the people were inside the shack. There was little warmth, and no escape from the persistent wind that carried cold straight down out of the Arctic. The loose slats of the walls left tiny gaps that admitted a steady stream of benumbing wind that cut across the room, slashing at everything in its path.

When Longarm and Sam Brown threw snow on the bonfire until it died out, they all protested. The minister said, "Name of God, Mr. Long, I'd have thought you'd leave the fire. At least we could go outside and get warm."

"No, Reverend." Longarm shook his head. "A bonfire uses up all the wood and cow chips too fast. It's going to be a long night and we need a fire that'll last till morning."

Kane and the Lobatos boys began carrying in armloads of wood and dropping them against the wall.

Amber came close to Longarm. When she touched his hand, her fingers were icier than death. "Jesus," he said. "Keep those hands up inside that fur coat."

"I just wanted to tell you. Anything we've got—if you want to burn it . . ." She shrugged, letting her unfinished statement hang there between them.

"We'll hold off as long as we can, Amber. But I may as well tell you, we may have to chop up your coaches for firewood before daybreak."

A feminine scream erupted in the night. Instantly, Longarm remembered the steam release at the boiling springs. But Amber was reduced to trembling, and her face was paler than ever. She caught Longarm's arms and clung to him, shaken. "Is that some woman out there?" she whispered.

Longarm held her close, reassuring her. He laughed, lifting his voice so everybody in the room heard him. "That's no woman. That's the lady who is going to save our lives."

Within minutes, Longarm had them all moving again. With Sam Brown carrying a lighted torch, they gathered all tubs, buckets, pots, pans—anything that would hold water. Longarm stationed Lobatos at the edge of the rock-enclosed pool. The sulfurous smell was overwhelming, but Lobatos seemed not to mind it. Steam rose from the boiling spring, which was so hot that its runoff creek was not even crusted over with ice, as far as they could see in the darkness.

The two actors and Reverend Forsley were set to carrying the buckets of hot water from the spring to the shack, where Longarm stationed Kane, the three Lobatos boys, and Sam on the coaches or beside the hut. As the first buckets of water were brought across the clearing from the rocks, Longarm took one, Sam took the other. They threw the water up against the side of the house as high as they could toss it.

The mineral-rich water steamed and sizzled and stank as it struck the crusted snow. The water started to run down the side of the aged structure, and turned to ice almost instantly.

"Keep slinging that water," Longarm shouted. "As high as you can, as long as you can, all the way around the shack."

Inside the house, Longarm set Amber, the other two actresses, and Mozelle to setting up the cots along the south wall as close to the stove as possible, but leaving a path around it.

"You got enough flour to make pancakes?" Longarm asked Nonnie.

"I got plenty of flour, Mr. Long. You tell me what to make, and I'll do it."

"Keep a big pot of snow on the fire, boiling at all times," Longarm told her. "Maybe Mozelle could keep the pot filled. We can use it to make coffee. But we want it filled and hot all the time."

"I'll take care of that," Mozelle told him.

"I'll start cooking up them pancakes," Nonnie said. "Pretty soon you can start sending the men in. I'll have hotcakes they can roll some honey in. And I got some fine fat hens that the cold is doing in. I could make soup out of them."

Longarm grinned at her. "You do that," he said. "The biggest pot you can make."

He stood for a moment in the sharp edge of the wind, watching the men run from the spring to the shack. Each time one of the men on the coaches or down below tossed a bucket of hot water, he yelled out his triumph, watching it run, crystallize, turn to thick-ribbed ice.

Longarm crossed the yard to the edge of the rockbed near the spring. He gathered smooth rocks and set them upon each other until he'd built a small concave shelter, high enough for a man to crouch in. He got a shovel then, and banked snow as high as he could over the stones. Then he brought buckets of water and poured it over the snow until the outer surface was ice-encrusted and wind-resistant. Inside, he piled hay up on the ground and then covered it with three folded horse blankets.

He stood back to admire his handiwork, thinking that this was probably as warm a crypt as a man could hope to be buried in. As he stood there, Nonnie Lobatos yelled from the lighted doorway of the shack.

"Come and see! Come and see!" she shouted. "It's warm in here. It's warm in here. There ain't no wind. There ain't no wind at all!"

The men came running from the darkness. Longarm crossed the yard, finding the snow up about his calves now, bogging him down as he tried to walk.

He grinned, pleased with what he found inside the shack. The hard physical labor the men had performed had renewed and invigorated them. Their faces were bright red, but their eyes glowed. Their trousers and coat sleeves were soaking wet, but they swung their arms, stamped their feet, and stood steaming as close to the stove as they could get.

Longarm drew a deep breath. For the first time he was sure they were all going to make it—at least through the night, at least until Fondis Estabrook came with his armed posse at dawn. Fondis had one little shock in store for him. He wasn't going to find corpses in this shack, as he had once before.

"We're going to make it," Longarm said, grinning at them.

Flagg Lobatos laughed. "Did you figger we wouldn't? Hell, this here ain't no storm a-tall. I was in a blue norther once. An old boy lit a candle during a blue. It was so cold that the flame froze 'n' busted plumb off the wick. That ol' boy picked it up anyway and used it to light his way out to the two-holer. When he was finished his duty—and he finished quick in that cold, I can tell you—he put the froze-up flame in his pocket and run back to the house. Well, he just disremembered all about that ol' wick till a couple of days later, when the weather changed. That flame burnt his rump somethin' awful, I can tell you."

"Praise the Lord," Reverend Forsley intoned. "Praise the Lord that He has seen fit to deliver us."

"I wouldn't count the delivery complete yet, preacher," Flagg Lobatos said. "This here storm ain't half as wild as your leadin' deacon, Mr. Fondis Estabrook, is going to be, come daylight."

"We ought to try to get some sleep," Longarm said. "I've set up a guard post overlooking the path into here. Any man can use a gun can take an hour's watch. Maybe Miss Austin would lend us her seal coat to huddle in."

"Of course," Amber agreed at once.

"The rest of you men get out of those wet clothes and into bed."

"You expect us to sleep naked?" Preacher Forsley demanded.

"That's right." Longarm nodded. "Sometimes you got to forget church rules and regulations if you hope to stay alive, Pastor Forsley. You wear your clothes to bed, you get warm, you sweat. The sweat dries and freezes. You wake up dead. You sleep naked, that's one way to wake up to be counted among the quick in the morning. And I suggest we all pair up—"

"Naked?" The pastor's voice shook.

"Body heat is body heat. Now, if you'd rather curl up with one of the dogs, you can see if one of them is willing to share a blanket with you."

"I'll share a cot with you, Reverend," the actress named Ellen said. She gave him a flat smile from her pretty face. "You won't be the first man of the cloth I've slept with, without any cloth between us. And I promise you, I won't rape you. I know you probably rape easy, but you're just not my type."

The minister stood red-faced, unable to speak, unable to reconcile what was going on with what he'd been taught to believe. Longarm said, "You better accept like a gentleman, Perkins. I think it's the best offer you're going to get."

Kane Estabrook spoke up suddenly in the laughter that swirled and danced in the room around the bewildered minister. "I'm going to sleep with Mozelle, Mr. Lobatos. Naked." He grinned, nodding. "I just know you're not going to stand for anything like that under your own roof—with your own daughter—unless there's a wedding first."

Flagg chewed that over a moment, then joined Kane in grinning broadly. "That shore is the truth, young feller! No man sleeps with my little Mozelle that don't marry her first."

"The minister is right here," Kane said.

"A wedding!" Nonnie Lobatos burst into tears. "A wedding. My own little girl."

Lobatos put his head back, laughing. "Our own little girl and Fondis Estabrook's only son! That there'll be another big hell of a surprise for ol' Fondis when he comes ridin' in here come morning."

They stood crowded together in the room, with the hot stove and its pot of boiling snow-water as the altar. Reverend Forsley stood before the stove, his damp clothes steaming. He held his pocket Bible dutifully in his hands, though he was totally unable to read the fine print in this poor lamplight.

The wind howled against the newly formed ice walls of the frame shack. The screaming and wailing along the eaves was almost a sobbing of mindless frustration. Along the north wall the horses stirred, warm and protected. Steam rose from the pot of chicken soup. During the ceremony, the Lobatos boys rolled chill-thickened honey in hot pancakes and munched quietly on them. Only Nonnie Lobatos cried. She sobbed her way through the entire ceremony.

Amber opened the rites by singing "O Promise Me." Longarm listened, amazed. Her singing voice was incredibly lovely. What was she doing in a place like this?

He heard Forsley saying with emphasis, ". . . For marriage is an honorable estate, instituted before God, and not to be entered upon lightly or irreverently . . ."

Longarm pulled his gaze from Amber's face long enough to see the radiance glowing in Mozelle Lobatos' eyes. It was all worth it, whatever it had cost them, whatever they had gone through, and whatever lay ahead. The happiness he saw glittering in Mozelle's eyes made it all worthwhile.

Then Forsley was saying, "I now pronounce you man and wife. You may kiss the bride."

Nonnie had ceased crying. She ran to Kane and Mozelle,

hugging them in her arms. Only Pastor Forsley looked as if he might weep now.

Longarm knew what the minister was thinking. Even if he lived through this blizzard tonight, he had to face Fondis Estabrook in the morning, knowing he had performed the ceremony uniting Fondis' son with the daughter of the wandering herder Flagg Lobatos. The minister could see no good in the world ahead of him. Longarm watched the man massage at his skinny throat with his trembling hands, looking sick.

Two of the Lobatos boys, yawning, started undressing, ready to share a mat and blanket together. The minister's reedy voice stopped them. "Just a minute, please. If we must undress to sleep, I am forced to insist that the lamp be put out first."

Lobatos laughed and consented. He turned down the wick and blew out the lamp. The glow from the fire illumined the room, but Forsley no longer complained. He didn't waste his energies fighting the inevitable. He undressed quickly, standing with his skinny legs bent and his arms stretched awkwardly across his body. Then he crawled quickly under the blanket he was to share with the actress.

Amber came to where Longarm stood with young J.C. Lobatos, near the front door. "I have a sleeping quilt to share, Custis. I have no scruples that prevent me from sleeping nude with a man without a ceremony."

"Praise God," Longarm whispered. He kissed her smiling lips. "As soon as I get a chance, I'll be there. You just keep a place warm for me."

J.C. Lobatos was near the fire. He held a honeyed pancake in one hand and was oiling his rifle with the other. Longarm stepped over the people on their mats. He touched J.C.'s arm. "For God's sake, J.C.," he whispered. "Don't oil that gun. If you had to use it out in that cold, you'd find it frozen solid—with oil."

"What do I do?"

"Use some of that hot water and soap. Wash all that oil out, every drop you can get. And dry it out on the stove top."

When J.C.'s gun was washed and dried, Longarm draped Amber's seal coat over his shoulders and walked out to the guard post with him.

Longarm crouched before the protected mouth of the small cave. "You're out of the wind," he said. "Hay and blankets between you and the ground. Under that seal fur, you'll be so warm your only trouble will be keeping from going to sleep."

"I won't sleep. I hate that old son of a bitch down there worse than anybody could—except maybe my old man."

Longarm grinned. "You shouldn't talk about ol' Fondis like that, J.C. He's in your family now."

J.C. crawled into the cave and settled there with the rifle across his knees. "In the family. Ol' Fondis Estabrook. In the family. Now, ain't that funny as hell?"

"Shoot him if he tries to sneak in here in the next hour."

J.C. laughed. "My pleasure. I mean, if you can't shoot your own family, where in hell can you start?"

Longarm left J.C. crouched out of the wind and watching the pass down from the mesa. Longarm walked a few yards down the narrow lane. The wind howled, tormented and twisted out of shape by the great shoulders of stone heaved up here in some prehistoric time.

He wanted to take a look at the soddy, built against a knoll in view of the road, but the snow blinded him, the darkness was almost suffocating. He turned and stamped his legs, hurrying back up the road to the ice-enclosed shack. He called out to J.C., "Be out to take your place in an hour."

He pushed open the shack door, stepped quickly inside, and shut it behind him, the wind howling at his heels like a pack of mindless animals. The room was quiet, and yet alive with movement, illumined by the red glow from the stove.

"Custis."

Longarm heard Amber's whisper and felt a tightening sensation in his groin as he stepped over reclining figures in the darkness. He sank to the mat beside Amber's lovely head. Her hair spilled out over the uncased pillow. He caught the tresses in his fist, caressing their richness.

"Get undressed," Amber whispered. "Quick. I saved a place for you. It's all warm. It's better than that . . . it's all hot."

Longarm grinned in the darkness. He tightened his fist on the side of her head. "There ought to be a law against you . . . I've got the next watch, in less than an hour . . . I can't undress now. I swear I'll come back as soon as I can." He drew her hand over to the throbbing rise below his belt. "Do you believe me?"

He sat beside Amber and smoked a cheroot. He used the cigar as a shield against her seductiveness, his desire for her. It wasn't enough to tell himself that Estabrook's armed men were just waiting for a chance to pounce. Amber was as near as she could be. She moved over and laid her head on his lap, which almost unhinged him and very nearly destroyed his strongest defenses against her. She rolled her head back and forth, blowing on him with her lips parted and her breath searing through the twill fabric.

The moments raced past, as if time were a horse out of control. At first, Longarm thought the cry came from Screaming Springs, the boiling geyser wailing ahead of schedule. Then he realized the sounds came from the mat shared by the Reverend Forsley and the actress. "Oh my God," the preacher sobbed. "Oh . . . my . . . God."

Longarm smiled. Apparently he wasn't the only one enduring the temptations of the devil in this strange, red-lit darkness. . . .

Carrying his gun, Longarm walked against the wind, bent low and wavering toward the guard post.

J.C. Lobatos saw him coming and crept out of the cave, stretching his arms and stamping his legs.

"Everything all right?" Longarm said.

"Yeah. Something funny happened, though. I almost shot the Sheriff."

Longarm felt himself tense. "Carr?"

"Yeah. He came up here. He just rode in about twenty minutes ago—he wasn't sneaking or anything. Just rode up here. If he'd of come sneaking, I'd of shot him. Started to anyway. But I held my fire. He looked around, then rode back. He never did spot me in the rocks, and I just let him go."

"You're a smart kid. J.C. Someday you may be President."

"Christ, I hope not."

Chapter 19

Longarm walked out of the ice-encased line shack. The first gray feelers of dawn slithered across the rim of the mesa. He noticed a difference at once. It was still cold, and the air he breathed burned his nostrils. But the wind had changed direction in the last hour before daybreak, and by now was blowing in from the west.

Sam Brown came around the corner of the shack. He gave Longarm a faint smile. "You have won, Marshal. You kept the wolf wind from getting your people. Fresh wind, feels like the Chinook. Warm wind. Indian wind."

"Yes," Longarm said. "We're still alive." He shook his head. "If we want to stay that way, we better get ready for company."

"What you want me to do?"

"You can stay in the house, Sam. You don't have to do anything. There may be gunplay and I don't want you to get mixed up in it."

"I *am* mixed up in it," Sam said. "I'm here. I'm on your side."

Longarm gave him a crooked grin. "There must be some other reason."

"Oh sure. It's been a long, cold night. Time for some action. Chinook gets a man's blood stirring."

The first rays of the sun glistened, dazzlingly white, on the ice covering the clapboard shack. Longarm brought the men out. He gave Desmond Bayne and his fellow actor the option of remaining in the shack or being staked out with a gun. Both elected to be hidden, and armed.

"I don't trust men with guns," Desmond Bayne said. "When

210

a man gets to shooting, sometimes he doesn't know when to stop. I'd hate to be unarmed against him."

Sam came out of the shack. "I've doused all signs of the fire, Marshal. There will be no smoke to alert your friends. I've told the ladies to keep much cover on to stay warm."

"Good." Longarm nodded. He sent Sam and the three Lobatos boys into the rocks that banked the geyser. "When you see them coming up the incline, hunker down. And stay there until I signal. I'll take a kerchief out of my coat pocket and blow my nose. That will be the signal for all of you to stand up at the same time. A show of guns is sometimes as good as gunfire."

The minister elected to stay in the shack with the women, and Longarm agreed this would be his best option. He wanted Flagg Lobatos as far from the controversy as he could get him, for as long as he could keep him there. So he stationed Flagg at the lean-to. "And stay out of sight," he warned. "We want them to come all the way in."

He stationed Desmond and the other actor on each side of the boulders that guarded the path onto the mesa. "Find rocks and stay behind them," he said. He smiled toward Desmond. "Unlike the villains in the plays you're in, these hombres will be using real bullets."

When all the men had been stationed and were crouched so that he could not see them, Longarm glanced at Kane Estabrook. "Kane, you can stay in the shack. There's no sense in you taking up a gun against your father."

"I don't want to fight him," Kane said. "I hope I won't have to. I know you'll try to talk some sense into his head. I hope you can, Marshal. But if you can't, these people will need every gun they can get. These are my people now."

Longarm nodded. "I was hoping you'd say that. I saved one of the carriages for you. I'll take the other one."

Desmond Bayne stood up from behind the rock outcropping and waved his rifle above his head. Then he immediately crouched behind the rocks again. Longarm exhaled heavily. "Well, Kane, here they come. If you know anybody who might talk some sense into your father's head, you might pray to them."

"I have been praying to them, all night." Kane started toward the second carriage. He stopped and grinned across his shoulder. "Well, most of the night."

Longarm laughed. They got into the carriages. Longarm pulled himself up so that he could see through the rear window. He found himself slightly troubled. The interior of the coach smelled strongly of Amber's perfume. It was heady stuff, and Longarm found his mind wandering.

He watched Estabrook ride up the snow-packed incline at the head of his armed posse. A quick count showed Longarm there were at least thirty mounted men, all carrying guns. An exact count wasn't important. The Screaming Springs people were badly outnumbered and outgunned.

Carr rode directly behind Estabrook, and three of his deputies flanked him.

Estabrook hesitated just inside the perimeter of the tableland. He sat straight in his saddle and sniffed the air, then he signaled the riders forward. He rode at their head, unhurried and confident.

Estabrook rode almost to the shack before he reined in and lifted his hand in a signal for his posse to halt.

Longarm exhaled heavily. The riders were all inside the rocks, sitting with rifles drawn, waiting for a signal from Estabrook.

Fondis Estabrook's voice rose triumphantly. "Well, it looks like I told you it would. I think we can dismount and look around."

Lawson's voice rattled against Estabrook's. "No, Fondis! It's a trap. They aren't dead. They're hid."

Estabrook hesitated for the space of one long breath, staring at the sheriff. His voice shattered the wind. "You let us ride into a trap?" He sat tall in his saddle and yelled, "Look to yourselves! The bastards are hiding. Blow them out of there. Find the sons. Kill them."

Longarm opened the door of the carriage and stepped out of it. He set himself, braced with both legs apart. He fixed the barrel of his Winchester on Estabrook. "Unless you want to to be the first to die, Estabrook, you might want to reconsider that order."

He took a kerchief from his greatcoat pocket. The signal

was hardly needed. Men stood up from their places of concealment, holding guns fixed on the riders.

Estabrook raised his arm, staring straight down at Longarm. Before Fondis could yell his defiant order, Kane leaped out of the second carriage. Carrying his rifle close against his leg, Kane ran to his father.

"Papa!" he yelled. "Don't do it!"

"Kane!" Estabrook's voice broke. "What in hell are you doing here with this . . . rabble?"

"These people didn't cut your fence or drive those cows on the graze, Papa. I know they didn't. I rode up here that morning."

"*You* warned them into hiding!"

"They hadn't done anything, Papa. None of them had left the mesa that morning."

"Jesus Christ, Kane, what kind of son are you?" Fondis shook his head. "Why do you try to protect this trash?"

"Because this trash is my family, Papa. You hear me? My family."

"You went over to them? Against me?"

Kane nodded, staring up at his father in the dazzling daylight. "I married Mozelle, Papa. If you kill them, you're going to have to kill me."

Fondis hesitated, for perhaps the first time in his life.

Longarm stepped forward. "I better tell you people. You're trespassing. You're threatening assault. You're resisting a U.S. marshal. I'll give you one chance to ride out of here, or you're all under arrest."

"You'd like to shoot us all in the back, wouldn't you, Long?" Carr said. "He's sold out to those people. You going to let them drive you off your own range, or are you going to fight for what is yours?"

Longarm spoke coldly. He kept his voice loud but level. "That's one hell of a way for a sheriff to talk, Carr. Are you inciting these people against the law? Again? You better look at this sheriff that you figured was your toady all these years, Estabrook. You better see him for what he really is."

"I'm trying to keep the law," Carr said. "There's only one way to do that. Get rid of the lawbreakers."

"You don't want law at all, Carr," Longarm said. "You'd

213

never get what you want, under the law. You want this whole range. You want to own it all. You want it all to yourself."

"What kind of insane talk is that?" Estabrook demanded.

"Ask Carr," Longarm said. "Only I better warn you, Lawson Carr sees you just about the way he sees Flagg Lobatos—as vermin standing in his way. You think you've been ordering Carr around all this time? Hell, he's been calling the shots. He's been leading you down the road that led straight here, where you and Lobatos were supposed to kill each other off. Then Lawson Carr would pick up the pieces and build the kind of kingdom he once had back home in Virginia."

"You have gone insane," Carr said.

"Have I? Have you ever told Estabrook any more than he needed to know to keep him stirred up against Lobatos? Hell, I almost forced Cody Boyle to tell who paid him three hundred dollars to take a shot at you so Lobatos could be blamed, but Carr cracked me over the head and killed Boyle to shut him up. He apologized all to hell for hitting me instead of Boyle, but we all know that whack on the head was perfectly aimed. It stopped me. It stopped Boyle. And it left Carr free to push you closer to a range war with Lobatos."

Carr's voice slashed down at Longarm. "Are you saying *I* rounded up those cattle and cut those fences? I was in that office—with you."

"You were. But your deputies and your hired hands in the Interior Department weren't. They rounded up Wolfhead cattle, and they cut their own fences."

Carr laughed loudly. "Are you charging government men with taking bribes? Are you the only honest government man?"

"I'm not even saying that they took bribes. Hell, you could *talk* them into trapping Lobatos. Paint him as a villain, promise the trouble will stop when he's out of the way. Only what you talked them into was entrapment."

Carr looked around wildly. His eyes were as empty as they must have been that morning when he rode in and found his palatial home destroyed, his wife brutally raped and slain. There was no sign of sanity left in his handsome, haggard face.

He raged, "These people may listen to your Yankee lies, but I've heard enough, you son of a bitch."

He leveled his rifle in the crook of his arm and spurred his horse, lunging straight toward Longarm.

As the horse plunged toward him, Longarm yelled from the depths of his lungs.

The horse squealed, threw its head up, and reared high. Carr fired at that instant. His shot went wild over Longarm's head as the tall marshal raised his Winchester and fired one round, which caught Carr squarely in the center of his ribcage.

The horse came forward, with Carr still fighting the reins, jerking its head down. As the horse's front paws struck the ground, legs rigid, Carr was thrown from the saddle. The rifle flew from his arms. He struck hard on his shoulder and then sagged over on his back. He tried to move, but he could not do it.

He sprawled on the ground, his face contorted. He seemed to be saying something. Longarm went to him and hunkered over him on one knee. "What is it, Carr?"

"Amber," Carr whispered. "I want to see Miss Amber."

Kane turned and ran to the door of the shack. Amber came out into the yard, wearing no coat. She came across to where Longarm knelt over Carr. She seemed unaware of the cold.

"She's here, Lawson," Longarm said.

"I'm here, Lawson," Amber said. She knelt beside Longarm.

Carr stared up at her as if he could see her only through an occluding haze. "I loved you, Amber . . . I truly loved you . . ."

"I know," she said.

He coughed, and blood bubbled in his throat. His eyes filled with tears and he lay for some moments, unmoving. At last he whispered to her. When he parted his lips, blood ran from the corner of his mouth. He could barely speak, and Amber bent closer to him.

"Oh . . . Amber . . . it could all have been . . . so beautiful."

He sagged, struggling, choking on his own blood. He was dead. Longarm lifted Amber and walked back to the line shack with her.

When he turned back, he found that the fight had gone out of the posse.

Fondis Estabrook said, "I'm not a stupid man, Marshal. I

see you are right. I was blind. Lawson was behind it all, poor devil."

"Yes," Longarm said. "It was his dream. A great estate out here, with Amber as his lady. His last dream." He hesitated a moment, and then said, "Your fences ought to stay intact for a while—until the next drive through here from Texas, anyhow."

Fondis nodded wearily. "Are we under arrest, Long? We been wrong."

Longarm shook his head. "Part of your crew has deserted you, Fondis. I see that Carr's deputies—and Carmel and Pierce—have kind of melted away."

"Maybe that's what we all ought to do," Estabrook said. He ordered his men to tie Lawson Carr across his own saddle, then turned back to Longarm. "Is that all right with you, Marshal?"

"Seems a great idea to me," Longarm said. "You got a long ride back to town, and I got no charges against you."

When they came into the line shack, Nonnie Lobatos had a fire going in the stove and she was making coffee, pancakes, and fried chicken. "We're going to have a lot of fried chicken around here for a while," she said.

Flagg and his boys grinned, and laughed suddenly without reason. Freedom was a stimulant, like strong whiskey. It took some getting used to. Flagg said, "What I can't understand, Marshal, is why you was so set on suspectin' a handsome, clean-cut, upstandin' citizen like Lawson Carr instead of a grimy old reprobate like me."

"That part was easy," Longarm said. "Mozelle was in love with Kane. I saw you were truly trying to start a new life—for her. I could believe that. And poor old Lawson, I suspected him from the first, because I knew he was the one who told Elliot I was in bed with Elliot's wife. He stirred up Elliot, because getting Elliot out of the way before he could take Amber away from Dirty Fork was the first part of Carr's plan. What I couldn't see until later was how big Lawson's plan really was. He wanted Flagg and Fondis to kill each other off, and he'd pick up the pieces—at a dime on the dollar."

"That has to be the way it is," J.C. said. "The sheriff rode in here last night. I told the marshal. Carr knew we weren't

216

dead. He brought Mr. Estabrook up here, hoping we'd open fire as they rode in."

Amber took a long sip of hot coffee. Her beautiful eyes brimmed with tears. She said, "It's all so sad, so senseless. But I guess that's how Lawson saw the slaughter of his family in Virginia—as senseless."

"A man goes crazy inside," Longarm said. "He's driven."

"We've got to be driven on to Denver." Amber gazed at Longarm. "We're due to appear in a theater there next week. No matter what, we've got to pick up our lives. We've got to go on." She turned to Sam. "Are you still going to drive one of my carriages?"

Sam smiled and nodded. "As far as the lady wants me to. For a dollar a day and found. Sam will be a rich Indian."

Desmond Bayne laughed. "A real Indian in our plays, Amber. Think of it. I'll teach him diction."

"That's the last thing you'll do," Amber said. "I refuse to go onstage with a red man who talks like you do."

They laughed, but after a moment, Amber returned to the subject nearest her heart. "I am still nervous and upset after all that happened in Dirty Fork. Elliot's death and all. And this nightmare up here. Poor Lawson's death. Even if Sam drives my carriage, Mr. Long, I need someone strong that I can depend on. Couldn't you tie your horse behind my carriage and ride with me to Denver? I know it would take a week to get there in this snow, but I do need you. I need someone who can help me through these next few days . . . and nights."

Longarm nodded. "It sounds like a rough job." He grinned. "But somebody's got to do it."

SPECIAL PREVIEW

Here are the opening scenes
from

LONGARM ON THE SANTA FE

thirty-sixth in the bold
LONGARM series from Jove

Chapter 1

When Longarm got to the crest of the low ridge that the long-legged cavalry roan had been mounting for the past half-dozen miles, he reined in and waited for his companion to draw abreast. The sun was an hour past noon and no longer shone into his eyes, as it had when they'd gotten their last glimpse of Hoodoo Jack Simms and Big Ed Slater.

While Longarm waited, he studied the expanse of winter-brown prairie that stretched from the ridge to a thin line of trees that marked a creek's bed, less than a mile away. In the bright early-afternoon sunlight, the terrain was bare and deserted. Not even a wintering bird could be seen in the vast canopy of the pale winter sky.

Second Lieutenant Bedford Wheeler, U.S. Cavalry, drew up at Longarm's side and scowled at the emptiness that he saw. There was disappointment in his youthful face as he slowly shook his head, keeping his eyes turned toward the barren reach of grassland in front of them.

An onlooker studying the two men as they sat in their saddles on the crest would have been hard put to find another pair that offered as great a contrast.

Deputy U.S. Marshal Custis Long, whose friends called him Longarm, had a well-tanned face that told of long periods in the saddle, facing all kinds of weather, and his gunmetal-blue eyes were at the moment as cold as the blue ice at the heart of an Arctic glacier. His well-groomed mustache, brown like the sideburns shaved square at the level of his earlobes, swept above his full lips like the horns of a Texas steer. Even in the restricted movements that were allowed a man on horseback, his big frame showed the muscular grace of a strong, active man.

Wheeler, wearing the regulation cavalry field uniform, was perhaps a bit more than half Longarm's age, but beside him Wheeler looked baby-callow. The lieutenant's face was clean-shaven, his skin the bright pink hue that shows before tanning on the face of a man who has spent little time outdoors. The lines that give a man's face character had not yet had time to form on the lieutenant's countenance. His brown eyes were soft, and his lips protruded in a babylike pout.

"Looks like we've lost them again," he said flatly.

Before answering, Longarm fished a cheroot from his pocket, flicked a horn-hard thumbnail across a matchhead, and touched the flame to the tip of the long, slim cigar. A freshening breeze from the north trailed the blue-gray smoke away from his face as he replied, "Not likely. They'll be holed up some-place along that draw. It's the first cover they've come to since we spotted them."

Lieutenant Wheeler gazed at the ragged line of young, leaf-less cottonwoods the ridge had hidden from them earlier. The trees straggled across the flat plateau in a narrow and often interrupted weaving line that stretched southward in the general direction of the South Platte River, still out of sight below the horizon. Between the cottonwood trunks there were low-lying sandplum bushes, almost as bare of leaves as the trees.

"Why do you think that?" he asked, then added quickly. "Even from here, I can see there's not enough brush to hide them."

"You ain't been out here long enough to know what a little bit of cover like that can hide," Longarm answered. "If I was Hoodoo Jack and his sidekick, I'd cut a shuck for those trees and wait till whoever was after me got in range. And from what your man with that payroll wagon said, Hoodoo Jack Simms is a man that won't stand and face a fight when there's anyplace he can hide and bushwhack you."

While he spoke, Longarm was sliding his Winchester out of its saddle scabbard. Wheeler looked at him, frowning.

"You really think those outlaws are as close as that?" he asked. "They had a good five-mile lead when we saw them just after daybreak, and we haven't gained on them all that much, Marshal Long. If you'll remember, they spurred up when they spotted us following them."

"Sure they did. Until they seen us, they didn't know there was anybody after 'em. When you're trailing a man and he sees you the first time, he just naturally kicks his horse up."

"They must've known somebody would chase them."

"Outlaws have got funny minds, Lieutenant. Most of 'em figure they're going to get away scot-free from whatever job they've pulled. Then, when they see they ain't, they got a way of running as fast as they can for a while. But it don't take long for 'em to shake off that first surprise, and that's when they remember they can't afford to get their horses winded. So they slow down."

Wheeler said thoughtfully, "What surprises me is that they were foolish enough to leave that man in Cheyenne. They should have been smart enough to foresee that somebody like you would find him, and that he'd talk. But regardless of that, if I was a criminal running with accomplices from a crime, I'd have taken that wounded man along, no matter what bad shape he was in."

"That's the army way," Longarm conceded. "Don't abandon your wounded, ain't that what the book says?"

"Of course. A primary rule, Marshal."

"Outlaws don't play by rules, Lieutenant. You better get wise to that sooner than later, or you'll be sorry."

Longarm nudged the roan forward in a slow walk. A bit reluctantly, the army officer followed him. Longarm kept his eyes moving along the line of trees and the clumps of sandplum bushes that became visible between their trunks as he drew closer. The range was still extreme, but he didn't know how nervous the fugitives might be getting after the long morning of pursuit. He did know that bushwhacking was Hoodoo Jack Simms' style, and the cover the creekbed offered gave him an opportunity the fugitive outlaw would welcome.

Longarm and Wheeler had been following the two outlaws since early the preceding day, after Longarm had picked up their trail in Cheyenne. Simms and Slater were the last survivors of an ambush in which they and four like them had trapped an army payroll wagon loaded with gold being sent to pay the soldiers manning the forts in northern Wyoming.

Half of the escorting cavalry detachment had been killed in the first volley fired by Simms and his band, and the rest of the escorting squad, as well as three of the bushwhackers, had died in the sharp, short fight that followed. The payroll clerks in the wagon had done their best, but only one of them had survived his wounds and gotten back to Fort Russell. It was this survivor who'd not only reported the payroll theft and murders, but had described the bushwhackers accurately enough to give Longarm the leads he needed to begin running them down.

And if Billy Vail hadn't known you were waiting for a train to Denver at the depot there in Cheyenne right when he got word from the paymaster at Fort Russell about those bastards getting away with the payroll chest, old son, you wouldn't be out here right now, his thoughts ran on, ignoring the presence of the lieutenant. *Out here with a green shavetail who don't know his ass from a hot rock, and ain't smart enough to understand how much he don't know, fresh as he is from the East.*

However, Vail's telegram assigning him to the case had gotten to Longarm before the train for Denver pulled in, and he'd wasted no time in pulling together the loose ends that faced him. After getting the story of the ambush from the surviving payroll clerk, he'd lost an argument with Colonel Blaisdell, the commanding officer of the provost marshal force at Fort Russell, who'd insisted on having Lieutenant Wheeler go with him.

To save time and get on the gang's trail quickly, Longarm had agreed. He'd requisitioned the long-legged roan from the fort's remount station and, with Wheeler accompanying him, had ridden the three miles from the fort to Cheyenne. There, over Wheeler's protests, Longarm had conducted a quick shakedown of the scabby red-light district south of the tracks, and before daylight he had pulled the wounded survivor of the outlaw gang out of one of the dives.

Very little persuasion had been required to get the captured outlaw to start talking. He'd blabbed the names of Simms and Slater and revealed their getaway plans. Because arguing with a greenhorn second lieutenant was easier than arguing with a chicken colonel, Longarm had been able to convince Wheeler that they'd be wasting valuable time by going back to the fort and mustering a squad to go with them. He and the lieutenant had been able to set out on the trail of Hoodoo Jack Simms and Big Ed Slater less than eight hours after the outlaws had ridden out of Cheyenne.

Now, as they neared the draw, a twitching in the yellowed, sere leaves of the sandplum bushes caught Longarm's eye and he shifted slightly in his saddle. In two places, the brush had started to lean against the chill wind that had come up fast in the few minutes since they'd stopped at the crest of the ridge.

Longarm reacted instantly when he saw the sandplum brush swaying in a manner the wind couldn't account for. "Split up and ride fast!" he called to Wheeler.

Without waiting to see whether the lieutenant obeyed, he kicked the cavalry horse into a forward leap just as a pair of smoke puffs blossomed above the low-hanging bushes and rifle slugs raised spurts of dust from the dry prairie soil a few yards beyond them.

Longarm heard the hoofbeats of Wheeler's horse at the same time the sound of the shots reached his ears, their sharp, cracking reports faint in the fast-rising wind. A split second later he sent an answering bullet from the Winchester into the brush where he'd seen the dry leaves shaking.

At the same time he toed the roan into a zigzag lope at an angle that would extend the distance between him and the hidden sniper. Gunsmoke rose from the brush again, and lead whistled past Longarm's head. Longarm didn't bother to reply, though he heard the flat blast of Wheeler's Springfield carbine behind him.

Experience hadn't yet taught the greenhorn that shooting at an invisible target did nothing but waste lead. Longarm concentrated on getting to the creekbed as fast as possible while opening up the range still more between himself and the outlaws who, his senses had told him, were likely to be hunkered down in the bushes.

Another quick shot zipped between the two men as they got to the edge of the draw leading to the creekbed and slid into the brush. There, in the cover of the sandplum bushes and with the trunks of a half-dozen cottonwoods between him and Hoo-doo Jack, Longarm reined in to take stock of the situation. At his side, the young officer was breathing hard, the air whistling out of his expanded nostrils.

"That was a close call," Wheeler commented, trying to keep his voice steady, but not quite succeeding.

"There's likely to be closer ones before we get those two fellows corraled," Longarm replied.

He took out a fresh cheroot, but the wind, whistling down the draw in which the winter-shallow creek lay, blew out the first match he struck before he could raise it to light the cigar. Twisting in the saddle to put his cupped hands to the wind before striking a second match, he saw the ominous gray of snow clouds, a high, threatening bank moving down from the northern mountains that were less than fifty miles distant.

"What we better do right now is shake a leg," Longarm went on. "If we lollygag around here and let 'em get too much of a lead on us before that storm hits, we're apt to have some real trouble, a kind we ain't counting on."

"What storm?" Wheeler asked, frowning. He looked at the sky. The clouds still appeared to be far distant, and ahead of them the sun was shining brightly through the bare limbs of the cottonwoods along the creek bank. The lieutenant jerked his head to indicate the blue sky above them and went on, "It's as clear as a bell, Marshal Long. I don't see anything to worry about."

"Maybe you don't, but I sure as hell do." Longarm pointed to the gray clouds sweeping down from the north. "That's a real weather-maker coming at us, and it's moving faster than we can. If we don't step fast, we might lose those two, because I'd imagine by now they're making tracks."

A trickle of water, barely deep enough to cover the stones in the center of its bed, ran in the creek. Longarm reined the roan into the center of the waterway and toed the horse into a walk. Behind him he heard the hooves of Wheeler's horse scraping over the bed of the little stream. The creek's course was almost straight, its banks bordered on each side by the sparse stands of young cottonwoods interspersed with thick growths of sandplum.

Above the splashing and the scraping, Wheeler called, "We're wasting time following the creek, Marshal! Those outlaws will have started on across the prairie by now! They'll be so far ahead that we'll never overtake them!"

Longarm didn't waste his breath explaining to the inexpe-

rienced young officer that he was trying to avoid a brush-fight.
He'd decided quickly to flush the fugitives out of their protecting cover. Had he been alone, or with a companion he knew
could be trusted to move silently, keep cool, and shoot fast and
straight, Longarm would have made a silent approach to the
outlaws and tried to take them by surprise. With a tyro like
Wheeler, he knew that surprising Simms and Slater was an
impossibility. Instead of answering the lieutenant, he simply
nodded and kept moving ahead.

Longarm's instincts, honed to a fine edge in countless con-
frontations like the one they now faced, told him that the outlaws would do one of two things. Either they'd stand ready to
shoot as he and the lieutenant approached along the creekbed,
or they'd pull out of the draw, rein in, and wait until he and
the lieutenant emerged from the gully. For the few moments
while their horses were pushing through the brush, he and
Wheeler would be sitting ducks. He was betting strongly that
the fugitives would choose to run.

When his judgment told him that they'd ridden far enough
in the cover of the creekbed to give the outlaws a chance to
get in position, while they were still far short of the spot where
Simms and Slater had been when they fired, Longarm led the
way up the east bank of the creek and out onto the prairie
again. Ahead of them, at extreme rifle range, the two outlaws
were galloping as fast as they could spur their horses. With a
sweep of his hand, Longarm motioned for Wheeler to follow
him and headed for the fugitives on a long slant that would
intercept them within the next few miles.

Engrossed in the chase, they had paid no attention to the
threat of the oncoming storm. Riding out of the draw, Longarm
glanced up long enough to see that the scudding cloudbank
coming from the north now covered almost the entire sky.
They'd ridden only a short distance when the clouds swallowed
the sun, and the sudden sharp bite of the air on his face set
Longarm's eyes to searching the sky.

He did not like what he saw. The slit of blue to the south
was closing fast, and when he looked to the north again he
found his vision cut off by an impenetrable haze. When they'd
stopped on the ridge, he'd been able to sweep twenty miles of
prairie with his eyes; now visibility to the north was only a

mile or so. Longarm knew the prairie's weather pattern like a book. He'd seen similar storms blow in on the prairie before, and knew the haze was not mist but heavy snow, blowing toward them at a pace faster than their horses could travel.

Swiveling in the saddle, he called to Wheeler, "That storm you didn't believe in is catching up to us. We're going to be up to our bellybuttons in snow before we got a hope of catching up to those men ahead of us."

"What do you think we should do, then?"

"Hell, there's not but one thing we can do. Keep moving!"

Almost before Longarm had finished speaking, the first snowflakes were swirling around them. The already sharp wind took on a cutting bite. Longarm folded the lapels of his coat together and buttoned them across his chest, then pulled his wide-brimmed hat down on his head more firmly. Wheeler was twisting in his saddle to get his greatcoat, which was in a compact roll strapped behind his saddle. He managed to free the long, heavy coat and get his arms into its sleeves without dismounting, and to don his gloves.

Suddenly the air was gray, the clouds so low they seemed to be pressing on their heads, the wind whipping big snowflakes into their faces, where the wet flakes stung like tiny bullets.

Above the whistle of the wind, Wheeler shouted, "How are we going to keep on a straight course? I can't see ten feet ahead!"

"Don't worry about that. I can keep us heading straight. Just don't get separated from me." Longarm put his head down and kneed the cavalry roan forward a bit faster.

Already, Simms and Slater were dark blobs moving through a thickening haze of whirling snowflakes. Their vaguely defined forms disappeared completely before Longarm and Wheeler had ridden another ten minutes. For all practical purposes, the two of them were alone, riding enclosed in an impenetrable veil that extended from sky to earth and imprisoned men and horses in a circle only a few yards in diameter. Underfoot, the ground was already a soft, featureless white.

"What do we do now?" Wheeler asked Longarm.

"We keep on riding straight ahead. That's all we can do. If we stop out here on this damn bare prairie, we'll freeze."

"How the hell do you know you're going straight?"

"If you don't know, Lieutenant, I do. I've been out in these blizzards before. Don't worry. Simms and Slater are in the same pickle barrel that we are. They got to keep moving, they can't go any faster than we do, or see where they're going any better than we can. We'll see 'em again as soon as the snow lets up."

"How long will that be, Marshal?"

"Maybe ten minutes, maybe ten hours, maybe ten days. The longest time I ever heard of a blizzard lasting in this part of the country was two weeks."

"Two weeks!" Wheeler exclaimed. "Why, if it goes on like this for more than a few hours, the snow'll be ten feet deep!"

Longarm nodded "It's been known to happen." His voice was calm. "And that means we better keep moving as fast as we can, while we can."

"It seems stupid to me to move without knowing where we're going. So far I haven't seen any kind of shelter, if that's what we're looking for."

"Like I already said, Lieutenant, if we don't keep moving, we're likely to freeze. And even if you didn't see anyplace up ahead that we can head for, there is one. I think I can find it, with a lot of luck."

"Well, I suppose you know the territory, Marshal. How far are we from this place you're talking about?"

"Maybe six or eight miles. It's an abandoned army post. I don't guess you ever heard of it. The place used to be called Fort Sedgewick. It was put in to guard a ford on the South Platte, in the days when there was a lot of emigrants moving along the Overland Trail."

Wheeler shook his head. "No. Maybe I've heard the name or seen it on a map, but I don't remember it if I have."

"Well, it never was much of a shucks as a fort, just a little outpost. Tents for the men, and two or three soddies for the headquarters and cookshack and stores. There's part of the soddies still standing, or was, last time I passed by the place. I'm guessing there's still enough left to shelter in."

"And you think we can make it there?"

"I think we *better* make it." Longarm didn't mention that he was already feeling the symptoms of freezing as the wind struck through his clothing. He went on, "I guess we can get there before it's too late, if our horses hold out."

They'd kept moving slowly during their conversation, which had been carried on in shouts made necessary by the increasingly shrill keening of the biting wind. Now Longarm reined in. He fumbled his bandanna out of his hip pocket, the wind stabbing him like an icicle, piercing his midsection when he opened his coat. With fingers that were already growing stiff, he unfolded the big red handkerchief and spread it on one thigh.

As he worked, he told Wheeler, "You better fix that pretty yellow scarf around your neck like I'm fixing my bandanna, Lieutenant."

Longarm had taken out his pocketknife; now he cut two eye-slits in the bandanna. Taking off his hat, he spread the kerchief over his face, positioning the eye openings carefully. The bandanna met and overlapped at the back of his head, and he pulled his hat over the top edge of the bandanna to hold it in place. Then he tucked the kerchief's bottom edge into the collar of his gray flannel shirt. The improvised facemask reduced his field of vision, but it helped to cut the wind's bite. More importantly, it trapped the warmth of his exhaled breath and protected the skin of his face from freezing.

Wheeler had watched carefully, and now he pulled off his cavalry gauntlets and arranged his yellow cavalry scarf as Longarm had fixed the bandanna. After a few moments he was surprised to find that the effect of his exhalations was to make his face feel warm, even though the thin cloth of the neckerchief provided no real warmth in itself.

"Keep opening and closing your hands on your reins, now," Longarm cautioned as he kneed the cavalry roan into motion again. "Those gauntlets you got on wasn't ever intended to keep a man's hands from freezing up."

Slowly they moved forward through the swirling snow, which was falling more thickly than ever. They'd gone only a short distance when Wheeler's horse began to toss its head and neigh plaintively. The young officer reined in after the animal began rearing, threatening to throw him.

"What's wrong with this damned beast?" he called to Longarm, his voice muffled by the snow-covered neckerchief covering his face. "He acts like he's gotten spooked over something."

"He has." Longarm reined in. "You stay where you are and keep a tight rein. I'll see if I can fix your critter's eyes."

"His eyes?"

"Yep. The snow's froze his lashes together. He's panicky because he can't see where he's going."

As he spoke, Longarm was pushing his way through the blanket of calf-deep snow to the head of Wheeler's mount. He fumbled his pocketknife from his pocket as he moved.

"Hold a tight rein, now," he told the lieutenant. "I got to trim his eyelashes so they won't be long enough to catch the snowflakes anymore."

Wheeler watched through the eye-slits of his neckerchief as Longarm pinched the horse's eyelids together and, with infinite care, trimmed away the animal's thick lashes close to the flesh, using the razor-sharp edge of the knife's small blade.

When the delicate job was completed, the horse grew calm once more. Longarm pushed through the snow to his own mount and led it close to Wheeler. He tossed the reins to the officer.

"Hold mine as steady as you can. Might as well fix him so he won't spook later on."

While Wheeler held the roan's head, Longarm trimmed its lashes. He put his knife back into his pocket and started pushing through the snow to mount the animal. A twinge of worry nipped at the edges of his mind as he moved; standing in snow that was almost knee-deep for the time required to tend the two horses had stiffened his legs, and he could feel a numbness creeping up from his thighs into his body. Longarm knew he must find shelter without delay.

With agonizing slowness he led the way toward the banks of the South Platte. The horses could not move faster than a deliberate walk in the deepening snow, and often it was necessary for the pair to detour around drifts, for by now the swirling wind was piling the snow so that in places it formed ridges as high as a tall man's head.

Even though he'd assured Wheeler that he could find the old army post, Longarm was beginning to doubt his own words as they moved forward ever more slowly and the snow continued to pile up deeper and deeper.

Time lost its meaning as they pushed on blindly through the almost impenetrable veil of thickly falling flakes. The horses moved more and more reluctantly, and Longarm could tell that the extreme cold was sapping their vitality almost as badly as it was his own. Though he tried to follow his own advice to Wheeler, and work his hands on the reins, his fingers responded less and less readily to his efforts to flex them and keep them useful.

Doggedly, Longarm led his companion forward in what he hoped was the right direction. He had no choice but to trust the instincts that had served him so well in the past, a sense of direction that he was trusting to lead them to the river, which they could then follow to the abandoned outpost.

As the horses moved slowly through the snow, floundering now and then in spite of the care with which they lifted and planted their hooves, he glanced at his companion from time to time. Though Wheeler's face was hidden by the yellow cavalry kerchief, now encrusted with ice around the mouth and nostrils, Longarm gave the lieutenant credit for a toughness that the young officer hadn't displayed earlier; in spite of their slow progress, Wheeler did not complain.

Old son, Longarm told himself as he stared through the eye-slits into a world of shifting white against a field of gray, *If you got turned around and ain't heading toward the river, you've took too big a bite to chew or swallow. But there ain't much else you can do except keep going, because if you were wrong, it's too damned late to do anything about it.*

Because there was no alternative, Longarm kept moving ahead. The snowstorm showed no signs of abating. The big flakes kept swirling from the sky as thickly as ever, while the horses picked their way forward at a slower and slower pace. There was no way Longarm could judge how much time they'd been moving; he knew that his time sense was disoriented, with the sun obscured and the invisible sky a uniform gray.

Wheeler's horse stumbled and almost went down. Then,

just as it found a footing, Longarm felt the hooves of the long-legged roan beginning to slip. He reined in hard and called to Wheeler, "Pull up! It looks like we've finally made it to the South Platte!"

Ride the High Plains with the hard-bitten, rough-and-tumble Infantrymen of Outpost Nine as their handsome lieutenant, Matt Kincaid, leads them into battle in the bloody Indian uprisings!

___ 05761-4	EASY COMPANY AND THE SUICIDE BOYS #1 John Wesley Howard	$1.95
___ 05804-1	EASY COMPANY AND THE MEDICINE GUN #2 John Wesley Howard	$1.95
___ 05887-4	EASY COMPANY AND THE GREEN ARROWS #3 John Wesley Howard	$1.95

And...
Watch for a new *Easy Company* adventure every month from Jove!

LONGARM

He's a man's man, a ladies' man—the fastest lawman around. Follow Longarm through all his shoot-'em-up adventures as he takes on the outlaws—and the ladies—of the Wild, Wild West!